THE CHILD
IN TIME

THE CHILD
IN TIME

Ian
McEwan

Houghton Mifflin Company

B O S T O N

ACKNOWLEDGMENTS

I am indebted to the following authors and books: Christina Hardyment, *Dream Babies,* Jonathan Cape; David Bohm, *Wholeness and the Implicate Order,* Routledge & Kegan Paul; Joseph Chilton Pearce, *Magical Child,* E. P. Dutton and Co.

Library of Congress Cataloging-in-Publication Data

McEwan, Ian.
The child in time.
I. Title.
PR6063.C4C45   1987   823'.914   87-8603
ISBN 0-395-42912-9

Printed in the United States of America

Q 10 9 8 7 6 5 4 3 2

A portion of this book previously appeared in *Esquire.*

TO PENNY

THE CHILD
IN TIME

1

"... and for those parents, for too many years misguided by the pallid relativism of self-appointed child-care experts ..."

— *The Authorized Child-Care Handbook,*
Her Majesty's Stationery Office

SUBSIDIZING PUBLIC TRANSPORT had long been associated in the minds of both government and the majority of its public with the denial of individual liberty. The various services collapsed twice a day at rush hour and it was quicker, Stephen found, to walk from his flat to Whitehall than to take a taxi. It was late May, barely nine-thirty, and already the temperature was nudging the eighties. He strode towards Vauxhall Bridge past double and treble files of trapped, throbbing cars, each with its solitary driver. In tone the pursuit of liberty was more resigned than passionate. Ringed fingers drummed patiently on the sill of a hot tin roof, white-shirted elbows poked through rolled-down windows. There were newspapers spread over steering wheels. Stephen stepped quickly through the crowds, through layers of car radio blather — jingles, high-energy breakfast DJs, news flashes, traffic "alerts." Those drivers not reading listened stolidly. The steady forward press of the pavement crowds must have conveyed to them a sense of relative motion, of drifting slowly backwards.

Jigging and weaving to overtake, Stephen remained as always, though barely consciously, on the watch for children, for a five-year-old girl. It was more than a habit, for a habit could be broken. This was a deep disposition, the outline experience had stenciled on character. It was not principally a search, though it had once been an obsessive hunt, and for a long time too. Two years on, only vestiges of that remained; now it was a longing, a dry hunger. There was a biological clock, dispassionate in its unstoppability, which let his daughter go on growing, extended and complicated her simple vocabulary, made her stronger, her movements surer. The clock, sinewy like a heart, kept faith with an unceasing conditional: she would be drawing, she would be starting to read, she would be losing a milk tooth. She would be familiar, taken for granted. It seemed as though the proliferating instances might wear down this conditional, the frail, semiopaque screen whose fine tissues of time and chance separated her from him; she is home from school and tired, her tooth is under the pillow, she is looking for her daddy.

Any five-year-old girl — though boys would do — gave substance to her continued existence. In shops, past playgrounds, at the houses of friends, he could not fail to watch out for Kate in other children, or ignore in them the slow changes, the accruing competences, or fail to feel the untapped potency of weeks and months, the time that should have been hers. Kate's growing up had become the essence of time itself. Her phantom growth, the product of an obsessive sorrow, was not only inevitable — nothing could stop the sinewy clock — but necessary. Without the fantasy of her continued existence he was lost, time would stop. He was the father of an invisible child.

But here on Millbank there were only ex-children shuffling to work. Further up, just before Parliament Square, was a group of licensed beggars. They were not permitted anywhere near Parliament or Whitehall or within sight of the square. But a few were taking advantage of the confluence of commuter routes. He saw their bright badges from a couple of hundred yards away. This was their weather, and they looked cocky with their freedom. The wage-earners had to give way. A dozen beggars were working both sides of the street, moving towards him steadily against the surge. It was a child Stephen was watching now, not a five-year-old but a skinny prepubescent. She had registered him at some distance. She walked slowly, somnambulantly, the regulation black bowl extended. The office workers parted and converged about her. Her eyes were fixed on Stephen as she came. He felt the usual ambivalence. To give money ensured the success of the government program. Not to give involved some determined facing-away from private distress. There was no way out. The art of bad government was to sever the line between public policy and intimate feeling, the instinct for what was right. These days he left the matter to chance. If he had small change in his pocket, he gave it. If not, he gave nothing. He never handed out banknotes.

The girl was brown-skinned from sunny days on the street. She wore a grubby yellow cotton frock and her hair was severely cropped. Perhaps she had been deloused. As the distance closed he saw she was pretty, impish and freckled, with a pointed chin. She was no more than twenty feet away when she ran forward and took from the pavement a lump of still glistening chewing gum. She popped it in her mouth and began to chew. The little head tilted back defiantly as she looked again in his direction.

Then she was before him, the standard-issue bowl held out

before her. She had chosen him minutes ago, it was a trick they had. Appalled, he had reached into his back pocket for a five-pound note. She looked on with neutral expression as he set it down on top of the coins.

As soon as his hand was clear, the girl picked the note out, rolled it tight into her fist, and said, "Fuck you, mister." She was edging round him.

Stephen put his hand on the hard, narrow shoulder and gripped. "What was that you said?"

The girl turned and pulled away. The eyes had shrunk, the voice was reedy. "I said, Fank you, mister." She was out of reach when she added, "Rich creep!"

Stephen showed empty palms in mild rebuke. He smiled without parting his lips to convey his immunity to the insult. But the kid had resumed her steady, sleepwalker's step along the street. He watched her for a full minute before he lost her in the crowd. She did not glance back.

The Official Commission on Child Care, known to be a pet concern of the prime minister's, had spawned fourteen subcommittees whose task was to make recommendations to the parent body. Their real function, it was said cynically, was to satisfy the disparate ideals of myriad interest groups — the sugar and fast-food lobbies; the garment, toy, formula milk, and firework manufacturers; the charities; the women's organizations; the pedestrian-controlled crosswalk pressure group people — who pressed in on all sides. Few among the opinion-forming classes declined their services. It was generally agreed that the country was full of the wrong sort of people. There were strong opinions about what constituted a desirable citizenry and what should be done to children to procure one for the future. Everyone was on a subcommittee. Even Stephen Lewis, an author of children's books, was on one, entirely through the influence of his friend, Charles Darke, who resigned just after the committees began their work. Stephen's was the Subcommittee on Reading and Writing, under the reptilian Lord Parmenter. Weekly, through the parched months of what was to turn out to be the last decent summer of the twentieth century, Stephen attended meetings in a gloomy room in Whitehall where, he was told, night bombing raids on Germany had been planned in 1944. He would have had much to say on the subjects of reading and writing at other times of his life, but at these sessions he tended to rest his arms on the big polished table, incline his head in an attitude of respectful attention, and say nothing. He was spending a great deal of time alone these days. A roomful of people did not lessen his introspection, as he had hoped, so much as intensify it and give it structure.

He thought mostly about his wife and daughter, and what he was going to do with himself. Or he puzzled over Darke's sudden departure from political life. Opposite was a tall window through which, even in midsummer, no sunlight ever passed. Beyond, a rectangle of tightly clipped grass framed a courtyard, room enough for half a dozen ministerial limousines. Off-duty chauffeurs lounged and smoked and glanced in at the committee without interest. Stephen ran memories and daydreams, what was and what might have been. Or were they running him? Sometimes he delivered his compulsive imaginary speeches, bitter or sad indictments whose every draft was meticulously revised. Meanwhile, he kept half an ear on the proceedings. The committee divided between the theorists, who had done all their thinking long ago, or had had it done for them, and the pragmatists, who hoped to discover what it was they thought in the process of saying it. Politeness was strained, but never broke.

Lord Parmenter presided with dignified and artful banality,

indicating chosen speakers with a flickering swivel of his hooded, lashless eyes, raising a feathery limb to subdue passions, making his rare, slow-loris pronouncements with dry, speckled tongue. Only the dark double-breasted suit betrayed a humanoid provenance. He had an aristocratic way with a commonplace. A long and fractious discussion concerning child development theory had been brought to a useful standstill by his weighty intervention — "Boys will be boys." That children were averse to soap and water, quick to learn, and grew up all too fast were offered up similarly as difficult axioms. Parmenter's banality was disdainful, fearless in proclaiming a man too important, too intact, to care how stupid he sounded. There was no one he needed to impress. He would not stoop to being merely interesting. Stephen did not doubt that he was a very clever man.

The committee members did not find it necessary to get to know one another too well. When the long sessions were over, and while papers and books were shuffled into briefcases, polite conversations began which were sustained along the two-tone corridors and faded into echoes as the committee descended the spiral concrete staircase and dispersed onto many levels of the ministry's subterranean car park.

Through the stifling summer months and beyond, Stephen made the weekly journey to Whitehall. This was his one commitment in a life otherwise free of obligations. Much of this freedom he spent in his underwear, stretched out on the sofa in front of the TV, moodily sipping neat Scotch, reading magazines back to front or watching the Olympic Games. At night the drinking increased. He ate in a local restaurant alone. He made no attempt to contact friends. He never returned the calls monitored on his answering machine. Mostly he was indifferent to the squalor of his flat, the meaty black flies and their leisurely patrols. When he was out he dreaded returning to the deadly alignments of familiar possessions, the way the empty armchairs squatted, the smeared plates and old newspapers at their feet. It was the stubborn conspiracy of objects — lavatory seat, bedsheets, floor dirt — to remain exactly as they had been left. At home too he was never far from his subjects: his daughter, his wife, what to do. But here he lacked the concentration for sustained thought. He daydreamed in fragments, without control, almost without consciousness.

The members made a point of being punctual. Lord Parmenter was always the last to arrive. As he lowered himself into his seat he called the room to order with a soft gargling sound which cleverly transformed itself into his opening words. The clerk to the committee, Peter Canham, sat on his right, with his chair set back from the table to symbolize his detachment. All that was required of Stephen was that he should appear plausibly alert for two and a half hours. This useful framework was familiar from his schooldays, from the hundreds or thousands of classroom hours dedicated to mental wandering. The room itself was familiar. He was at home with the light switches in brown Bakelite, the electric wires in dusty piping tacked inelegantly to the wall. Where he had gone to school, the history room had looked much like this: the same worn-out, generous comfort, the same long battered table which someone still bothered to polish, the vestigial stateliness and dozy bureaucracy mingling soporifically. When Parmenter outlined, with reptilian affability, the morning's work ahead, Stephen heard his teacher's soothing Welsh lilt croon the glories of Charlemagne's court or the cycles of depravity and reform in the medieval papacy. Through the window he saw not an enclosed car park and baking limousines but, as from two

floors up, a rose garden, playing fields, a speckled gray balustrade, then rough, uncultivated land which fell away to oaks
and beeches, and beyond them the great stretch of foreshore
and the blue tidal river, a mile from bank to bank. This was
a lost time and a lost landscape — he had returned once to
discover the trees efficiently felled, the land plowed, and the
estuary spanned by a motorway bridge. And since loss was
his subject, it was an easy move to a frozen, sunny day outside
a supermarket in south London. He was holding his daughter's
hand. She wore a red woolen scarf knitted by his mother and
carried a frayed donkey against her chest. They were moving
towards the entrance. It was a Saturday, there were crowds.
He held her hand tightly.

Parmenter had finished, and now one of the academics was
hesitantly arguing the merits of a newly devised phonetic alphabet. Children would learn to read and write at an earlier
age and with greater enjoyment, the transition to the conventional alphabet promised to be effortless. Stephen held a pencil
in his hand and looked poised to take notes. He was frowning
and moving his head slightly, though whether in agreement
or disbelief it was hard to tell.

Kate was at an age when her burgeoning language and the
ideas it unraveled gave her nightmares. She could not describe
them to her parents but it was clear they contained elements
familiar from her storybooks — a talking fish, a big rock with
a town inside, a lonely monster who longed to be loved. There
had been nightmares through this night. Several times Julie
had got out of bed to comfort her, and then found herself
wakeful till well after dawn. Now she was sleeping in. Stephen
made breakfast and dressed Kate. She was energetic despite
her ordeal, keen to go shopping and ride in the supermarket
cart. The oddity of sunshine on a freezing day intrigued her.

For once she cooperated in being dressed. She stood between his knees while he guided her limbs into her winter underwear. Her body was so compact, so unblemished. He picked her up and buried his face in her belly, pretending to bite her. The little body smelled of bed warmth and milk. She squealed and writhed, and when he put her down she begged him to do it again.

He buttoned her woolen shirt, helped her into a thick sweater, and fastened her dungarees. She began a vague, abstracted chant which meandered between improvisation, nursery rhymes, and snatches of Christmas carols. He sat her in his chair, put her socks on, and laced her boots. When he knelt in front of her she stroked his hair. Like many little girls she was quaintly protective towards her father. Before they left the flat she would make certain he buttoned his coat to the top.

He took Julie some tea. She was half asleep, with her knees drawn up to her chest. She said something which was lost to the pillows. He put his hand under the bedclothes and massaged the small of her back. She rolled over and pulled his face towards her breasts. When they kissed, he tasted in her mouth the thick, metallic flavor of deep sleep. From beyond the bedroom gloom Kate was still intoning her medley. For a moment Stephen was tempted to abandon the shopping and set Kate up with some books in front of the television. He could slip between the heavy covers beside his wife. They had made love just after dawn, but sleepily, inconclusively. She was fondling him now, enjoying his dilemma. He kissed her again.

They had been married six years, a time of slow, fine adjustments to the jostling principles of physical pleasure, domestic duty, and the necessity of solitude. Neglect of one led to diminishment or chaos in the others. Even as he gently pinched Julie's nipple between his finger and thumb he was making his calculations. Following her broken night and a shopping expedition, Kate would be needing sleep by midday. Then they could be sure of uninterrupted time. Later, in the sorry months and years, Stephen was to make efforts to re-enter this moment, to burrow his way back through the folds between events, crawl between the covers, and reverse his decision. But time — not necessarily as it is, for who knows that, but as thought has constituted it — monomaniacally forbids second chances. There is no absolute time, his friend Thelma had told him on occasions, no independent entity. Only our particular and weak understanding. He deferred pleasure, he caved in to duty. He squeezed Julie's hand and stood. In the hall Kate came towards him talking loudly, holding up the scuffed toy donkey. He bent to loop the red scarf twice around her neck. She was on tiptoes to check his coat buttons. They were holding hands even before they were through the front door.

They stepped outdoors as though into a storm. The main road was an arterial route south; its traffic rushed with adrenal ferocity. The bitter, cloudless day was to serve an obsessive memory well with a light of brilliant explicitness, a cynical eye for detail. Lying in the sun by the steps was a flattened Coca-Cola can whose straw remained in place, still three-dimensional. Kate was for rescuing the straw; Stephen forbade it. And there, as though illuminated from within, a dog by a tree was shitting with quivering haunches and uplifted, dreamy expression. The tree was a tired oak whose bark looked freshly carved, its ridges ingenious, sparkling, the ruts in blackest shadow.

It was a two-minute walk to the supermarket, over the four-lane road by a crossing. Near where they waited to cross was a motorbike salesroom, an international meeting place for bikers. Melon-bellied men in worn leathers leaned against or sat astride their stationary machines. When Kate withdrew the knuckle she had been sucking and pointed, the low sun illuminated a smoking finger. However, she found no word to frame what she saw. They crossed at last, in front of an impatient pack of cars that snarled forward the moment they reached the center island. There were crowds, he held her hand tightly as they moved towards the entrance. Amid voices, shouts, the electromechanical rattle at the checkout counters, they found a cart. Kate was smiling hugely to herself as she made herself comfortable in her seat.

The people who used the supermarket divided into two groups, as distinct as tribes or nations. The first lived locally in modernized Victorian terraced houses which they owned. The second lived locally in tower blocks and public housing projects. Those in the first group tended to buy fresh fruit and vegetables, brown bread, coffee beans, fresh fish from a special counter, wine, and spirits, while those in the second group bought tinned or frozen vegetables, baked beans, instant soup, white sugar, cupcakes, beer, spirits, and cigarettes. In the second group were old-age pensioners buying meat for their cats, biscuits for themselves. And there were young mothers, gaunt with fatigue, their mouths set hard round cigarettes, who sometimes cracked at the checkout and gave a child a spanking. In the first group were young, childless couples, flamboyantly dressed, who at worst were a little pressed for time. There were also mothers shopping with their au pairs, and fathers like Stephen, buying fresh salmon, doing their bit.

What else did he buy? Toothpaste, tissues, dishwashing liquid, and best bacon, a leg of lamb, steak, green and red peppers, radicchio, potatoes, tinfoil, a liter of Scotch. And who was there when his hand reached for these items? Someone who followed him as he pushed Kate along the stacked aisles, who stood a few paces off when he stopped, who pretended to be interested in a label and then continued when he did? He had been back a thousand times, seen his own hand, a shelf, the goods accumulate, heard Kate chattering on, and tried to move his eyes, lift them against the weight of time, to find that shrouded figure at the periphery of vision, the one who was always to the side and slightly behind, who, filled with a strange desire, was calculating odds, or simply waiting. But time held his sight forever on his mundane errands, and all about him shapes without definition drifted and dissolved, lost to categories.

Fifteen minutes later they were at the checkout. There were eight parallel counters. He joined a small queue nearest the door because he knew the girl at the till worked fast. There were three people ahead of him when he stopped the cart, and there was no one behind him when he turned to lift Kate from her seat. She was enjoying herself and was reluctant to be disturbed. She whined and hooked her foot into her seat. He had to lift her high to get her clear. He noted her irritability with absent-minded satisfaction — it was a sure sign of her tiredness. By the time this little struggle was over, there were two people ahead of them, one of whom was about to leave. He came round to the front of the cart to unload it onto the conveyor belt. Kate was holding onto the wide bar at the other end of the cart, pretending to push. There was no one behind her. Now the person immediately ahead of Stephen, a man with a curved back, was about to pay for several tins of dogfood. Stephen lifted the first items onto the belt. When he straightened he might have been conscious of a figure in a dark coat behind Kate. But it was hardly an awareness at all, it was the weakest suspicion brought to life by a desperate memory.

The coat could have been a dress or a shopping bag or his own invention. He was intent on ordinary tasks, keen to finish them. He was barely a conscious being at all.

The man with the dogfood was leaving. The checkout girl was already at work, the fingers of one hand flickering over the keypad while the other drew Stephen's items towards her. As he took the salmon from the cart, he glanced down at Kate and winked. She copied him, but clumsily, wrinkling her nose and closing both eyes. He set the fish down and asked the girl for a shopping bag. She reached under a shelf and pulled one out. He took it and turned. Kate was gone. There was no one in the queue behind him. Unhurriedly he pushed the cart clear, thinking she had ducked down behind the end of the counter. Then he took a few paces and glanced down the only aisle she would have had time to reach. He stepped back and looked to his left and right. On one side there were lines of shoppers, on the other a clear space, then the chrome turnstile, then the automatic doors onto the pavement. There may have been a figure in a coat hurrying away from him, but at that time Stephen was looking for a three-year-old child, and his immediate worry was the traffic.

This was a theoretical, precautionary anxiety. As he shouldered past shoppers and emerged onto the broad pavement, he knew he would not see her there. Kate was not adventurous in this way. She was not a strayer. She was too sociable, she preferred the company of the one she was with. She was also terrified of the road. He turned back and relaxed. She had to be in the shop, and she could come to no real harm there. He expected to see her emerging from behind the lines of shoppers at the checkouts. It was easy enough to overlook a child in the first flash of concern, to look too hard, too quickly. Still, a sickness and a tightening at the base of the throat, an unpleasant lightness in the feet, were with him as he went back. When he had walked past all the tills, ignoring the girl at his, who was irritably trying to attract his attention, a chill rose to the top of his stomach. At a controlled run — he was not yet past caring how foolish he looked — he went down all the aisles, past mountains of oranges, toilet rolls, soup. It was not until he was back at his starting point that he abandoned all propriety, filled his constricted lungs, and shouted Kate's name.

Now he was taking long strides, bawling her name as he pounded the length of an aisle and headed once more for the door. Faces were turning towards him. There was no mistaking him for one of the drunks who blundered in to buy cider. His fear was too evident, too forceful, it filled the impersonal, fluorescent space with unignorable human warmth. Within moments all shopping around him had ceased. Baskets and carts were set aside, people were converging and saying Kate's name, and somehow, in no time at all, it was generally known that she was three, that she was last seen at the checkout, that she wore green dungarees and carried a toy donkey. The faces of mothers were strained, alert. Several people had seen the little girl riding in the cart. Someone knew the color of her sweater. The anonymity of the city store turned out to be frail, a thin crust beneath which people observed, judged, remembered. A group of shoppers surrounding Stephen moved towards the door. At his side was the girl from the checkout, her face rigid with intent. There were other members of the supermarket hierarchy, in brown coats, white coats, blue suits, who suddenly were no longer warehousemen or submanagers or company representatives but fathers, potential or real. They were all out on the pavement now, some crowding round Stephen asking questions or offering consolation while others, more usefully, set off in different directions to look in the doorways of nearby shops.

The lost child was everyone's property. But Stephen was alone. He looked through and beyond the kindly faces pressing in. They were irrelevant. Their voices did not reach him, they were impediments to his field of vision. They were blocking his view of Kate. He had to swim through them, push them aside to get to her. He had no air, he could not think. He heard himself pronounce the word *stolen*, and the word was taken up and spread to the peripheries, to passersby who were drawn to the commotion. The till girl with the fast fingers who had looked so strong was crying. Stephen had time to feel momentary disappointment in her. As if summoned by the word he had spoken, a white police car spattered with mud cruised to a halt at the curb. Official confirmation of disaster nauseated him. Something was rising in his throat and he bent double. Perhaps he was sick, but he had no memory of it. The next thing was the supermarket again, and this time rules of appropriateness, of social order, had selected the people at his side — a manager, a young woman who might have been an assistant, a submanager, and two policemen. It was suddenly quiet.

They were heading briskly towards the rear of the vast floor space. It was some moments before Stephen realized that he was being led rather than followed. The shop had been cleared of customers. Through the plate-glass window on his right he saw another policeman outside, surrounded by shoppers, taking notes. The manager was talking quickly into the silence, partly hypothesizing, partly complaining. The child — he knows her name, Stephen thought, but his status prevents him from using it — the child might have wandered into the loading bay area. They should have thought of that first. The cold-store door was sometimes left open, however often he remonstrated with his subordinates.

They quickened their pace. An unintelligible voice spoke in

short bursts over a policeman's radio. By the cheese section they passed through a door into an area where all pretenses were dropped, where the plastic-tiled floor gave way to one of concrete in which mica sparkled coldly, and where light came from high, bare bulbs hung from an invisible ceiling. There was a fork lift parked by a mountain of flattened cardboard boxes. Stepping over a dirty puddle of milk, the manager was hurrying towards the cold-store door, which stood ajar.

They followed him into a low, cramped room in which two aisles stretched away into semidarkness. Tins and boxes were piled untidily into racks along the sides, and down the center, suspended from meat hooks, were giant carcasses. The group divided into two and set off down the aisles. Stephen went with the policemen. The cold air penetrated drily to the back of the nose and tasted of chilled tin. They walked slowly, looking into the spaces behind the boxes in the racks. One of the policemen wanted to know how long someone could last in here. Through the chinks in the meat curtain which divided them, Stephen saw the manager glance at his subordinate. The younger man cleared his throat and answered tactfully that as long as you kept moving you had nothing to worry about. The vapor billowed from his mouth. Stephen knew that if they found Kate in here she would be dead. But the relief he felt when the two groups met at the far end was abstract. He had become detached in an energetic, calculating way. If she was to be found, then they would find her, because he was prepared to do nothing else but search; if she was not to be found, then in time that would have to be faced in a sensible, rational manner. But not now.

They stepped out into an illusory tropical warmth and made for the manager's office. The policemen took out their notebooks and Stephen told his story, which was energetic both in delivery and in attention to detail. He was sufficiently removed from his own feelings to take pleasure in succinctness of expression, the skillful marshaling of relevant facts. He was watching himself, and saw a man under stress behaving with admirable self-control. He could forget Kate in the meticulous detailing of her clothing, the accurate portrayal of her features. He admired also the dogged, routine questioning of the policemen, the oil and leather smell of their polished gun holsters. They and he were men united in the face of unspeakable difficulty. One of the policemen spoke his description of Kate into the radio and they heard a distorted answer from a patrol car in the neighborhood. That was all very reassuring. Stephen was entering a state close to elation. The manager's assistant was speaking to him with a concern he felt was quite misplaced. She was pressing her hand against his forearm and urging him to drink the tea she had brought. The manager was standing just outside his office, complaining to an underling that supermarkets were the favored territory of child-snatchers. The assistant pushed the door shut briskly with her foot. The sudden movement released perfume from the folds of her sober clothes and caused Stephen to think of Julie. He confronted a blackness that emanated from inside the front of his head. He took hold of the side of his chair and waited, let his mind empty, and then, when he felt he had gained control, stood. The questioning was over. The policemen were folding away their notebooks and standing too. The assistant offered to escort him home, but Stephen shook his head vigorously.

Then, without any apparent interval, any connecting events, he was outside the supermarket, waiting at the crossing with half a dozen other people. In his hand was a full shopping bag. He remembered that he had not paid. The salmon and tinfoil were free gifts, compensation. The traffic slowed reluctantly and stopped. He crossed with the other shoppers and tried to absorb the insult of the world's normality. He saw how rigorously simple it was — he had gone shopping with his daughter, lost her, and was now returning without her to tell his wife. The bikers were still there, and so too, further on, was the Coca-Cola can and its straw. Even the dog was under the same tree. On his way up the stairs he paused by a broken step. There was loud crashing music in his head, a great orchestral tinnitus whose dissonance faded as he stood there holding the banister and started up again the moment he continued.

He opened the front door and listened. The air and light in the flat told him that Julie was still asleep. He took off his coat. When he lifted it to hang it up, his stomach contracted and a bolt — he thought of it as a black bolt — of morning coffee shot into his mouth. He spat into his cupped hands and went into the kitchen to wash. He had to step over Kate's discarded pajamas. That seemed relatively easy. He entered the bedroom with no thought for what he was about to do or say there. He lowered himself onto the edge of the bed. Julie rolled over to face him but she did not open her eyes. She found his hand. Hers was hot, unbearably so. She said something sleepily about how cold his hand was. She drew it towards her and tucked it under her chin. Still she did not open her eyes. She luxuriated in the security of his presence.

Stephen gazed down on his wife and certain stock phrases — "a devoted mother," "passionately attached to her child," "a loving parent" — seemed to swell with fresh meaning; these were useful, decent phrases, he thought, tested by time. A neat curl of black hair lay on her cheekbone, just below her eye. She was a calm, watchful woman, she had a lovely smile, she loved him fiercely and liked to tell him. He had built his life round their intimacy and come to depend on it. She was a violinist, she taught at the Guildhall. With three friends she had formed a string quartet. They were getting bookings and they had had one small, favorable notice in a national newspaper. The future was, had been, rich. The fingers of her left hand with their pads of toughened skin were stroking his wrist. He was looking down at her from an immense distance now, from several hundred feet. He could see the bedroom, the Edwardian apartment block, the tarred roofs of its back additions with their lopsided, crusty cisterns, the mess of south London, the hazy curvature of the earth. Julie was barely more than a speck among the tangle of sheets. He was rising still higher, and faster. At least, he thought, from up here where the air was thin and the city below was taking on geometric design, his feelings would not show, he could retain some composure.

It was then that she opened her eyes and found his face. It took her some seconds to read what was there before she scrambled upright in the bed and made a noise of incredulity, a little yelp on a harsh intake of breath. For a moment explanations were neither possible nor necessary.

In general, the committee was not well disposed towards a phonetic alphabet. Colonel Jack Tackle of the End Domestic Violence Campaign had said it sounded like a bloody nonsense. A young woman called Rachael Murray had delivered a tense rebuttal whose reliance on the language of professional linguistics could not disguise her quivering contempt. Now Tessa Spankey beamed about her. She was a publisher of children's books, a large woman with dimples at the base of each finger. Her face was double-chinned and friendly, all freckles and crow's-feet. She took care to include each of them in her tender gaze. She spoke slowly and reassuringly, as though to a group of nervous infants. There was no language in the world, she said, which was not arduous to learn to read and write. If learning could be fun, that was all very well. But fun was peripheral. Teachers and parents should embrace the fact that at the heart of language learning was difficulty. Triumph over difficulty was what gave children their dignity and a sense of mental discipline. The English language, she said, was a minefield of irregularity, of exceptions outnumbering rules. But it had to be crossed, and crossing it was work. Teachers were too afraid of unpopularity, too fond of sugaring pills. They should accept difficulty, celebrate it, and make their pupils do likewise. There was only one way to learn to spell and that was through exposure, immersion in the written word. How else — and she rattled off a well-rehearsed list — do we learn the spellings of *through, tough, bough, cough,* and *though?* Mrs. Spankey's maternal gaze raked the attentive faces. Diligence, she said, application, discipline, and jolly hard work.

There was a murmur of approbation. The academic who had proposed the phonetic alphabet began to talk of dyslexia, the sale of state schools, the housing shortage. There were spontaneous groans. The mild-mannered fellow pressed on. Two thirds of eleven-year-olds in inner-city schools, he said, were illiterate. Parmenter intervened with lizardlike alacrity. The needs of special groups were beyond the committee's terms of reference. At his side, Canham was nodding. Means and ends, not pathologies, were the committee's concerns. The discussion became fragmentary. For some reason a vote was proposed.

Stephen raised his hand for what he knew to be a useless alphabet. It hardly mattered, for he was crossing a broad strip of cracked and potholed asphalt that separated two tower blocks. He carried with him a folder of photographs and lists of names and addresses, neatly typed and alphabetically ordered. The photographs — enlarged holiday snaps — he showed to anyone he could interest. The lists, compiled in the library from back numbers of local newspapers, were of parents whose children had died in the preceding six months. His theory, one of many, was that Kate had been stolen to replace a lost child. He knocked on doors and spoke to mothers who were first puzzled, then hostile. He visited baby sitters. He walked up and down the shopping streets with his photographs displayed. He loitered by the supermarket, and by the entrance to the drugstore next door. He went further afield till his search area was three miles across. He anesthetized himself with activity.

He went everywhere alone, setting out each day shortly after the late winter dawn. The police had lost interest in the case after a week. Riots in a northern suburb, they said, were stretching their resources. And Julie stayed at home. She had special leave from the college. When he left in the morning she was sitting in the armchair in the bedroom, facing the cold fireplace. That was where he found her when he came back at night and turned on the lights.

Initially there had been bustle of the bleakest kind: interviews with senior policemen, teams of constables, tracker dogs, some newspaper interest, more explanations, panicky grief. During that time Stephen and Julie had clung to one another, sharing dazed rhetorical questions, awake in bed all night, theorizing hopefully one moment, despairing the next. But that was before time, the heartless accumulation of days, had clarified the absolute, bitter truth. Silence drifted in and thickened. Kate's clothes and toys still lay about the flat, her bed was still unmade. Then one afternoon the clutter was gone. Stephen found the bed stripped and three bulging plastic sacks by the door in her bedroom. He was angry with Julie, disgusted by what

he took to be a feminine self-destructiveness, a willful defeat-
ism. But he could not speak to her about it. There was no
room for anger, no openings. They moved like figures in a
quagmire, with no strength for confrontation. Suddenly their
sorrows were separate, insular, incommunicable. They went
their different ways, he with his lists and daily trudging, she
in her armchair, lost to deep, private grief. Now there was no
mutual consolation, no touching, no love. Their old intimacy,
their habitual assumption that they were on the same side, was
dead. They remained huddled over their separate losses, and
unspoken resentments began to grow.

At the end of a day on the streets, when he turned for home,
nothing pained Stephen more than the knowledge of his wife
sitting in the dark, of how she would barely stir to acknowledge his return, and how he would have neither the good will
nor the ingenuity to break through the silence. He suspected —
and it turned out later he was correct — that she took his efforts
to be a typically masculine evasion, an attempt to mask feelings
behind displays of competence and organization and physical
effort. The loss had driven them to the extremes of their per-
sonalities. They had discovered a degree of mutual intolerance
which sadness and shock made insurmountable. They could
no longer bear to eat together. He ate standing up in sandwich
bars, anxious not to lose time, reluctant to sit down and listen
to his thoughts. As far as he knew she ate nothing at all. Early
on he brought home bread and cheese, which over the days
quietly grew their separate molds in the unvisited kitchen. A
meal together would have implied a recognition and acceptance
of their diminished family.

It came to the point where Stephen could not bring himself
to look at Julie. It was not only that he saw haggard traces of
Kate or himself mirrored in her face. It was the inertia, the

collapse of will, the near ecstatic suffering which disgusted him and threatened to undermine his efforts. He was going to find his daughter and murder her abductor. He had only to keep walking, remain attentive, and he would surely enter the force field that would warn him that she was nearby. He had only to act on the correct impulse and show the photograph to the right person and he would be led to her. If there were more daylight hours, if he could resist the temptation which was growing each morning to keep his head under the blankets, if he could walk faster, maintain his concentration, remember to glance behind now and then, waste less time eating sandwiches, trust his intuition, go up side streets, and move faster, cover more ground, run even, run . . .

Parmenter was standing, faltering as he clipped his silver pen into the inside pocket of his jacket. As he made towards the door which Canham was holding open for him, the old man smiled a general farewell. The committee members shuffled their papers and began the customary measured conversations that would see them out of the building. Stephen walked down the hot corridor with the academic who had been so convincingly voted down. His name was Morley. In his civilized, tentative manner he was explaining how the discredited alphabet systems of the past made his work all the harder. Stephen knew that soon he would be alone again. But even now he could not help drifting off, could not prevent himself reflecting that the situation had deteriorated to such an extent that he felt no particular emotion when he returned from his searching one late February afternoon and found Julie's armchair empty. A note on the floor gave the name and phone number of a retreat in the Chilterns. There was no other message. He wandered about the flat, turning on lights, staring in at neglected rooms, little stage sets about to be struck.

Finally he arrived back at Julie's chair, loitered by it a moment, resting his hand lightly on its back as if calculating the odds of some dangerous act. At last he stirred himself, took two paces round the chair and sat down. He stared into the dark grate where spent matches lay at odd angles by a piece of tinfoil; minutes went by, time in which to feel the chair's bunched material yield Julie's contours for his own, empty minutes like all the others. Then he slumped, he was still for the first time in weeks. He remained that way for hours, all through the night, sometimes dozing briefly, when awake never stirring or shifting his gaze from the grate. All the while, it seemed, there was something gathering in the silence about him, a slow surge of realization mounting with a sleek, tidal force which did not break or explode dramatically but which bore him in the small hours to the first full flood of understanding of the true nature of his loss. Everything before had been fantasy, a routine and frenetic mimicry of sorrow. Just before dawn he began to cry, and it was from this moment in the semidarkness that he was to date his time of mourning.

❧ 2 ❧

"Make it clear to him that the clock cannot be argued
with and that when it is time to leave for school, for
Daddy to go to work, for Mummy to attend to her
duties, then these changes are as incontestable as the
tides."

— from *The Authorized Child-Care Handbook*, HMSO

THAT STEPHEN LEWIS had a lot of money and was famous
among schoolchildren was the consequence of a clerical error,
a moment's inattention in the operation of the internal post at
Gott's, which had brought a parcel of typescript onto the wrong
desk. That Stephen no longer mentioned this error — it was
many years old now — was partly due to the royalty checks
and advances that had flowed from Gott's and his many foreign
publishers ever since, and partly to the acceptance of fate that
comes with one's first aging. In his mid-twenties it had seemed
arbitrarily humorous that he should be a successful writer of
children's books, for there were still many other things he
might yet have become. These days he could not imagine being
anything else.

What else could he be? The old friends of his student days,
the aesthetic and political experimenters, the visionary drug-
takers, had all settled for even less. A couple of acquaintances,

once truly free men, were resigned to a lifetime of teaching English to foreigners. Some were facing middle age exhaustedly teaching remedial English or "life skills" to reluctant adolescents in far-flung secondary schools. These were the luckier ones who had found jobs. Others cleaned hospital floors or drove taxis. One had qualified for a begging badge. Stephen dreaded ever meeting her in the street. All these promising spirits, nurtured, brought to excited life by the study of English literature, from which they culled their quick slogans — Energy is perpetual delight; Damn braces, bless relaxes — had been disgorged from libraries in the late sixties and early seventies intent on inward journeys, or eastward ones in painted buses. They had returned home when the world grew smaller and more serious to service Education, now a dingy, shrunken profession; schools were up for sale to private investors, and the attendance requirements were soon to be reduced.

The idea that the more educated the population was, the more readily its problems could be solved had quietly faded away. It belonged with the demise of a more general principle, that on the whole life would be better for more and more people and that it was the responsibility of governments to stage-manage this drama of realized potential, widening possibilities. The cast of improvers had once been immense, and there had always been jobs for types like Stephen and his friends. Teachers, museum keepers, mummers and actors, itinerant storytellers — a huge company, and all bankrolled by the state. Now governmental responsibilities had been redefined in simpler, purer terms: to keep order, and to defend the state against its enemies. For a while Stephen had kept alive a vague ambition to be a teacher in a state school. He saw himself, tall and craggy by the blackboard, before him a silent, respectful class intimidated by his tendency to sudden sarcasm, leaning forward to catch his every word. Now he knew how lucky he had been. He remained the author of children's books, and half forgot that it was all a mistake.

One year after leaving University College, Stephen had returned to London with amoebic dysentery after a hashish-befuddled tour of Turkey, Afghanistan, and the Northwest Frontier Province to discover that the work ethic he and his generation had worked so hard to destroy was still strong within him. He craved order and purpose. He took a cheap room, found a job as a filing clerk in a news-clipping agency, and set about writing a novel. Each evening he worked four or five hours, delighted by the romance, the nobility of the undertaking. He was impregnable against the dullness of his job; he had a secret which was growing at one thousand words a day. And he had all the usual fantasies. He was Thomas Mann, he was James Joyce, perhaps he was William Shakespeare. He added to the excitement of his endeavor by working by the light of two candles.

It was his intention to write of his travels, in a novel called *Hashish,* about hippies stabbed to death in their sleeping bags, a nicely brought-up girl sentenced to a lifetime in a Turkish jail, mystic pretentiousness, drug-enhanced sex, amoebic dysentery. First of all he needed to get down the background of his main character, something about his childhood to show the physical and moral distance he had to travel. But the opening chapter stubbornly refused to end. It took on a life of its own, and this was how Stephen came to write a novel based on a summer holiday he had spent in his eleventh year with two girl cousins, a novel of short trousers and short hair for the boys and Alice bands and frocks tucked into underpants for the girls, with unspoken yearnings, coyly interlacing fingers in place of crazed sex, bicycles with wicker hampers instead of Day-Glo Volkswagen buses, and set not in Jalalabad but just outside Reading. It was all done in three months and he called it *Lemonade*.

For a week he fingered and shuffled his typescript, worrying that it was too short. Then one Monday morning he pleaded ill, made a photocopy, and delivered it personally to the Bloomsbury offices of Gott, the famous literary publisher. As is usual, he heard nothing for a very long time. When the letter finally arrived it was not from Charles Darke, the young senior editor profiled in the Sunday newspapers, rescuer of Gott's faltering reputation. It was from a Miss Amanda Rien, pronounced, she said with a squeaky laugh when she ushered him into her office, not as a French word, but to rhyme with *mean*.

Stephen sat with his shins pressed tight against Miss Rien's desk, for the room had once been a broom closet. There were no windows. On the walls, instead of framed black-and-white photographs of the early-twentieth-century giants who had made great the name of Gott, was a portrait not of Evelyn Waugh, surely, but of a frog in a three-piece suit leaning on a cane by the balustrade of a country house. Elsewhere, tacked to the few feet of wall space, there were pictures of teddy bears, half a dozen of them at least, attempting to jump-start a fire engine, a mouse in a bikini holding a gun to its head, and a grim-faced crow with a stethoscope round its neck, taking the pulse of a pale young boy who appeared to have fallen out of a tree.

Miss Rien sat less than four feet away, gazing at Stephen with proprietorial wonder. He smiled back uncomfortably, and lowered his gaze. Was this really his first, she wanted to know. Everyone at Gott's was thrilled, absolutely thrilled. He nodded, suspecting a terrible mistake. He did not know enough about publishers to speak out, and the last thing he wanted was to appear foolish. He was reassured when Miss Rien said that Charles knew he was here and was dying to meet him. Minutes later the door snapped open and Darke, without leaving the corridor, leaned in and shook Stephen's hand. He spoke rapidly, and without introduction. It was a brilliant book, and of course he wanted to do it. Of course he did. But he had to dash. New York and Frankfurt were on the line. But they would have lunch. And soon. And congratulations. The door snapped shut and Stephen turned to find Miss Rien studying his face for the first signs of adulation. She spoke solemnly and with lowered voice. A great man. A great man and a great publisher. There was nothing to do but agree.

He returned to his room excited and insulted. As a potential Joyce, Mann, or Shakespeare he belonged without question to the European cultural tradition, the grown-up one. It was true that from the start he had been anxious to be understood. He had written in a simple, precise English. He had wanted to be accessible, but not to everyone. After much thought he decided to do nothing until he had met Darke again. In the meantime, to complicate his feelings further, there arrived in the post a contract and the offer of an advance for two thousand pounds, the equivalent of two years' wages. He made inquiries and discovered this to be an exceptional sum for a first novel. The press-clipping agency was unbearably tedious now that he had finished writing. For eight hours a day he cut articles out of newspapers, stamped them with the date, and filed them. The people in the office were stupefied by the work they did. He was longing to give his notice. Several times he took out his pen, preparing to sign and take the money, but out of the corner of his eye he saw a jeering, ironic crowd of teddy bears, mice, and crows welcoming him to their ranks.

And when at last the time came for him to put on the tie

he had bought for the occasion, the first he had worn since leaving school, and voice his confusion to Darke in the discreet quiet of a restaurant, over the most expensive meal Stephen had ever eaten, nothing was clarified at all. Darke listened, nodding impatiently whenever Stephen neared the end of a sentence. Before Stephen had finished, Darke set down his soup spoon, placed his small, smooth hand on the younger man's wrist, and explained in a kindly manner, as though to a child, that the distinction between adult and children's fiction was indeed a fiction itself. It was entirely false, a mere convenience. It was bound to be, when the greatest of writers all possessed a childlike vision, a simplicity of approach, however complicatedly stated, that made adult genius at one with infancy. And conversely — Stephen was pulling his hand free — the greatest so-called children's books were precisely those that spoke to both children and adults, to the incipient adult within the child, to the forgotten child within the adult.

Darke was enjoying his speech. To be in a famous restaurant making expansive remarks to a young writer was one of the more desirable perquisites of his profession. Stephen finished his shrimp cocktail and sat back to watch and listen. Darke had sandy hair with an ungovernable plume that rose from the back of the crown. It was a habit with him to feel for this tuft and press it flat with his palm while he spoke. It sprang up when he let it alone.

For all his worldly confidence, dark suit, and handmade shirt, Darke was only six years older than Stephen. It was a crucial six years, however, dividing, on Darke's part, a reverence for maturity that had made it a teenage ambition to appear twice one's age, from Stephen's conviction that maturity was treachery, timidity, fatigue, and that youth was a blessed state to be embraced for as long as was socially and biologically feasible. At the time of their first lunch together, Darke had been married to Thelma seven years. The big house in Eaton Square was solidly established. The then almost-valuable oil paintings of sea battles and hunting scenes were already in place. So too were the thick clean towels in the guest bedroom, the cleaning lady who came four hours every day and spoke no English. While Stephen and his friends were in Goa and Kabul with their Frisbees and their hashish pipes, Charles and Thelma had a man who parked their car, a telephone answering service, dinner parties, hardback books. They were grown-ups. Stephen lived in a room and could get all his stuff into two suitcases. His novel was suitable for children.

And there was more than the Eaton Square house. Darke had already owned and sold a record company. By the time he left Cambridge it had been clear to all but the commercially astute that popular music was the exclusive preserve of the young. The astute remembered middle England, the parents who had lived through the Depression and had fought in a world war. With these nightmares behind them they needed sweetness, warmth, and an occasional wistfulness in their music. Darke specialized in "easy listening," favorite classics, evergreen melodies orchestrated for two hundred strings.

He was also unfashionably successful in his choice of a wife twelve years his senior. Thelma was a lecturer in physics at Birkbeck with a respected thesis recently completed on — as far as any gossip columnist could tell — the nature of time. She was not the obvious wife for a young millionaire in the kitsch music business, a man young enough, some said cruelly, to be her son. Thelma talked her husband into starting a literary book club and the success of this brought him to the dusty firm of Gott's, which within two years was profitable for the first time in a quarter of a century. It was in his fourth year there that Darke took Stephen to lunch, but a further five were to pass —by which time Darke was the head of an independent television company and Stephen was something of a limited success himself — before the two men were close friends and Stephen, his claim on youth relinquished, became a regular visitor at Eaton Square.

The arrival of fresh plates, the perfunctory sampling of a different wine did not interrupt for one moment Darke's urgent, kindly, self-loving speech. He spoke rapidly, with a kind of hunted assurance, as though he were addressing a meeting of skeptical shareholders, as though he feared the silence that would return him to his own thoughts. It was a long time before Stephen understood from what depth of feeling he was speaking. At the time it felt like a hard sell in which the publisher made good and instinctive use of his author's Christian name.

"Stephen, listen. Stephen, talk to a ten-year-old in midsummer about Christmas. You could be talking to an adolescent about his retirement plans, his pension. For children, childhood is timeless. It's always the present. Everything is in the present tense. Of course they have memories. Of course time shifts a little for them and Christmas comes round in the end. But they don't *feel* it. Today is what they feel, and when they say 'When I grow up . . .' there's always an edge of disbelief — how could they ever be other than what they are? Now you say *Lemonade* wasn't written for children, and I believe you, Stephen. Like all good writers, you wrote it for yourself. And this is my point. It was your ten-year-old self you addressed. This book is not for children, it's for a child, and that child is you. *Lemonade* is a message from you to a previous self which will never cease to exist. And the message is bitter. That is what makes it such a disturbing book to read. When Mandy

Rien's daughter read it, she wept — bitter tears, but useful tears too, Stephen. Other kids have reacted in the same way. You've spoken directly to children. Whether you wanted to or not, you've communicated with them across the abyss that separates the child from the adult and you've given them a first, ghostly intimation of their mortality. Reading you, they get wind of the idea that they are finite as children. Instead of just being told, they really understand that it won't last, it can't last, that sooner or later they're finished, done for, that their childhood is not forever. You put over to them something shocking and sad about grown-ups, about those who have ceased to be children. Something dried up, powerless, a boredom, a taking for granted. They understand from you that it's all heading towards them, as certain as Christmas. It's a sad message, but it's a true one. This is a book for children through the eyes of an adult."

Charles Darke took a hearty pull of the wine he had tested with such absent-minded discernment a couple of minutes before. He cocked his head, savoring the implications of his own words. Then, raising his glass, he emptied it and repeated, "A sad message, but very, very true." Stephen looked up sharply at what sounded like a catch in his publisher's voice.

Apart from the two weeks that were the subject of his novel, Stephen's childhood had been pleasantly dull, despite its exotic locations. If he were to send back a message now, it would be one of dour encouragement: things will improve — very slowly. But was there a message for adults too?

Darke's mouth was crammed with sweetbreads. He waved his fork in the air in tight little circles, desperate to speak; he succeeded finally through a garlic-scented gasp which temporarily altered the flavor of Stephen's salmon. "Of course. But it won't change lives. I'll sell three thousand copies and

you'll get some decent reviews. But package it for kids . . ."
Darke flopped back in his seat and raised his glass.

Stephen shook his head and spoke softly. "I won't permit
it. I'll never permit it."

Turner Malbert did the illustrations in tasteful, limpid wa-
tercolors. In the week of publication, a famous child psy-
chologist appeared on television to make an impassioned attack
on the book. It was more than any child should be expected
to deal with, it would unhinge latently unstable minds. Other
experts defended it; a handful of librarians boosted its currency
by refusing to stock it. For a month or two it was a topic at
dinner parties. *Lemonade* sold a quarter of a million copies in
hardback, and eventually several million around the world.
Stephen gave up his job, bought a fast car and a cavernous,
high-ceilinged flat in south London, and generated a tax bill
that two years later made it a virtual necessity to publish his
second novel as a children's book too.

In retrospect, the events of Stephen's year, the committee year,
were to seem organized round a single outcome. Living through
that year, however, he felt it to be empty time, dry of meaning
or purpose. His usual diffidence was spectacularly heightened.
For example, the second day of the Olympic Games brought
a sudden threat of global extinction; for twelve hours things
went quite out of control, and Stephen, sprawling on the
sofa in his underwear for the heat, did not much care either
way.

Two sprinters, a Russian and an American, quivering, whip-
petlike men, rubbed shoulders at the starting blocks and became irritable. The American struck out with a clenched fist,
the other lashed back and seriously scratched the first man's
eye. Violence, and the idea of violence, spread outward then

upward through an intricate system of command. First team-mates, then coaches tried to intervene, lost their tempers, and became involved in the fighting. The few Russian and American spectators in the stands sought one another out. There was an ugly scene with a broken bottle, and within minutes a young American — unfortunately an off-duty soldier — had bled to death. On the track two high officials representing the opposing powers were pulling at one another's blazers and a lapel was badly torn. A starting pistol was fired in a Russian woman's face and a second eye was lost, an eye for an eye. There was shoving and snarling in the press box.

Within half an hour both teams had withdrawn from the games and at rival press conferences were exchanging insults of scatological intensity. Very soon the murderer of the soldier was apprehended and allegations were made that he had KGB connections and military motives. Between the respective embassies there was an exchange of fiercely worded notes. The American president, newly installed and with something of a sprinter's constitution himself, was anxious to demonstrate that he was not the weakling in foreign policy that his opponents frequently claimed, and was casting about for something to do. He was still pondering when the Russians astonished the world by closing the border crossing at Helmstedt.

In the United States this act was blamed on the prevarications of a docile president, who now silenced his critics by bringing his country's nuclear forces to their most advanced state of readiness. The Russians did likewise. Nuclear submarines slid quietly to their allotted firing points, silos gaped open, missiles bristled in the hot shrubbery of rural Oxfordshire and in the birch forests of the Carpathians. Newspaper columns and television screens filled with professors of deterrence who urged the importance of getting the missiles in the air before they were destroyed on the ground. In a matter of hours the super-markets of Great Britain were emptied of sugar, tea, baked beans, and soft toilet rolls. The confrontation lasted half a day, until the nonaligned nations initiated a supervised, simultaneous scaling-down of nuclear readiness. Life on earth was to continue after all and so, with much fanfaring of the Olympic spirit, the hundred-meters heat was resumed, and there was planetary relief when it was won by a neutral Swede.

It may have been the freakishly good summer or the Scotch he drank from late morning on that made him feel better than he knew he really was, but Stephen honestly did not mind that life on earth was to continue. It was much like a soccer final played between two foreign teams. The drama held him while it unfolded, but he had no stake in the result; for him it could go either way. The universe was enormous, he thought wearily, intelligent life was spread thinly, but the planets involved were probably innumerable. Among those who stumbled across the convertibility of matter and energy there were bound to be quite a few who blew themselves to bits, and they were likely to be the ones who did not deserve to survive. The dilemma wasn't human, he thought lazily, scratching himself through his underpants, it was in the very structure of matter itself, and there was nothing much to be done about that.

Similarly, other, more personal events, some of which were rather odd or intense, fascinated him while they were happening, but at one remove, as though someone else, not he, were involved, and afterwards he gave them little thought and certainly made no connections between them. They were background to the real business of steady, supine drinking, of avoiding friends and work, of failing to concentrate whenever he was drawn into conversation, of being unable to read more than twenty lines of print before wandering again, fantasizing, remembering.

And when Darke resigned — the official announcement came
two days after the Parmenter Committee launch — Stephen
went round to Eaton Square because Thelma phoned and asked
him. He became involved not because he was an old friend
and naturally concerned, nor because he owed Charles and
Thelma favors. He made, or seemed to make, no decision in
the matter at all; his friends needed a witness, someone they
could explain themselves to, who could stand in for the outside
world. Although he was chosen, he was later to question the
extent of his own passivity; the Darkes had many friends, after
all, but perhaps Stephen was the only suitable observer of what
Charles was to enact.

Two hours after Thelma phoned, Stephen set out to walk to
Eaton Square from Stockwell by way of Chelsea Bridge. The
warm early-evening air was smooth in the throat, and the
pavements outside pubs were thick with beer drinkers, dark-
skinned and talkative, apparently carefree. The national character had been transformed by a two-month heat wave. Halfway across the bridge he stopped to read the evening newspaper.
The resignation had made the front page, but not the headlines.
A boxed inset at the foot of the page spoke of ill health and,
self-consciously scandalous, hinted at some kind of breakdown. The prime minister was said to be "vaguely annoyed"
at not having been warned. The gossip column ran a short
paragraph which said that Darke was too unpolitical, too relaxed in his attitude ever to have expected high office. The
prime minister distrusted his past connection with books. Only
close friends, the piece concluded, would be much moved by
his departure. Aware of two beggars bearing down on him,
men in long coats despite the warmth, Stephen folded his paper
and continued across the bridge.

There had been an evening in a Greek restaurant many years

before when Darke had initiated a parlor game. He was contemplating moving out of television management, at which he had been a qualified success, and into politics. But which party should he join? Elated, Darke sat next to Julie, pouring wine, making a show of being firm with the waiter, doing everyone's ordering. The conversation was joky and mock cynical, but embodied some truth. Darke had no political convictions, only managerial skill and great ambition. He could join any party. A friend of Julie's from New York was taking the matter seriously and insisting that the choice lay between an emphasis on the collectivity of experience or its uniqueness. Darke spread his hands and said that he could argue for both. For the support of the weak, for the advancement of the strong. The more fundamental question was — and here he paused while someone else completed his sentence — *Who do you know who can get you selected as a candidate?* Darke laughed louder than anyone.

By the time the coffees came, it was decided that he should make his career on the right. The arguments were straightforward. It was in power and likely to remain so. From his business days Darke knew a good number of people with connections in the party machine. On the left the selection procedures were tortuously democratic and unreasonably weighted against those who had never been members of the party. "It's all very simple, Charles," Julie said as they were leaving the restaurant. "All you have to fear is the lifelong contempt of all your friends." Again Darke laughed boisterously.

There were initial difficulties, but it was not too long before he was offered a candidacy in rural Suffolk, where he managed to halve his predecessor's majority with some thoughtless remarks about pigs. He and Thelma sold their weekend cottage in Gloucestershire and bought a weekend cottage on the edge of the constituency. Politics brought out something in Darke that the record industry, publishing, and television management had barely touched. Within weeks he was on television himself, ostensibly to comment on some irregularity in his constituency — an old-age pensioner whose electricity supply had been cut was dead from hypothermia. Breaking the unspoken rule, Darke talked to camera rather than to interviewer, and managed to insert quick summaries of recent government successes. He was a barrage-of-words man. He was in a studio two weeks later, ably refuting some self-evident truth. The friends who had helped him were impressed. He was noticed at party headquarters. At a time when the government was in difficulties with its own back benches, Darke was a ferocious defender. He sounded reasonable and concerned while advocating self-reliance for the poor and incentives for the rich. After long consideration and more parlor games at the supper table, he decided to speak against hanging in the annual punishment debate at the party conference. The idea was to be tough but caring, tough *and* caring. He spoke well to that theme on a law-and-order radio panel discussion, earning three solemn bursts of applause from the studio audience, and was quoted in a *Times* editorial.

For the next three years he attended dinners and made himself knowledgeable in fields where he thought there might be jobs going — education, transport, agriculture. He kept himself busy. He made a parachute jump for charity and cracked his shin. Television cameras were there. He was on a panel of judges for a famous literary prize and made indiscreet remarks about the chairman. He was chosen to present a bill to outlaw curb-crawling. It was lost for lack of time, but it made him popular with the tabloids. And all the time he kept talking, jabbing his forefinger in the air, uttering opinions he never thought he had, developing the oracular high style of the spokesman: "I think I speak for all of us when I say . . ." and "Let no one deny . . ." and "The government has made its position clear . . ."

He wrote a piece for the *Times* reviewing the first two years of licensed begging, which he read aloud to Stephen in the magnificent drawing room at Eaton Square. "By removing the dross of prelegislation days, and aiming for a leaner, fitter public charity sector, the government has provided itself in microcosm with an ideal towards which its economic policies should aspire. Tens of millions have been saved in social security payments and a large number of men, women, and children have been introduced to the pitfalls and strenuous satisfactions of self-sufficiency long familiar to the business community in this country."

Stephen never doubted that sooner or later his friend would tire of politics and begin another adventure. He kept up a show of wry distance, mocking Charles for his opportunism.

"If you had decided to go with the other side," Stephen said to him, "you'd be arguing just as passionately now for taking the stock market into public ownership, lower defense spending, and the abolition of private education."

Darke smacked his own forehead, feigning astonishment at his friend's naiveté. "You idiot! I stood for *this* program. A majority elected me because of it. It doesn't matter what I think. I have my mandate — unrestricted investment, more weapons, good private schools."

"You're not in it for yourself, then."

"Of course not. I serve!" And the two men laughed into their drinks.

In fact Stephen's own cynicism concealed a fascination with

the unfolding story of Charles's career. Stephen did not know any other members of Parliament. This one was already quite famous in a modest way, and brought back insiders' tales of drunkenness, even violence, in the House of Commons bar, of the minor absurdities of parliamentary ritual, of vicious Cabinet gossip. And when at last, after three years' toil in television studios and dining rooms, Darke became a junior minister, Stephen was truly elated. To have an old friend in high office transformed government into an almost human process and made Stephen feel rather worldly. Now a limousine — albeit a rather small and dented one — called at Eaton Square each morning to take the minister to work, and a certain weary authoritativeness had crept into his manner. Stephen sometimes wondered whether his friend had finally succumbed to the opinions he had effortlessly assumed.

It was Thelma who answered the door to Stephen.

"We're in the kitchen," she said, and led him across the hall. Then she changed her mind and turned.

He gestured at the bare walls, where smudged gray rectangles hung in place of paintings.

"Yes, the removal people started work this afternoon." She had steered him into the drawing room and spoke quickly and softly. "Charles is in a fragile state. Don't ask him any questions, and don't make him feel guilty about leaving you with that committee."

Since Darke's rise in politics, Stephen had seen a great deal more of Thelma. He had kept her company in the evenings and tried to learn a little about theoretical physics. She liked to pretend that he was closer to her than her husband was, that they had a special, conspiratorial understanding. It was not treachery so much as flattery. It was embarrassing and irresistible. He nodded now, as always happy to please her. Charles was her difficult child, and she had enlisted Stephen's help many times: on one occasion, to help curb the minister's drinking on the eve of a parliamentary debate; on another, to distract him at the dinner table from needling a young physicist friend of hers who was a socialist.

"Tell me what's happened," Stephen said, but she was moving back in the echoing hall and putting on a mock stern voice.

"Have you just got out of bed? You look awfully pale." She nodded briskly as he protested, implying that she would get the truth out of him later. They set off again across the hallway, down some steps, and through a green baize door, an item Charles had installed not long after he was offered his job in government.

The ex-minister was sitting at the kitchen table drinking a glass of milk. He stood and came towards Stephen, wiping away a milk mustache with the back of his hand. His voice was light, oddly melodious. "Stephen . . . Stephen, many changes. I hope you'll be tolerant."

It had been a long time since Stephen had seen his friend without a dark suit, striped shirt, and silk tie. Now he was in loose corduroy trousers and a white T-shirt. He looked suppler, younger; without the padding of a tailored jacket, his shoulders appeared to be delicately constructed. Thelma was pouring Stephen a glass of wine, Charles was guiding him towards a wooden chair. They all sat with their elbows on the table. There was quiet excitement, news in the air that was difficult to break. Thelma said, "We've decided that we can't tell you it all at once. In fact, we think we'd rather show you than tell you. So be patient, you'll know it all sooner or later. You're the only one we'll be taking into our confidence, so . . ."

Stephen nodded.

Charles said, "Did you see the television news?"

"I saw the evening paper."

"The story is I'm having a breakdown."

"Well?"

Charles looked at Thelma, who said, "We've made some well-considered decisions. Charles is giving up his career, and I'm resigning. We're selling the house and moving into the cottage."

Charles went to the fridge and refilled his glass with milk. He did not return to his chair but stood behind Thelma's, with one hand resting lightly on her shoulder. For as long as Stephen had known her, Thelma had wanted to give up university teaching, move out to the country somewhere, and write her book. How had she got round Charles? She was looking at Stephen, waiting for a reaction. It was difficult not to read triumph into the slight smile, and difficult to follow her instructions and not ask questions.

Stephen spoke past Thelma to Charles. "What are you going to do in Suffolk? Breed pigs?"

Charles smiled wryly.

There was a silence. Thelma patted her husband's hand and spoke without turning to face him. "You promised yourself an early night." He was already straightening. It was barely eight-thirty. Stephen watched his friend closely, marveling at how much smaller he appeared, how slight in build. Had high office really made him larger?

"Yes," he was saying, "I'll go up." He kissed his wife on the cheek and said to Stephen from the doorway, "We really would like you to come and see us in Suffolk. It will be easier than explaining." He raised his hand in ironic salute and left.

Thelma refilled Stephen's glass and pursed her lips into an efficient smile. She was about to speak, but she changed her mind and stood. "I'll be back in a minute," she said as she crossed the kitchen. Moments later he heard her on the stairs calling after Charles, and the sound of a door opening and closing. Then the house was quiet but for the baritone hum of kitchen equipment.

The day after Julie left for her retreat in the Chilterns, Thelma had arrived in a snowstorm to collect Stephen. While he fumbled about the bedroom for clothes and a bag to put them in, she cleaned up the kitchen, bagged the rubbish, and carried it down to the garbage cans. She gathered up handfuls of unopened bills and stuffed them into her handbag. In the bedroom she supervised Stephen's packing. She worked with brisk, maternal thoroughness, speaking to him only when it was necessary. Did he have enough pairs of socks? Pants? Was this sweater really thick enough? She took him into the bathroom and made him select items for a washbag. Where was his toothbrush? Was he going to grow a beard? If not, where was his shaving soap? There was no single action for which Stephen could generate a motive. He saw no point in being warm, or in having socks or teeth. He could carry out simple commands so long as he did not have to reflect on their rationale.

He followed Thelma down to the car, waited while she opened the passenger door for him, and sat motionless on the scented leather seat while she returned to the flat to turn off the water and gas. He stared ahead at the large flakes melting on contact with the windshield. There came to him images of a Dickensian melodrama in which his shivering three-year-old daughter beat a path through the snow to her home, only to find it locked and deserted. Should they leave a note on the door, he asked Thelma when she came down. Rather than argue that Kate could not read and was never coming back,

Thelma returned upstairs and pinned her address and phone number to his front door.

Forgotten weeks passed in the carpeted, marble-and-mahogany tranquillity of the Darkes' guest bedroom. He experienced a chaos of emotion amid the impeccable order of monogrammed towels, potpourri on waxed, dustless surfaces, laundered sheets which smelled of lavender. Later on, when he was steadier, Thelma spent evenings with him and told tales of Schrödinger's cat, backward-flowing time, the right-handedness of God, and other quantum magic.

She belonged to an honorable tradition of women theoretical physicists, though she claimed she had not made a single discovery, not even an insignificant one. Her task was to reflect and teach. Discoveries, she said, were now the rat-race end of science, and besides, they were for the young. There had been a scientific revolution this century and hardly anyone, even among the scientists themselves, was thinking it through. During the cold evenings of a disappointing spring she sat with him by the fire and told him how quantum mechanics would feminize physics, all science, make it softer, less arrogantly detached, more receptive to participating in the world it wanted to describe. She had pet topics, set pieces which she developed each time round. On the luxury and challenge of solitude, the ignorance of so-called artists, how informed wonder would have to become integral to the intellectual equipment of scientists. Science was Thelma's child (Charles was another), for whom she held out great and passionate hopes and in whom she wished to instill gentler manners and a sweeter disposition. This child was on the point of growing up and learning to claim less for itself. The period of its frenetic, childish egotism — four hundred years! — was drawing to a close.

She took him step by step, using metaphors in place of

mathematics, through the fundamental paradoxes, the kinds of things, she said, her first-year students were expected to know: how it could be demonstrated in the laboratory that something could be a wave and a particle at the same time; how particles appeared to be "aware" of each other and seemed — in theory at least — to communicate this awareness instantaneously over immense distances; how space and time were not separable categories but aspects of one another, and likewise matter and energy, matter and the space it occupied, motion and time; how matter did not consist of tiny hard bits and was more like patterned movement; how the more you knew about something in detail, the less you knew about it in general. A lifetime's teaching had instilled useful pedagogic habits. She paused regularly to find out if he was following her. As she spoke, her eyes scanned his face for total concentration. Inevitably she would discover that not only had he failed to understand, he had been daydreaming for fifteen minutes. This in turn could provoke another set piece. She would press forefinger and thumb to her forehead — a certain amount of play-acting was in order.

"You ignorant pig!" she might begin, as Stephen set his face round contrition. Perhaps these were their moments of greatest intimacy. "A scientific revolution, no, an intellectual revolution, an emotional, sensual explosion, a fabulous story just beginning to unfold for us, and you and your kind won't give it a serious minute of your time. People used to think the world was held up by elephants. That's nothing! Reality, whatever that word means, turns out to be a thousand times stranger. Who do you want? Luther? Copernicus? Darwin? Marx? Freud? None of them has reinvented the world and our place in it as radically and bizarrely as the physicists of this century have. The measurers of the world can no longer detach themselves.

They have to measure themselves too. Matter, time, space, forces — all beautiful and intricate illusions in which we must now collude. What a stupendous shakeup, Stephen. Shakespeare would have grasped wave functions, Donne would have understood complementarity and relative time. They would have been excited. What richness! They would have plundered this new science for their imagery. And they would have educated their audiences too. But you arts people, you're not only ignorant of these magnificent things, you're rather proud of knowing nothing. As far as I can make out, you think that some local, passing fashion like modernism — modernism! — is the intellectual achievement of our time. Pathetic! Now stop smirking and get me a drink."

She appeared ten minutes later in the kitchen doorway and indicated he should follow her into the drawing room. Two giant Chesterfields faced each other across a low, pitted marble-topped table. A sealed Thermos and coffee cups had been set out by Thelma or the housekeeper. The sea battles too had been replaced by rectangular gray smudges. She followed his gaze and said, "Pictures and ornaments go separately. Something to do with insurance."

They settled side by side as they always did when Charles was working late at the ministry or in the Commons. She had never taken his political career seriously. She had tolerated from a benign distance the bustle around the house as he advanced and secured his position. The government post had revived in her talk of retirement, of her book, of making a proper home of the cottage. But how to remove Charles now that he was a minor fixture of national life, now that a *Times* editorialist had parenthetically spoken of him as "prime minister material"? What feminine quantum magic had she worked?

She was kicking her shoes off with the carelessness of a teenager and tucking her slender legs beneath her. She was almost sixty-one. She kept her eyebrows plucked. The high cheekbones gave her a bright, pert look which made Stephen think of a highly intelligent squirrel. Intelligence shone from her face, and the severity of her manner was always playful, self-mocking. The salt-and-pepper hair was drawn back in a straggly bun — de rigueur, she claimed, for women physicists — and secured with an antique comb.

She tucked some loose strands of hair behind her ear, no doubt arranging her methodical thoughts. The windows were wide open and through them came the distant, airy sound of heavy traffic and the whine and warble of patrol cars.

"Put it this way," she said at last. "No one would guess it for a moment, but Charles has an inner life. In fact, more than an inner life — an inner obsession, a separate world. You'll have to take that on trust. Most of the time he denies it's there, but it's with him all the time, it consumes him, it makes him what he is. What Charles desires, if that's the word — what he needs is quite at odds with what he does, what he's been doing. It's the contradictions that make him so frantic, so impatient about success. This move, at least as far as he is concerned, has to do with resolving these." She smiled hurriedly. "Then there are my needs, but that's another matter, and you know all about that." She sat back, apparently satisfied that all had been made clear.

Stephen let half a minute go by. "Well, what exactly is this inner life?"

She shook her head. "I'm sorry if it sounds obscure. We'd rather you came and visited us. See for yourself. I don't want to explain it ahead of time."

She described her resignation from her job and her pleasure

in the prospect of writing her book. It would consist of elaborations on her many set pieces. He saw them, Thelma in the upstairs study with the creaking floorboards, at her desk where sunlight brightened her scattered papers and from where, through the open latticed window, she would have a view of Charles in shirtsleeves, idling with his wheelbarrow. Beyond the garden telephones were ringing, ministers were crossing town in limousines to important lunches. Charles was on his knees, patiently firming up soil round the base of a sickly shrub.

Later she brought in a tray of cold food. While they ate, Stephen described the committee meetings, trying to make them more amusing than they were. The evening flagged, and dwindled into talk of mutual friends. Thelma's manner was apologetic towards the end, as if she were worried that he thought he had made a wasted journey. She had little idea how most of his evenings were spent.

Because he would not be visiting the house again before it was sold, he accepted her invitation to stay the night. Well before midnight, he was facing a familiar cornflower wallpaper while he sat on the edge of the bed removing his shoes. He regarded the things in this room as his own. He had spent so much time staring at them — the blue glazed bowl of crushed flowers on an oak and brass chest of drawers, a small bust of Dante in pewter, a lidded glass pot for keeping cufflinks in. He had served three or four catatonic weeks in here. Now, as he removed his socks and crossed the room to open the window wider, he expected the worst kinds of memories. It had been a mistake to stay. The constant urban rumble could not mitigate the burdensome silence that emanated from the carpet's deep pile, the fleecy towels on the wooden stand, the granite folds of velvet curtain. Still dressed, he lay on his back on the bed. He was waiting for the pictures, the ones he could only dispel by jerking his head.

What came was not his daughter showing him her head-over-heels, but his parents, in a random moment from his last visit. His mother stood by the kitchen sink, her hands encased in rubber gloves. His father was at her side, with a clean beer glass in one hand and a dishcloth in the other. They were turning to look where he stood in the doorway. She held herself awkwardly, keeping her hands in the sink. She did not want suds on the floor. Nothing important had happened. He thought that his father had been about to speak. In her uncomfortable position, his mother cocked her head on one side as she prepared to listen. It was a habit Stephen himself had adopted. He could see their faces, the lined expressions of tenderness and anxiety. It was the aging, the essential selves enduring while the bodies withered away. He felt the urgency of contracting time, of unfinished business. There were conversations he had not yet had with them and for which he had always thought there would be time.

He had an unplaced memory, for example, a small thing that only they could explain. He was in the child's seat of a bicycle. In front of him was his father's massive back, the creases and folds of his white shirt switching with the rise and fall of the pedals. To the left was his mother on her bicycle. They were traveling along a concrete road. At intervals they bumped over the fine tar strips that joined the sections. By a great shingle bank they dismounted. The sea was on the other side; as they began the steep climb, he could hear the roar and rattle of stones. He remembered nothing of the sea itself, only the fearful anticipation as his father dragged him by the arm towards the top. But when was this, and where? They had never lived near the sea or taken holidays on beaches like this. His parents had never had bicycles.

When he visited them now, conversation moved in familiar ways. It was hard to break out to pursue the useless, important details. His mother had trouble with her eyes, and pains at night. His father's heart murmured and beat irregularly. Lesser illnesses were crowding in. There were bouts of flu he heard of only when they were over. There was a harsh undoing in progress. The telegram could arrive for him, the leaden phone call, and he would confront the frustration and guilt of a conversation never begun.

Only when you are grown up, perhaps only when you have children yourself, do you fully understand that your own parents had a full and intricate existence before you were born. He knew only outlines and details from stories — his mother in a department store, praised for the neatness of the bow she could tie behind her back; his father walking through a ruined town in Germany, or crossing the tarmac of an airfield to give the official news of victory to the squadron leader. Even when their stories began to concern himself, Stephen knew next to nothing of how his parents met, what attracted them, how they decided to get married, or how he had come about. It is difficult to step outside the moment on any given day and ask the unnecessary, essential question, or to realize that however familiar, parents are also strangers to their children.

He owed it to his love for them not to let them slip away with their lives forgotten. He was ready to get up from the bed, tiptoe from the Darkes' house, and take a long taxi ride through the night to their place, to arrive clutching his questions, his brief to prosecute the vandalizing erasures of time. Certainly he was ready, he was reaching for a pen, he would leave a note for Thelma and set out this minute, he was reaching for his socks and shoes. All that was holding him back was the need to close his eyes and take time for further thought.

❦ 3 ❧

"There is, however, evidence to suggest that the more intimately a father is involved in the day-to-day care of a small child, the less effective he becomes as a figure of authority. The child who feels himself to be loved by a father who strikes the proper balance between affection and distance is well on the way to being prepared emotionally for the separations to come, separations which are an inevitable part of all growing up."

— from *The Authorized Child-Care Handbook*, HMSO

FOLLOWING AN EXCHANGE of neutrally worded postcards with his wife, Stephen set out one morning in mid-June to visit her. He had not seen her in several months. She had come back from her retreat — a monastery that rented rooms to troubled outsiders — and within weeks had moved out of the flat and bought a place of her own. For the first time since April the day was overcast. It was something of a novelty, a reassertion of good taste, to walk everywhere in cool shade. He carried with him a set of scrawled directions. Because he did not wish to contemplate his motives too closely, he concentrated instead on the journey itself, which turned out to have a pleasing shape, tapering purposefully and consistently from the din of central London to a cottage in a pine plantation less than thirty miles away. At each stage of the journey he encountered fewer people. A ride on the crowded Underground brought him to Victoria. From here the train rumbled out across the river's broad white sky. He walked the length of every carriage looking for the most secluded seat. A disruptive minority of humankind regarded journeys, even short ones, as the occasion for pleasant encounters. There were people ready to inflict intimacies on strangers. Such travelers were to be avoided if you belonged to the majority for whom a journey was the occasion for silence, reflection, daydreams. The requirements were simple: an unobstructed view of a changing landscape, however dull, and freedom from the breath of other passengers, their body warmth, sandwiches, and limbs.

He found an empty first-class compartment and closed the door firmly. They were traveling from the past into the present. They ran along the rear gardens of Victorian terraces whose back additions offered glimpses through open doors into kitchens, past Edwardian and prewar semidetached houses, and then they were threading through suburbs, southward then eastward, past encampments of minute new houses with dirty, well-thumbed scraps of country in between. The train slowed over a tangle of junctions and shuddered to a halt. In the abrupt, expectant silence exuded by railway lines, he realized how impatient he was to arrive. They had stopped by a new housing development of raw, undersized houses, starter homes for first-time buyers. There were dumper trucks still at work. The front gardens were still rutted earth; out the back, fluttering white diapers proclaimed from diagrammatic metal trees a surrender to a new life. Two infants, hand in hand, staggered beneath the washing and waved at the train.

Shortly before his stop it began to rain. His station, barely more than a halt for commuters, was at the end of a long tunnel of nettles. Despite the rain, he took his time on the footbridge watching the black-buttoned roof of his train slip through a frail proscenium of signals and, foreshortened, click slowly out of sight round a curve. With that there settled a velvety country silence against which other small sounds seemed precision-cut and polished: the brisk departing steps of another passenger, complex birdsong and simpler human whistling. He remained on the footbridge, taking childish — or boyish — pleasure in the polished rails pointing away in both directions into the silence. As a child he had once stood on a larger bridge with his father waiting for a train to come through. Stephen had stared at the receding lines and had asked why they grew together as they got farther away. His father looked down at him, eyes narrowed, mock serious, and then squinted into the distance where question and answer converged. He always seemed to be standing at attention. He was holding Stephen's hand, their fingers were interlaced. His were stubby, with matted black hair across the knuckles. In games he used to move his fingers scissorlike, clamping Stephen's till the boy danced with agony and delight at such irresponsible power. Stephen's father looked from the horizon to explain that trains got smaller and smaller as they moved away, and that to accommodate them the rails did the same. Otherwise there would be derailments. Shortly after that an express shook the bridge as it shot beneath their feet. Stephen marveled then at the intricate relation of things, the knowingness of the inanimate, the deep symmetry that conspired to narrow the rail's gauge precisely in keeping with the train's diminishment; no matter how fast it rushed, the rails were always ready.

He stood outside the station reading Julie's instructions. The rain had broken into a fine mist and the handwriting was smudged, almost illegible. He followed the road out of the village along what she described as the old bus route. He passed a hypermarket with a crowded ten-acre car park, and crossed a motorway on an elegantly curving concrete bridge. After half a mile he turned down a paved track which cut a straight line through forestry land. Now that he was in real, open country he was lighthearted. On both sides were planted lines of conifers with their flashing parallax as one row ceded to the next, a pleasing effect which conveyed a false sense of speed. It was a geometrical forest uncomplicated by undergrowth or birdsong. The road gleamed white in the rain. Its single-mindedness pleased him, he wanted to run. Half a mile in there was a clearing in the plantation where a high barbed-wire fence ran round a nodding donkey. It was a gray beast languidly lifting its blunt, heavy head with a steady purr. There were others, spaced at regular intervals along the road. Outside one was an oil tanker making its collection from the reservoir tank. The driver was up in his cab with his feet on the dashboard, drinking beer from a tin can and reading a newspaper. He smiled and lifted his hand as Stephen passed, and this cheered Stephen further. He had forgotten how friendly people were in the country.

As Julie had promised, the road came to an end after half an hour's walking. The pine forest gave way abruptly to an unbounded prairie of wheat. Stephen rested against an aluminum five-barred gate. The only indication that the yellow field, which resembled a desert, was finite was a line on the horizon where the plantation resumed. Perhaps it was a mirage. The plain was cut neatly in two by an access track, a continuation of the paved road and equally straight. He set off, and within minutes found satisfaction in this new landscape. He was marching across a void. All sense of progress, and therefore all sense of time, disappeared. The trees on the far side did not come closer. This was an obsessive landscape — it thought only about wheat. The lack of hurry, the disappearance of any real sense of a destination, suited him.

Julie had returned from her monastery in the Chilterns after six weeks. Stephen left Eaton Square, timing his arrival at the flat to coincide with hers. They greeted one another cautiously. There was a touch of the old, easy affection. They stood side by side in the center of their living room, fingers loosely linked. How rapidly a home perishes through neglect, and how indefinably; it wasn't the dust, or the dead air, or the newspapers turned yellow so soon, or the withered pot plants. They said all these things as they dusted, opened windows, and carried things to the garbage cans. Stephen assumed that they were really talking about their marriage. For the next week or two they circled warily, sometimes polite, at others genuinely, sweetly affectionate, and once even making love. For a while it seemed they would soon begin to touch on the subjects they were at such pains to avoid.

But it could go the other way too, and it did. As Stephen saw it, the problem was desire. They had no need of comfort from one another, or advice. Their loss had set them on separate paths. There was nothing to be shared. Julie had lost weight and cut her hair short. She was reading mystical or sacred texts — St. John of the Cross, Blake's longer poems, Lao-tsu. Her penciled annotations crowded the margins. She worked hours each day at a Bach partita. The rasp of double-stopped notes, the spiraling frenzy of semiquavers warned him away. For his part, he made the first approaches to a serious drinking habit and indulged the books of his adolescence, reading of unencumbered, solitary men whose troubles were the world's. Hemingway, Chandler, Kerouac. He toyed with the idea of packing a light suitcase, taking a taxi out to the airport, and choosing a destination, drifting about with his melancholy for a few months.

Being together heightened their sense of loss. When they sat down to a meal, Kate's absence was a fact they could neither mention nor ignore. They could not give or receive comfort, therefore there was no desire. Their one attempt was routine, false, depressing for them both. Afterwards Julie put on her dressing gown and went to the kitchen. He heard her crying and knew he could not go to her. She would not welcome him anyway. They managed five weeks. The only serious conversations they had during that time were towards the end when they began to play with the idea of parting; it was not a divorce, of course, nor a separation, but "a time apart." And so a representative from a real-estate agent came to value the flat. He was a big man with a kind, authoritative manner who commented intelligently as he measured rooms and recorded original features.

They asked, implored the man to stay to tea. While he took his second cup they told him about Kate, the supermarket, the police, the monastery, the difficulty of being back. He propped his elbows on the kitchen table and rested his head on his hands. He nodded solemnly throughout — what he heard confirmed what he had always feared. When they had finished he dabbed at his lips with a handkerchief. Then he pushed his arms out across the table and took their hands. The grip was powerful, his hands were hot and dry. After a silence he told them they were not to blame each other. For a moment they felt elated, released.

But that moment passed. A real-estate agent could do more than they could for each other. What did that mean? They learned later that their man had once been a priest and had lost his faith. The flat was valued and Stephen gave Julie a check for two thirds the amount. She found her cottage and moved out, taking her violins, their bed, and a handful of possessions. She refused to install a telephone. They kept in touch with occasional postcards and met once or twice in restaurants in central London where nothing much was said. If there was love it was buried beyond their reach.

The rain moved across the great space in fine columns of mist towards him. For twenty minutes the ground had sloped away imperceptibly till the distant trees were sunk and his horizon was entirely wheat. It was curiosity and unease that brought him across this drenched plain when he could have been watching the men's ten thousand meters. Julie could set about transforming herself, purposefully evolve some different understanding of life and her place within it. She would have been on long walks through the symmetrical pines, reassessing her past, their past, shuffling priorities, making arrangements for a new future; the walking boots he had given her one birthday would have been pounding the straight concrete road. Before he could unearth his own feelings, and without his being a witness to the process, she could metamorphose into a complete stranger, someone he would not know how to talk to. He did not want to get left behind, he did not want to lose his place in her story.

She was not beyond confusion or irrationality, but she had an inviolably useful way of understanding and presenting her own morasses within the terms of a sentimental or spiritual education. With her, previous certainties were not jettisoned so much as encompassed, rather in the way, according to Thelma, scientific revolutions were said to redefine rather than discard all previous knowledge. What he frequently regarded in Julie as contradictory *(But that's not what you said last year!)*

she maintained was development *(Because last year I hadn't yet understood!)*. She did not simply inhabit her inner life, she ran it, directed it; the terrain ahead was mapped out. The course of study was not to be left to blind chance, to what might simply come her way. The role of fate, on the other hand, she would not deny. The work, the responsibility, was to fulfill one's destiny.

Such faith in endless mutability, in remaking yourself as you came to understand more or changed your version, he had come to see as an aspect of her femininity. Where once he had believed, or thought he ought to believe, that men and women were, beyond all the obvious physical differences, essentially the same, he now suspected that one of their many distinguishing features was precisely their attitudes to change. Past a certain age, men froze into place; they tended to believe that, even in adversity, they were somehow at one with their fates. They were who they thought they were. Despite what they said, men believed in what they did and they stuck at it. This was a weakness and a strength. Whether they were scrambling out of trenches to be killed in their thousands, or doing the firing themselves, or putting the final touches to a cycle of symphonies, it only rarely occurred to them, or occurred only to the rare ones among them, that they might just as well be doing something else.

To women this thought was a premise. It was a constant torment or comfort, no matter how successful they were in their own or other people's eyes. It was also a weakness and a strength. Committed motherhood denied professional fulfillment. A professional life on men's terms eroded maternal care. Attempting both was to risk annihilation through fatigue. It was not so easy to persist when you could not believe that you were entirely the thing that you did, when you thought you could find yourself, or find another part of yourself, expressed through some other endeavor. Consequently, women were not taken in so easily by jobs and hierarchies, uniforms and medals. Against the faith men had in the institutions they and not women had shaped, women upheld some other principle of selfhood, in which being surpassed doing. Long ago men had noted something unruly in this. Women simply enclosed the space that men longed to penetrate. The men's hostility was aroused.

At last he reached the pines on the other side. He climbed a second aluminum gate which brought him, as his map had promised, onto a narrower concrete track bounded by barbed-wire fences curving through the green gloom. Afterwards, Stephen tried to recall what was on his mind as he walked the three hundred yards between the gate and a well-used minor road. But it was to remain inaccessible, a time of mental white noise. He was aware perhaps of his wet clothes. He might have considered how he would set about drying them when he arrived.

He was all the more vulnerable then to what happened when he emerged from the plantation and took in his new surroundings. He stood still, transfixed. A quick, breathy sigh escaped him. The road made a right-angled bend, and stretched away from him roughly along the line of the path. A small convoy of cars passed and seemed to make no sound. He knew this spot, knew it intimately, as if over a long period of time. The trees around him were unfolding, broadening, blossoming. One visit in the remote past would not account for this sense, almost a kind of ache, of familiarity, of coming to a place that knew him too, and seemed, in the silence that engulfed the passing cars, to expect him. What came to him was a particular day, a day he could taste. Here it was, just as it should be, the heavy, greenish air of a wet day in early summer, the misty, tranquil rain, the heavy drops which formed on and fell from the unblemished horse chestnut leaves, the sense of the trees being magnified, and purified by a rain so fine it displaced the air. It was on just such a day, he knew, that this place gained its importance.

He stood still, afraid that movement would destroy the spaciousness, the towering calm he felt about him, the vague longing in him. He had never been here before, not as a child, not as an adult. But this certainty was confused by the knowledge that he had imagined it just like this. And he had no memory of imagining it at all. With this, he knew that if he stepped from the grass verge and looked to his left he would see a phone box and, opposite, a pub set back in a gravel car park. He went forward quickly.

He had to step out into the middle of the road before he could see round its curve. It was the way the compact red-brick building fulfilled his expectations that gave him the first touch of fear. It was happening too quickly. How could he have expectations without memory? He was a hundred yards away with a three-quarters view of the façade. The well-kept building looked as it should. It was a simple late-Victorian rectangular structure with a sloping red-tiled roof and a back addition that gave the whole the shape of the letter *T*. Out the back there was a derelict, once-white trailer, now a gardening shed. Some dishcloths were out to dry on a sagging line. At the front of the pub, to one side of the front porch, was a broken but usable wooden bench.

It all conformed. Its familiarity mocked him. A high, free-standing white post supported a sign which announced with picture and words "The Bell." The name meant nothing to him. He stood for many minutes looking, tempted to turn back, come another time and explore more closely. But it was not just a place he was being offered, it was a particular day, *this* day. He could taste the gravel's dustiness released by rain. He was aware that the gentle, soaking spray had produced around him another countryside of once common trees — elms, chestnuts, oaks, beeches, old giants lost to the cash-crop plantations, magnificent trees whose ascendancy over the landscape was restored, settled cumuli of foliage rolling unhindered towards the North Downs.

Stephen stood on the edge of a minor road in Kent on a wet day in mid-June, attempting to connect the place and its day with a memory, a dream, a film, a forgotten childhood visit. He wanted a connection which might begin a process of explanation and allay his fear. But the call of the place, its knowingness, the longing it evinced, the rootless significance — all this made it seem quite certain, even before he could tell himself why, that the loudness — this was the word he fixed on — of this particular location had its origins outside his own existence.

He waited for fifteen minutes, then he began to walk slowly in the direction of The Bell. A sudden movement could dispel this delicate reconstruction of another time. It was difficult to take in the tumbling chaos of so many deciduous trees in full leaf, and the way the misty rain magnified the bright ferns at their base to equatorial size, making rare species out of cow parsley and nettles. If he shook his head hard, he would be back among the orderly pines. He kept his gaze fixed on the building ahead. It was just past midday. The Bell would be open for its first lunchtime customers, and yet there were no cars parked on the gravel outside to diminish the impression of everything being correct, accurate in relation to a master copy.

There were no cars, but leaning by the wooden bench out front were two old-fashioned black bicycles. One was a lady's, both had wicker baskets. Fear was lightening his step, making his breathing shallow. He could have turned back. Julie was expecting him, he needed to do something about his wet clothes. He had to get home soon and work on the reading list for the committee. He slowed, but he did not stop. Cars passed close by. If he stepped in their path he could not be touched. The day he now inhabited was not the day he had woken into. He was lucid, determined to advance. He was in another time but he was not overwhelmed. He was a dreamer who knows his dream for what it is, and though fearful, lets it unfold out of curiosity.

He came closer to the silent building. He was an intruder. This place both concerned and excluded him, there was a delicate negotiation whose outcome he might affect adversely. He was crossing the gravel now, placing each step carefully. From a corner of the pub came the clipped sound of rain trickling into a water barrel. At a distance of thirty feet the windows of the pub showed black. The building looked deserted until he shifted his position and made out dim lights inside. He had stopped in front of the small porch. The bicycles were propped against the wall, sheltered by the eaves from the rain. Their back wheels just touched the arm of the broken bench. The man's bike was against the wall of the pub. The lady's leaned into an awkward intimacy. The front wheels were splayed, the pedals clumsily engaged. The machines were black and new, the maker's name was on the uprights in unblemished gold Gothic. The front baskets were clean wicker. The saddles were wide and well sprung and gave off the delicate fecal odor of quality leather. The handlebars had off-white rubber grips, and black beads of rain gathered on the chrome. He did not touch the bicycles. There was a movement inside, a figure passed in front of a light. He stepped to one side of the window, aware that he was visible to people he could not see.

It had stopped raining, but the sound of water was louder. It spilled from the cracked, mossy guttering and sounded in the rain barrel, it ticked away among the leaves. He was close to the pub's wall, with an oblique view through the window into the saloon. A man was carrying two glasses of beer from the bar towards a small table where a young woman sat waiting. The table was set into a bay, and light from its windows silhouetted the couple. The man was settling himself, sedately lifting the creases of his loose gray flannel trousers before sitting in close to the woman. They were on a bench seat built into three sides of the bay. Not recognition so much as its shadow, not its familiar sound but a brief resonance, caused Stephen to steady himself against the dry wall. His vision pulsed with the beating of his heart. Had the couple glanced up and to their left, towards the window by the door, they might have seen a phantom beyond the spotted glass, immobile with the tension of inarticulated recognition. It was a face taut with expectation, as though a spirit, suspended between existence and nothingness, attended a decision, a beckoning or a dismissal.

But the young man and woman were engrossed. He gulped his beer, a pint to her half, and talked earnestly, while her drink remained untouched. She was listening solemnly, plucking at the sleeve of her print dress, adjusting with unconscious precision the pretty clasp that kept her trim, straight hair clear of her face. They touched hands and made determined, weak smiles; then the hands came apart and they spoke at once. The matter — for it was clearly one single subject — was not yet resolved.

As far as Stephen could see, there were no other customers.

The barman, a broad, slow man, had his back turned and was fiddling with something on a shelf. The obvious thing was to enter, buy a drink, and take a closer look. The idea was unattractive. Stephen kept his hand on the wall, which was warm and reassuring to the touch. Quite suddenly, with the transforming rapidity of a catastrophe, everything was changed. His legs weakened, a chill spread downwards through his stomach. He was looking into the eyes of the woman, and he knew who she was. She had glanced up in his direction. The man was talking, making an insistent point, while the woman continued to stare. Her face showed no curiosity or shock; she simply returned Stephen's gaze as she listened to her partner. She nodded vaguely, glanced away to reply, and then looked again towards Stephen. But she could not see him. There was nothing to suggest she had registered him in any way at all. She was not ignoring him, she was looking through him at the trees across the road. She was not looking at all, she was listening. Absurdly, he raised his hand and made an awkward gesture, something between a wave and a salute. There was no response from the young woman whom he knew, beyond question, was his mother. She could not see him. She was listening to his father speak — how he recognized that way his father had of making a point with an open hand — and could not see her son. A cold, infant despondency sank through him, a bitter sense of exclusion and longing.

Perhaps he was crying as he backed away from the window, perhaps he was wailing like a baby waking in the night; to an observer he may have appeared silent and resigned. The air he moved through was dark and wet; he was light, made of nothing. He did not see himself walk back along the road. He fell back down, dropped helplessly through a void, was swept dumbly through invisible curves, and rose above the trees, saw the horizon below him even as he was hurled through sinuous tunnels of undergrowth, dank, muscular sluices. His eyes grew large and round and lidless with desperate, protesting innocence, his knees rose under him and touched his chin, his fingers were scaly flippers, gills beat time, urgent, hopeless strokes through the salty ocean that engulfed the treetops and surged between their roots; and for all the crying, calling sounds he thought were his own, he formed a single thought: he had nowhere to go, no moment that could embody him, he was not expected, no destination or time could be named; for while he moved forward violently, he was immobile, he was hurtling round a fixed point. And this thought unwrapped a sadness that was not his own. It was centuries, millennia old. It swept through him and countless others like the wind through a field of grass. Nothing was his own, not his strokes or his movement, not the calling sounds, not even the sadness, nothing was nothing's own.

When Stephen opened his eyes he was lying on a bed, Julie's bed, under an eiderdown, clasping against his chest a tepid hot-water bottle. Across the little room, most of whose space was taken by the bed, was an open door to the bathroom, from which rolled a cloud of steam, yellowish in the electric light, and the thunder of running water. He closed his eyes. This bed was a wedding gift from friends he had not seen in years. He tried to remember their names, but they were gone. In it, or on it, his marriage had begun and, six years later, ended. He recognized a musical creak when he moved his legs, he smelled Julie on the sheets and banked-up pillows, her perfume and the close, soapy essence that characterized her newly washed linen. Here he had taken part in the longest, most revealing, and, later, most desolate conversations of his life.

He had had the best sex ever here, and the worst wakeful nights. He had done more reading here than in any other single place — he remembered *Anna Karenina* and *Daniel Deronda* in one week of illness. He had never lost his temper so thoroughly anywhere else, nor been so tender, protective, comforting, nor, since early childhood, been so cared for himself. Here his daughter had been conceived and born. On this side of the bed. Deep in the mattress were the traces of pee from her early-morning visits. She used to climb between them, sleep a little, then wake them with her chatter, her insistence on the day beginning. As they clung to their last fragments of dreams, she demanded the impossible: stories, poems, songs, invented catechisms, physical combat, tickling. Nearly all evidence of her existence, apart from photographs, they had destroyed or given away. All the worst and the best things that had ever happened to him had happened here. This was where he belonged. Beyond all immediate considerations, like the fact that his marriage was more or less finished, there was his right to lie here now in the marriage bed.

When next he opened his eyes Julie was sitting on the edge of the bed looking down at him. The room was silent but for the heavily accented, echoing drip of a bathroom tap. There was restrained amusement in the tension around her lips, which she held pressed together against the temptation to say something wryly unsympathetic. Her clear gray eyes moved in steady, unpredictable triangles, from his left to his right eye and back, comparing them, measuring truth by the faint differences she detected, then down to his mouth to gauge the expression there and make further comparisons. He pushed himself into a sitting position and took her hand. It was responsive, yet cool to touch.

He said, "I'm sorry to be a nuisance."

She smiled instantly. "It's all right." Her lips closed up again, and bulged once more with the effort of retaining a humorous observation. It was not her way to ask him directly why he had arrived at her house in a state of shock. Questions, ordinary inquisitiveness did not suit her at all. She never insisted on the answer to a question. She might ask once, and if there was no reply, then she would match the silence. There was a pleasing depth to her silence. It was difficult not to tell her things in order to draw her from her steady self-communion, to bring her closer.

He said, "It's wonderful to lie in this bed again."

"It drives me mad," Julie said promptly. "It sags in the middle and squeaks every time you move."

Without meaning to, he said lightly, "I'll have it then," and Julie shrugged.

"If you like. Take it."

This was too bleak. Their hands disengaged and there was a silence. Stephen wanted to return to the intimacy he had woken up to, and he was tempted to explain everything as well as he could. But he could not trust himself with a long account, it could just as easily push them further apart. He kicked the bedclothes clear, leaned forward, and placed his hands on her shoulders, pressing firmly as if to make sure she was there. She was frail to touch, the body heat through her cotton blouse was fierce and endearing. She was watchful, but the suppressed smile was there.

"I'll explain what happened," he said, still pressing.

He released her and was about to rise from the bed when she put her hand on his arm. She spoke firmly. "You're not to get up. I've brought some tea. And I've made a cake." She pulled the covers back over his legs, to his waist, and stood to tuck him in. She did not want him to leave the marriage bed. From the floor she picked up a tray and set it before him. "For once," she said, "you can stop pretending everything's all right. You're my patient."

She cut the cake and poured the tea. The cups were fine bone china. She had gone to the trouble of finding saucers that matched the side plates. Undeniably, it was an occasion. They chinked cups and said, "Cheers." When he asked what time it was she said, "Bath time." She pointed at the streaks of dried mud along his arm. In the bedroom's half-light the whites of her eyes flashed repeatedly as she glanced up from her plate to his face, as though checking it against a memory. She would not hold his gaze now. When he smiled at her she looked down. She was wearing long earrings of colored crystal. Untypically, her hands would not keep still.

Small talk was not easy. After some time Stephen said, "You're looking very beautiful."

The reply came back immediately in an even tone. "So do you." She smiled at him and said, "Now . . ." through an efficient sigh and cleared away the tea things. She stood at the head of the bed, stroking his hair. He was holding his breath, the moment was holding its breath. They confronted two possibilities, equally weighted, balanced on a finely honed fulcrum. The moment they inclined towards one, the other, while never ceasing to exist, would disappear irrevocably. He could rise from the bed now, giving her an affectionate smile as he moved past her on his way to his bath. He would lock the door behind him, securing his independence and pride. She would wait downstairs, and they would resume their careful exchanges until it was time for him to walk across the field to catch his train. Or something could be risked, a different life unfolded in which his own unhappiness could be redoubled or eliminated.

Their hesitation was brief, delicious before the forking paths. Had he not seen two ghosts already that day and brushed against the mutually enclosing envelopes of events and the times and places in which they occurred, then he would not have been able to choose, as he did now, without deliberation and with an immediacy that felt both wise and abandoned. A ghostly, fading Stephen rose, smiled, crossed the room, and closed the bathroom door behind him, and innumerable invisible events were set in train. As Stephen took Julie's hand and felt the sinuous compliance of her body communicated along the length of her arm, and as he drew her across his lap and kissed her, he did not doubt that what was happening now, and what would happen as a consequence of now, was not separate from what he had experienced earlier that day. Obscurely, he sensed a line of argument was being continued. Here, however, there was nothing but delight as he held Julie's head, the dear head, between his hands and kissed her eyes, where earlier, outside The Bell, he had felt terror; but the two moments were undeniably bound, they held in common the innocent longing they provoked, the desire to belong.

The homely and erotic patterns of marriage are not easily discarded. They knelt face to face in the center of the bed undressing each other slowly.

"You're so thin," said Julie. "You're going to waste away." She ran her hands along the pole of his collarbone, down the bars of his ribcage, and then, gratified by his excitement, held him tight in both hands and bent down to reclaim him with a long kiss.

He too felt proprietorial tenderness once she was naked. He registered the changes, the slight thickening at the waist, the large breasts a little smaller. From living alone, he thought, as he closed his mouth around the nipple of one and pressed the other against his cheek. The novelty of seeing and feeling a familiar naked body was such that for some minutes they could do little more than hold each other at arm's length and say, "Well . . ." and "Here we are again . . ." A wild jokiness hung in the air, a suppressed hilarity that threatened to obliterate desire. All the coolness between them now seemed an elaborate hoax, and they wondered how they had kept it going for so long. It was amusingly simple: they had to do no more than remove their clothes and look at one another to be set free and assume the uncomplicated roles in which they could not deny their mutual understanding. Now they were their old, wise selves, and they could not stop grinning.

Later, one word seemed to repeat itself as the long-lipped opening parted and closed around him, as he filled the known dip and curve and arrived at a deep, familiar place, a smooth, resonating word generated by slippery flesh on flesh, a warm, humming, softly consonated, roundly voweled word . . . *home,* he was home, enclosed, safe and therefore able to provide, home where he owned and was owned. Home, why be anywhere else? Wasn't it wasteful to be doing anything other than this? Time was redeemed, time assumed purpose all over again because it was the medium for the fulfillment of desire. The trees outside edged in closer; needles stroked the small panes, darkening the room, which rippled with the movement of filtered light. Heavier rain sounded on the roof, and later receded. Julie was crying. He wondered, as he had many times before, how anything so good and simple could be permitted, how they were allowed to get away with it, how the world could have taken this experience into account for so long and still be the way it was. Not governments or publicity firms or research departments, but biology, existence, matter itself had dreamed this up for its own pleasure and perpetuity, and this was exactly what you were meant to do, it wanted you to like it. His arms and legs were drifting away. High, in clean air, he hung by his fingers from a mountain ledge; fifty feet below was the long smooth scree. His grip was loosening. Surely then, he thought as he fell backwards into the exquisite, dizzy emptiness and accelerated down the irresponsibly steep slope, surely at heart the place is benevolent, it likes us, it wants us to like it, it likes itself.

Then everything was different. They squeezed into the narrow, lukewarm bath, taking with them wine which they drank from the bottle. Satiated desire brought on a speedy, reckless clarity. They talked and laughed loudly and were careless with one another. Julie told a lengthy anecdote about life in the nearby village. Stephen gave an exaggerated account of the committee members. They made harsh summaries of the recent lives of mutual friends. Even as the animated talk proceeded they were uneasy because they knew there was nothing underpinning this cordiality, no reason for bathing together. There was an indecisiveness which neither dared voice. They were talking freely, but their freedom was bleak, ungrounded. Soon their voices began to falter, the fast talk began to fade. The lost child was between them again. The daughter they did not have was waiting for them outside. Stephen knew he would be leaving soon. The awkwardness grew when they were back in their clothes. The habits of separation are not easily discarded. They were losing their voices, they were dismayed. The old, careful politeness was re-establishing itself, and they were helpless before it. They had exposed themselves too easily, too quickly, they had shown themselves to be vulnerable.

Downstairs, he watched as Julie knelt to spread a damp towel in front of a smoky log fire. There should have been something affectionate to say that would neither be flippant nor expose him further. But all there remained was small talk. He could think only of taking her hand, and yet he didn't. They had used up the possibilities, the tension of touch, they had been to the limits. For now everything was neutralized. Had they been together still, they could have fallen back on other resources, ignored each other for a while, or undertaken some task, or faced the loss somehow. But here there was nothing. A sad pride pinned them to little exchanges over a final pot of tea. He had a glimpse of the kind of life she was leading. Pine trees grew right up to the house and the windows of the cottage were small, so all the rooms were gloomy, even on a sunny day. She kept a fire in right through the summer to control the damp. In a corner of the room was a scrubbed kitchen table on which stood her various notebooks in neat piles, candles to read by at night and on cloudy days, and a jam jar of weeds and what few wildflowers she could find on the edges of the plantation. Another jar contained sharpened pencils. Her violins were in a corner on the floor, fastened in their cases, and the music stand was not in sight. He imagined her wandering the rural concrete tracks, thinking, or trying not to think about Kate, and coming back to practice in the hissing silence.

Any minute he would be setting off across the machine-efficient prairie to return to his own hermitage. Sitting across from her, watching as she hunched over her tea, warming her hands round the cup, he was emotionless. He could begin to learn how to detach himself from his wife. Her fingernails were bitten down, her hair was unwashed, her face had a pinched look. He could learn not to love her, just so long as he could see her from time to time and be reminded that she was mortal, a woman in her late thirties, intent on solitude, on making sense of her own troubled life. Later he might be taunted by the memory of her thin, bare arms protruding from the torn sweater, endearingly too large, which he recognized as his own, and the huskiness in the voice as she kept her feelings down.

It was inevitable that as he stood they should exchange the briefest of goodbyes. She opened the door for him, there was a little squeeze of hands, and he was no more than three steps up the path before he heard the front door close behind him. By the wicket gate he turned to look back. It was a house such as a child might draw. It was box-shaped with its front door dead center, four small windows near each corner, and constructed of the same red bricks as The Bell. A path made out of leftover bricks made a shallow S-shape between the gate and the front door. The cottage stood in a clearing barely fifty feet across. The plantation trees were pressing in on all sides. For a moment he considered going back, but he had no idea what it was he wanted to say.

And so, by a perverse collusion in unhappiness, many months passed before they saw each other again. In his better moments, Stephen felt that what had taken place had happened too soon; they had been unprepared. In his worst, he was furious at himself for undoing what he saw as careful progress in separation. For years afterwards he would be baffled by his insistence on not returning to see her. At the time he argued it this way: Julie had never summoned him. He had initiated the visit himself. She was happy enough to see him, just as happy to see him go and to resume her solitude. If what had happened meant anything at all to her, then she would break the silence. If he heard nothing, then he could take it that she still wanted to be left alone.

The rain had long ceased. Stephen crossed the road near The Bell briskly, determined to resist further drama or significance. He hurried along the concrete path towards the big field. He had accepted a dinner invitation from a couple in London renowned for their elaborate meals and interesting friends, and he was going to be late.

❧ 4 ❧

"We could do worse than conclude, as have many before us, that from love and respect for home we derive our deepest loyalties to nation."

— from *The Authorized Child-Care Handbook*, HMSO

It was late morning and impressively hot, and the committee was taking evidence. The day before, the temperature had passed the one-hundred-degree Fahrenheit mark, inspiring patriotic exultation in the popular press. Responsible opinion judged the weather to be serving the government well, and today even higher temperatures were expected. Ten minutes into the morning session, at Canham's instigation, a clerk had brought an electric fan and plugged it in close to the chairman, at whom it was deferentially pointed. Over the weekend workmen had prized free the sash windows, which now stood wide open to the drone of sluggish traffic in Whitehall. A bluebottle, trapped between parallel panes of hot glass, buzzed intermittently. As the morning wore on the pauses became longer. On the surface of the enormous table, which was moist to the touch, loose papers stirred lazily in a faint stream of warm air.

For more than an hour Stephen had been staring at his hands

on his lap. Lately, the smell and feel of his own skin in this heat had brought back to him the taste of an only childhood in hot countries — of perspiration, and the pervasive sweet scent of mangoes, English vegetables boiling in the kitchen and spices in tins painted with dragons and palm trees, kept in the outbuilding by the amah girl. He had once lifted a lid and inhaled the essence of a brown flaky substance. When he went back indoors and stood in the deserted living room under the slow-moving ceiling fan, the bitter, putrid taste was a secret he had to keep from the lavender-polished, RAF-issue furniture.

This was his East: the manly scent of cigarettes and Flit, the fly-killer; bulky armchairs in floral casings, his father's with a brass ashtray held in place by leather-thonged straps, around his mother's the scent of pink soap, the knitting she pressed on with in the sticky heat, and *Woman's Realm;* on the walls, clever silhouettes in black painted tin of palm trees with sunsets; the pretty amah who, it was said, slept at the end of his bed at night, though he never saw her; the water snakes who lived between his sheets, held at bay by prayers; his first classroom, where the heat drew the fragrance of cedar from the pencil between his fingers, and the tiger under the palm tree, emblem of his school and of his father's beer.

One humid afternoon he followed his mother up the stairs and lay down beside her on the ribbed expanse of candlewick bedspread, on the ashtray side, by the ticking alarm. Her outlandish proposal was that they should fall asleep in broad daylight, hours before bedtime. He lay on his back, watching the fan.

"Close your eyes, son," she instructed him. "Close your eyes." He did so, and when he woke it was a long time later. She was gone, he could hear her downstairs talking and drinking tea with women friends. He was impressed; sleep need not simply happen, it was something people controlled by closing their eyes. What else could they control?

He liked to listen to his mother and her friends. The talk was of things going wrong, of people saying and doing the wrong things, and of illnesses and the wrong things doctors did. No one talked to children about things going wrong. The tea things were cleared away, and the women dispersed before his father came home. He wore baggy shorts, and there were damp stains on his khaki shirt. As soon as he was home he sought Stephen out and pretended to be an ogre chasing him, growling, "Fee fi fo fum, I smell the blood of an Englishman!" and tickled him and hurled him dangerously high in the air. When Flight Sergeant Lewis had showered and had had a beer made of tiger's blood, which Stephen was allowed to pour, they sat down to tea and more talk of interestingly wrong things: a young officer who knew too little, what another flight sergeant had done wrong, or how the politicians were telling the RAF to do the wrong things. Then his mother would tell of the things she had heard that afternoon. Afterwards it was Stephen's job to help clear the table while his mother washed, and his father dried.

It occurred to Stephen that if he could control events in the way his mother controlled sleep, then he would make his parents king and queen of the entire world, and they could set right all the wrongs they described so wisely. For was not his father stronger than any ogre? At the intersquadron games he pedaled his legs to a blur and came close to unpowered flight in the hop, skip, and jump; he carried Stephen on his back down to the beach where, they later learned, there were sharks, and came churning out of the surf, head and shoulders draped with seaweed, a roaring sea monster; the young officers asked him what to do even though he had to call them sir, while the men under his command dreaded his disfavor, as did Stephen and his mother. And was she not more beautiful than the queen of England, with the additional gifts of being able to remain twenty-one every birthday, of hitting bull's-eyes with a .22 rifle at shooting matches, of hearing sounds at night that no one else could hear, of knowing when he was having a bad dream, for she was always there when he woke in the dark?

They often went out to a special do at the sergeants' mess. His mother wore long satin dresses which she sewed herself. His father wore his uniform and always had a beer before they set out. Sometimes they danced in the living room to the music of the Forces Broadcasting Service, a waltz, a fox trot, or a two-step, moving confidently in the space between the furniture with their backs held straight and their feet pivoting neatly. Then they were like the elegant dancing couple who revolved on his mother's jewelry box to the tinkle of "Für Elise," dream figures whose features dissolved into pink blobs when you put your face up close.

Dreams were dangerous; was it only a bad dream when the plate of lunchtime mashed potato missed his father's head and smashed against the wall, when later his mother cried as she collected the crockery pieces in her apron and wiped the wall with a wet cloth? Did he dream the raised voices downstairs at night, was it a nightmare when he saw through the open kitchen door his father with a carving knife, when he put his red and angry face close to Stephen's and said he was a mother's boy or, worse, picked him up in front of visitors to hold him like a babe-in-arms and rocked and shushed him?

Perhaps he was a mother's boy. A few years later he still slept in her bed whenever his father, now a warrant officer, was away on training. This was when they had been posted to North Africa. When Stephen joined the Cubs and had to earn his proficiency badge in handicrafts, his mother helped him make a set of toy furniture. She ended up doing all the work herself. He carried the results — a blue three-piece suite, a matchbox sideboard, a standard lamp — in their shoebox living room to the weekly meeting in the Nissen hut, confident that her work was his by right.

She was a frail and beautiful insomniac who quietly worried about everyone except herself, and whose worrying was a subtle form of possessiveness, inseparable from love, it seemed, when it was directed against himself. She confronted him with a dangerous world of invisible germs and pneumonia-bearing drafts of air in certain rooms. She warned against the perils of wearing unaired clothes, of missing a meal, of not wearing a cardigan in the evening. While he was bound by loyalty to submit to her little strictures, he learned to scoff at them like his father did.

For Stephen was also a father's boy. During the Suez crisis, all the families were moved into military camps for protection against the local Arabs. Mrs. Lewis was in England visiting relatives and there followed heady weeks of disruption from the routines of school and beach. There was the novelty of ceasing to be the immediate focus of parental attention, of living in large tents with his friends, who all appeared in memory as freckly, short-haired, jug-eared boys like himself. There was the smell of lorry oil on hot sand, the military vehicles, faithful reproductions of his Dinky toys, neat, whitewashed stones lining every path, barbed wire and sandbagged machine gun nests. Above all, there was the officer with direct responsibility for the families — his father, a distant figure striding from one meeting to another, a service revolver strapped about his waist.

When that was over, there were other jaunts. They left his mother at home and raced the black Morris Oxford across the semidesert, along the empty roads, inland towards the airfield, to find out just how fast the new car would go. They went out with a jam jar to hunt for a scorpion. His father heaved aside a rock, and there it was, yellow and fat, lifting its pincers towards them in supplication. He used his foot to encourage it into the jar, and Stephen was ready with the perforated lid. They laughed — Stephen uneasily — when his mother said she could not sleep at night for fear that it would escape and roam the house in the dark. Later it was taken into the workshops and pickled in formaldehyde.

Each morning before school his father took him into the bathroom, scooped two fingersful from the Brylcreem jar, and worked it into Stephen's short-back-and-sides with fanatical vigor. Then he took his steel comb and, holding the boy's jaw in a tight grip, combed the obedient hair flat and made a straight gray parting of military precision. Within an hour this construction had melted in the sun. Most afternoons during the nine-month summer they spent on the beach, where the officers and their families sat at one end, the airmen, sergeants and warrant officers included, at the other. His father would stand chest-deep in the water counting slowly while Stephen stood unsupported on his shoulders until laughter or the slippery haircream underfoot caused him to fall. The count was interrupted when a wave washed over his father's head, but only momentarily. The record stood at forty-three when the game ceased, not long before Stephen left for boarding school.

North Africa was a five-year idyll. Angry voices no longer broke into his dreams. His time was divided between school, which ended at lunch, and the beach, where he met his friends, who were all sons of his father's colleagues, men who had risen through the ranks. It was where his mother met her friends, who were the wives of the same men. Just as his little family enclosed him with its fierce, possessive love, so the RAF enclosed their family, choosing and defining friends, entertainment, doctors and dentists, schools and teachers, the house, its furniture, even the cutlery and bed linen. When Stephen spent a night at a friend's house, he slept between familiar sheets. It was a secure and ordered world, hierarchical and caring. Children had to know their place and submit, as their parents did, to the demands and limitations of military life. Stephen and his friends — though not their sisters — were encouraged to call their fathers' colleagues "sir," like the American boys from the airbase. They were taught to let ladies precede them through doors. But they were generously indulged, encouraged, virtually ordered, to have fun. After all, their parents had grown up during the Depression, so now there was to be no shortage of lemonades, ice creams, cheese omelets, and chips. On the terrace of the Beach Club the parents sat round the tin tables laden with beer glasses marveling at the difference between their lives then and their lives now, between their childhoods and their children's.

Stephen's first term at boarding school was a blur of complex rites, brutalities, and constant noise, but he was not particularly sad. He was too silent and watchful to be singled out for bullying. In fact he was hardly noticed at all. He remained at heart a member of his little family group, and ticked off the ninety-one days till the Christmas holidays, determined to survive. Back home at last with the brilliant light, the view from his bedroom window of date palms leaning into the pale blue winter sky, he resumed his place easily enough in the triangle. It was only when it was time to return to England, the day after his twelfth birthday, to start again at the foot of another mountain of days, that he began to feel keenly for what he was about to leave. A quick arithmetic demonstrated that from now on three quarters of his life was to be spent away. He had, in fact, left home. His parents must have made the same calculations, for as they drove across the desert scrub to the airfield, the talk was unnaturally cheery with plans for the next holiday, and there were long silences which they could not break without repeating themselves.

In the airplane an elderly lady kindly moved across to let him have the window seat so he could wave to his parents. He could see them more clearly than they could see him. They were a dozen yards from the tip of the wing, standing arm in arm just where the tarmac met the sand. They were smiling, and waving hard, then resting their arms, then waving again. The propellers on his side of the plane started up. He saw his mother turn and dab at her eyes. His father put his hands in his pockets and took them out again. Stephen was old enough to know that a period of his life, a time of unambiguous affinities, was over. He pressed his face against the window and began to cry. His Brylcreem was all over the glass. When he tried to wipe it clear his parents mistook the movement of his hand and waved again. The plane was edging forward, and they slipped quite suddenly from his view. Turning towards the cabin, he was confirmed in his worst intimations when he saw that the old lady had been watching him and was crying too.

The presence of a stranger in the room, a gaunt young man who appeared to have declined the offer of a chair, had aroused Stephen from uneasy daydreams. The man had been speaking for half an hour already. He stood hunched like a penitent with blueish pale fingers clasped in front of him. His jaws and upper lip were smudged with closely shaved stubble which gave him the saddened, honest appearance of a chimpanzee, an impression furthered by large brown eyes and the black tangle of chest pelt, as thick as pubic hair, visible through his thin white nylon shirt and sprouting irreverently between its buttons. It seemed to Stephen that he held his hands still while he spoke to avoid exposing the unnatural length of his arms, whose elbows occurred an inch or two before they should have. The voice was a strained tenor, the words enunciated with precision and caution as though language, a dangerous weapon, had only recently been acquired and might explode in its user's face. Dazed from introspection, Stephen was so struck by the man's appearance that he had yet to take in what he was saying. The rest of the committee sat in silence, apparently attentive, faces politely wiped of all expression. Rachael Murray and one of the academics were taking notes. To aid his concentration, Lord Parmenter had closed his eyes and was breathing slowly and rhythmically through his nose.

After Stephen had registered the man's appearance, he became aware of a stirring among the committee members, a restlessness that could not be put down to boredom and the heat. Heads were turning in his direction. Eyes that met his slid away, and here and there — Rachael Murray, Tessa Spankey — was a suppressed smile. Even Lord Parmenter had shifted position and was inclining his leathery head in Stephen's direction. Was he expected to speak? Had he already been asked? He forced his wheeling, unruly attention on the tensed monotone, its straining, pleading note of *But surely, surely you will agree that this is so.* He found himself looking straight into the honest brown eyes. Was he expected to intervene? Now? He nodded faintly and gave a wry smile to indicate both total comprehension and a reasonable, knowing reticence.

"It has been shown beyond any doubt" — *and please,* the eyes seemed to say, *do not take issue here* — "that we use but a fraction of this limitless intellectual, emotional, intuitive resource. Only recently a case has come to light of a young man who did outstandingly well in a university degree course and was discovered to have virtually no brain at all, merely a wafer-thin band of neocortex lining the skull. It is clear we get by on very little, and the consequence of this underuse is that we are divided, deeply divided from ourselves, from nature and its myriad processes, from our universe. Members of the committee, we have undernourished our capacity for empathic and magical participation in creation, we are both alienated and stunted by abstraction, removed from the profound and immediate apprehension — which is the hallmark of a whole person — of the dancing interpenetration of the physical and the psychic, their ultimate inseparability."

The man who resembled an ape paused and surveyed his listeners with bright eyes. He fondled his earlobe. "If these are the punitive consequences, what then is the cause, what prevents the growing mind from achieving wholeness? As we have seen, the brain as a physical organ has its own quite definable pattern of development. In just the way that molar teeth and secondary sexual characteristics make their appearances at roughly the same times in the lives of individuals, so the brain has its spurts of growth, and there can be no doubt that these in turn are associated with quite definable surges in mental development and capability. By forcing literacy onto children between the ages of five and seven, we introduce a degree of abstraction that shatters the unity of the child's world view, drives a fatal wedge between the word and the thing that the word names. For as we have seen, the human brain at that age has simply not developed the higher logical abilities to deal easily and happily with the self-enclosed system of written language. Literacy should not be introduced to a child until it has made, of its own accord, in line with the genetic programming of the brain's growth, the vital separation of the self from the world. It is for this reason, Mr. Chairman, I urge that children should not begin to learn to read until they are eleven or twelve, when their brains and minds undergo the important surge of growth that makes this separation possible."

Stephen straightened his back, an ancient mammalian ploy to make himself larger. He was expected to justify himself as a writer of children's books, a shatterer of tiny worlds.

The speaker had clasped his hands again, the knuckles showed white. "Dance and movement of all kinds," he said, "the sensual exploration of the world, music — for, surprisingly enough, musical symbols are not abstractions so much as precise instructions for physical movements — painting, discovering through manipulation how things work, mathematics, which is more logical than abstract, and all forms of intelligent play — these are the appropriate, essential activities of the younger child, enabling its mind to remain in harmony with, to flow with, the forces of creation. To inflict literacy at this stage, to dissolve the enchanted identification of word and thing and through that, self and world, is to bring about a premature self-consciousness, a harsh isolation which we like to explain away to ourselves as individuality.

"It is in effect, Mr. Chairman, nothing less than a banishment from the Garden, for its effects are lifelong. Premature literacy makes for adults in whom an unforced, intelligent empathy with the natural world, with their fellow beings, with social processes, is stunted; adults for whom the apprehension of the unity of creation will remain a difficult, elusive concept, understood dimly, if at all, through the study of mystical texts. Whereas" — and here the stranger dropped his voice and settled his gaze again on Stephen — "whereas this apprehension is a gift to us in childhood. We must not wrench it from our children with our anxious, competitive education, with our busy, intrusive books."

Towards the end of these remarks there were smiles around the table. The committee was enjoying the presence of what it had decided was a crank. Canham, who was responsible for checking the credentials of those who made representations, was looking uncomfortable as he scribbled on a pad. One of the academics, not Morley, was wiping his nose with a tissue to conceal laughter. Colonel Jack Tackle had folded his arms across his chest and bowed his head. He was vibrating slightly. These furtive signs aroused Stephen's sympathy for the speaker. Now that he had delivered his talk, he seemed to regret his refusal of a chair. He stood awkwardly at the head of the table, arms dangling, waiting to be questioned or dismissed. He was not to know that the government did not intend a magical citizenry. His eyes had lost their challenge and he was staring at a point several feet above the chairman's head. Stephen wanted to shake the man's hand. In the spirit of contrariness, he wanted to lend support. But he had his own corner to fight now. Lord Parmenter had inquisitively gargled his surname.

"Only cynics," Stephen said, glaring round the room, "would dispute the desirability of being whole in the way it has been described, or of realizing whatever potential we have. The issue is surely the means."

He paused, hoping for another thought, then began again, unsure of what it was he was going to say. "I'm not a philosopher, but it seems to me . . . that there are some problems to be considered."

He stopped again, and then proceeded quickly through a sigh of relief. "You could describe writing in much the same way as you've just described musical symbols — in this case, a set of instructions on what to do with lips, tongue, throat, and voice. It's only later that children learn to read quietly to themselves. But I'm not sure that either description, of musical notation or writing, is correct. Both activities seem highly abstract, and perhaps abstraction of a certain kind is precisely what we're good at from our earliest days. The problems come when we try to reflect on the process and define it. A tune has a kind of meaning. It's hard to say what it is, but a child has no difficulty understanding it. Reading and writing are abstract activities, but only to the extent that language-speaking is. The two-year-old who is beginning to speak whole sentences is making use of a fabulously complex set of grammatical rules.

"I remember Kate, my daughter . . . but no . . . the written word can be the very means by which the self and the world connect, which is why the very best writing for children has about it the quality of invisibility, of taking you right through to the things it names, and through metaphors and imagery can evoke feelings, smells, impressions for which there are no words at all. A nine-year-old can experience this intensely. The written word is no less a part of what it names than the spoken word — think of the spells written round the rim of the necromancer's bowl, the prayers chiseled on the tombs of the dead, the impulse some people have to write obscenities in public places and that others have to ban books that contain obscenities, of always spelling god with a capital G, of the special importance of a written signature. Why keep children from all this?"

Stephen held the standing man's eyes in his. Lord Parmenter had closed his eyes again. Canham was on his feet, talking in a murmur through the open door to someone in the corridor.

"The written word is a part of the world into which you wish to dissolve the childlike self. Even though it describes the world, it's not something separate from it. Think of the delight with which a five-year-old picks out street signs, or the total surrender of a ten-year-old to an adventure novel. It's not words he sees, or punctuation or rules of grammar, it's the boat, the island, the suspicious figure behind the palm tree."

He blinked to repulse an image of his daughter, older than he had ever known her, sitting up in bed engrossed in a novel. She turned a page, frowned, turned back. It could have been a book he had written for her. He formed a resolution; then it faded and he continued.

"The literate child reads and hears a voice in her head. It's immediate, intimate, it nourishes her fantasy life, it frees her from the whims and inclinations of grown-ups who might or might not have time to read to her." He was sitting on the edge of Kate's bed reading to her. He was not sure which of the two images he preferred. He was not even sure, — in fact it might be a rather fine thing, to pass the first eleven years of life playing the accordion, dancing, taking old clocks apart, listening to stories. In the end, it probably made no difference either way, nor was there any way of telling. It was that old business of theorizing, taking up a position, planting the flag of identity and self-esteem, then fighting all comers to the end. There was no evidence to be had, it was all down to mental agility, perseverance.

And there was no richer field for speculation assertively dressed as fact than child care. He had read the background material, the extracts compiled by Canham's department. For three centuries generations of experts, priests, moralists, social scientists, doctors — mostly men — had been pouring out instructions and ever-mutating facts for the benefit of mothers. No one doubted the absolute truth of his judgments, and each generation knew itself to stand on the pinnacle of common sense and scientific insight to which its predecessors had merely aspired.

He had read solemn pronouncements on the necessity of binding the newborn baby's limbs to a board to prevent movement and self-inflicted damage; of the dangers of breast feeding or, elsewhere, its physical necessity and moral superiority; how affection or stimulation corrupts a young child; the importance of purges and enemas, severe physical punishment, cold baths, and, earlier in this century, of constant fresh air, however inconvenient; the desirability of scientifically controlled intervals between feeds, and, conversely, of feeding the baby whenever it is hungry; the perils of picking a baby up whenever it cries (that makes it feel dangerously powerful) and of not picking it up when it cries (dangerously impotent); the importance of regular bowel movements, of potty training a child by three months, of constant mothering all day and night, all year, and elsewhere of the necessity of wet nurses, nursery maids, twenty-four-hour state nurseries; the grave consequences of mouth-breathing, nose-picking, thumb-sucking, and maternal deprivation, of not having your child expertly delivered under bright lights, of lacking the courage to have it at home in the bath, of failing to have it circumcised or its tonsils removed, and, later, the contemptuous destruction of all these fashions; how children should be allowed to do whatever they want so that their divine natures can blossom, and how it is never too soon to break a child's will; the dementia and blindness caused by masturbation, and the pleasures and comfort it affords the growing child; how sex can be taught by reference to tadpoles, storks, flower fairies, and acorns, or not mentioned at all, or only with lurid, painstaking frankness; the trauma imparted to the child who sees its parents naked, the chronic disturbance nourished by strange suspicions if it only ever sees them clothed; how to give your nine-month-old baby a head start by teaching it math.

Here was Stephen now, a foot soldier in this army of experts, asserting as energetically as he knew how that the proper time for children to become literate was between the ages of five and seven. Why did he believe this? Because it had long been standard practice, and because his livelihood depended on ten-year-olds reading books. He was arguing like a politician, a government minister, passionately, seemingly innocent of self-interest. The stranger was listening, head politely cocked, the tips of the fingers of his right hand brushing the table's surface.

"The young child who can read," Stephen said, "has power, and through that acquires confidence."

While he was talking on in this manner, and while a complicating voice was telling him that his agnosticism was only another aspect of his own parched emotional state, Canham hurried across and whispered into the ear of the chairman. At the gargling sound, Stephen broke off midsentence and turned to see Lord Parmenter raise a weary finger. "The prime minister will be passing down the corridor in less than a minute and wants to step in and meet the committee. Any objections?"

Canham shifted from one foot to the other while keeping his left hand on his tie knot. He made a few steps into the room as if to rearrange the furniture, then changed his mind and returned to the door. Finally there was a stir of muffled no's around the table. Of course there were no objections. Committee members were making small adjustments to dress, tucking in shirts, patting hair, fiddling with makeup. Colonel Tackle was putting his tweed jacket back on.

Two men in blue blazers shouldered into the room, scanning

faces with a neutral glare as they made their way to the windows. Here they took up positions with their backs to the room, scowling out at a couple of lounging off-duty chauffeurs who turned away unconcernedly and went on smoking. Thirty seconds passed before three tired men in rumpled suits came in and nodded at the committee. Immediately after them came the prime minister and, behind, more aides, some of whom could not find enough space and remained in the doorway. There was a stir round the table to rise, which Lord Parmenter quelled with a movement of his hand. Canham was silently, earnestly offering a chair, but he was ignored. The prime minister preferred to stand, and took up a position just to one side of the chairman, deftly usurping him.

Directly opposite, at the far end of the table, stood the man who resembled an ape, whose gaze expressed friendly curiosity. His disposition represented a violation of protocol to Canham. He was waving and mouthing at the stranger to stand aside or sit down, but again he was ignored, and now Lord Parmenter was beginning the introductions.

Stephen had heard that there was a convention in the higher reaches of the civil service never to reveal, by the use of personal pronouns or other means, any opinion as to the gender of the prime minister. The convention undoubtedly had its origins in insult, but over many years it had passed into a mark of respect, as well as being a test of verbal dexterity and a display of good taste. It was his impression now that Lord Parmenter was following form in his impeccable welcoming remarks, in which he paid tribute to the fact that the current examination of child-care practices by numerous expert committees was due entirely to the personal interest taken in these matters by their distinguished visitor, to whom generations of parents and children were certain to be grateful.

He then introduced the members in turn, never faltering for a moment in his recall of Christian and surnames, titles or background. At each name the prime minister inclined minimally. Stephen was the last to be introduced and had time to notice how Rachael Murray blushed when her name was spoken. Colonel Jack Tackle snapped to attention in his seat. Stephen discovered that the stranger's name was Professor Brody from the Institute of Development, and that one member, Mrs. Hermione Sleep, had been introduced before but was not remembered. The fan of tendons round the neck of Emma Carew, a cheerful, anorexic headmistress, tightened like umbrella struts when her name was remembered and spoken aloud.

Every member of the committee, however worldly wise, was a little awed. For years Stephen had dealt only scathing or derisive words, imputed only the most cynical intentions, and had declared on a number of occasions feelings of pure hatred. But the figure standing before him now, unlit by studio lights, unframed by a television set, was neither institution nor legend, and bore little resemblance to the caricatures of political cartoonists. Even the nose was much like any other. This was a neat, stooped sixty-five-year-old with a collapsing face and filmy stare, a courteous rather than an authoritative presence, disconcertingly vulnerable. Stephen wanted to disguise himself. His impulse was to be civil, to be liked, to protect the prime minister from his critical opinions. This was the nation's parent, after all, a repository of collective fantasy. And so when the time came for Parmenter to announce his name, he found himself bobbing and even smiling eagerly, like an attendant lord in a Shakespeare play. Because he was last to be introduced he was honored with a question.

"Are you the writer of children's books?"

Speechless, he nodded.

"The foreign secretary's grandchildren are avid readers."

He said thank you before he had time to appreciate that no compliment had been paid. The prime minister addressed a few expressionless remarks to the committee, reminding it of the importance of the undertaking and to keep up the good work.

The men in blue blazers were stepping back from the windows, and the aides and two of the men in creased suits were moving towards the door, which was held wide open. The committee heard coughing and shuffling in the corridor from those who had been waiting outside. The third man was edging his way round the chairs with a message for Stephen. The envoy's breath smelled of chocolate. "The prime minister would like a word with you in the corridor, if you wouldn't mind."

Watched by his colleagues, Stephen followed the man out. Most of the retinue were moving away in the direction of the stairs at the far end of the corridor. Those remaining stood in a huddle several feet away, waiting. A senior-looking civil servant who was offering a document for signature received a set of instructions. He made a humming noise at each one. Finally the document was signed and he withdrew. The chocolate-eater pushed Stephen forward. There was no handshake or introductory remark.

"I understand you are a close personal friend of Charles Darke's."

Stephen said, "That's right." Because his words sounded too direct, he added, "I've known him since he was in publishing."

They had turned and were moving along the corridor at a ruminative pace. The tread of the two bodyguards was close behind.

The next question was slow in coming. "And what news do you have of him?"

"He's moved to the country with his wife. They sold their house."

"Yes, yes. But has he had a breakdown, is he ill?"

Stephen resisted an urge to make himself important by telling everything of the little he knew. "His wife sent me a postcard inviting me down. She said they were happy."

"Was it his wife who made him resign?"

They arrived at the head of the stairs and stood, flanked by the two bodyguards, looking down into the broad marbled stairwell.

For a moment he looked straight into the prime minister's face. He did not know whether this conversation was important or trivial. He shook his head. "Charles spent a long time in public life."

"Quite. No one gives it up without a very good reason."

On the way back to the committee door the tone changed. "I liked Charles Darke. More than most people imagined. He's a talented man, and I had hopes for him." They were almost within earshot of the waiting aides and their pace slowed. "Personal information becomes rather bland by the time it reaches me, do you see what I mean?"

"You want to persuade him to come back?" But it was not in order for Stephen to ask the questions.

The prime minister raised a small hand, on one finger of which was a plain gold ring. An aide detached himself from the group. "Perhaps after your visit you could let me know how you found him." The aide had reached into a leather document-holder and was passing a small card to Stephen.

He was about to say that he could not promise much, but a signal had gone out that their interview was at an end. Another of the retinue was at the prime minister's side and was opening an appointment book as they and all the others headed back at speed towards the stairs.

Stephen found his seat amid silence. Only Lord Parmenter seemed genuinely uninterested, even mildly irritated at the interruption. He waited till Stephen was settled, then suggested that Professor Brody might like to speak again.

The gaunt young man nodded and with a deft, barely conscious movement of his fingers tucked away some black strands between his shirt buttons before clasping his hands before him and announcing that if the committee did not mind, he would take the points in the order in which they had been raised.

Restrictions on water use had reduced the front gardens of suburban west London to dust. The interminable privets were crackling brown. The only flowers Stephen saw on the long walk from the Underground station — the end of the line — were surreptitious geraniums on window ledges. The little squares of lawn were baked earth from which even the dried grass had flaked away. One wag had planted out a row of cacti. Stronger representations of pastoral were to be found in those gardens that had been cemented over and painted green. The little men in red coats and rolled-up sleeves who turned the windmills were motionless, sunstruck.

The street in which his parents lived ran straight and shopless for a mile and a half, part of a single 1930s development, once despised by those who preferred Victorian terraces and made desirable now by migrations from the inner city. They were squat, grubbily rendered houses, dreaming under their hot roofs of open seas; there was a porthole by each front door, and the upper windows, cased in metal, attempted to suggest the bridge of an ocean liner. He walked slowly through the hazy silence toward number 763. A lozenge of dog turd crumbled underfoot. He wondered, as he did each time he came, how there could be so little activity in a street where there were so many houses close together — no kids kicking a ball around or playing hopscotch on the pavement, no one stripping down a gearbox, no one even leaving or entering a house.

Twenty minutes later he was sitting on a shaded patio with his father, drinking a beer from the fridge and feeling quite at home. The orderliness of cleaned, sharpened garden tools stowed in their proper place, the pink flagstones recently swept and the hard brush hanging between its rightful pegs on the wall, the garden hose neatly and tightly wound onto its drum and the proscribed garden tap with its hint of brass polish — details that had oppressed him as an adolescent now cleared the mind and left it uncluttered for more essential things. Indoors and out, there was an orderly concern for objects, their cleanliness and disposition, which he no longer took to be the exact antithesis of all that was human, creative, fertile — key words in his furious teenage notebooks. From where they sat with their beers there was a view of similarly ordered gardens, brown lawns, creosoted fences, orange roofs, and right above, against a blueish-black sky, just two arms of a pylon whose body was out of sight, straddling the unfortunate house next door.

The mind was freed to talk about the weather.

"Son," his father said, reaching from his folding chair with a gasp to top up Stephen's beer, "I don't remember a hotter summer than this in seventy-four years. It's hot. In fact, I'd say it was too hot."

Stephen said that that was better than too wet and his father agreed.

"I'd have this anytime, whatever they're saying about the reservoirs or what's happened to our lawn. You can sit out. All right, in the shade if need be, but you're sitting outside, not indoors. Those wet summers we had — when you get to our age, your mum and I, they're no good for anything but an ache in the bones. Give me the heat anytime." Stephen was about to speak, but his father continued, a little irritably. "The fact is, people are never satisfied. It's too hot, it's too cold, it's too wet, it's too dry. They're never bloody satisfied. They don't know what they want. No, this will do me. We never complained about weather like this in the old days, eh? On the beach there every day, beautiful water, swimming." And with his usual good humor restored, he raised his glass and took a long pull while he tapped out with his slippered feet a triumphant rhythm.

They sat for a few minutes in homely, unawkward silence. From the kitchen, where Stephen's mother was cooking a roast, came the lulling sounds of the oven door being opened and closed, a heavy spoon ladling from a saucepan. Later, at his father's insistence, she came out to join them and drink her sherry. She removed her apron before sitting down and folded it carefully across her lap. The numerous small anxieties associated with preparing a three-course meal animated her face. She kept her head tilted towards the kitchen window, listening out for the vegetables.

The conversation about the weather resumed, this time with reference to its effect on the garden, her special love.

"It's such a shame," she said. "We had so much in, didn't we. It was going to be beautiful."

Stephen's father was shaking his head. "I was just saying to Stephen. It's better than sitting indoors all day watching it tip down and saying to yourself, Maybe it will be all right tomorrow. And then it isn't."

"I know," she said. "But I like to see things grow. I don't like to see them die." She finished her sherry and said, "How long are you two going to be?"

Stephen's father glanced at his watch. "We'll have another beer."

"So shall I serve up at half past?"

He nodded.

Frowning at a stab of pain as she rose from her chair, she said, "Good. As long as I know what I'm doing." She patted her son's knee and walked quickly back indoors.

His father followed her and returned with two fresh cans of beer. The loud groan he gave after he had lowered himself into his chair was less an expression of pain than self-mockery. Supporting the cans on the armrests, he slumped down and smiled, pretending for a moment to be worn out by his exertions. After they had refilled their glasses, he asked Stephen about the committee and listened patiently to an account of the meetings.

He was unimpressed by Stephen's interview with the prime minister. "They're all out for what they can get, son. I've told you before, you're wasting your time there. This report's already been written in secret and the whole thing's a load of rubbish anyway. These committees are a lot of flannel as far as I can see. Professor So-and-So and Lord So-and-So! It's to make people believe the report when they read it, and most people are such bloody fools, they will believe it. Lord So-and-So put his name to this so it must be true! And who is this lord? Some Joe who's said the right things all his life, offended no one, and made himself some money. The right word in the right ear and he's on the honors list, then suddenly he's a god, his word is law. He's a god. Lord So-and-So said this, Lord So-and-so thinks that. That's the trouble with this country, too much bowing and scraping, everyone kowtowing to lords and sirs, no one thinking for themselves! No, I'd jack it in if I were you, son. You're wasting your time there. Get on and write a book. It's time you did. Kate's not coming back, Julie's gone. You might as well get on with it."

The speech was not planned, and it surprised both of them. Stephen shook his head, but he could think of nothing to say. Mr. Lewis settled back in his chair. The two men raised their glasses and drank deeply.

There was a minute or two, just before dinner, when Stephen was alone indoors. His father had gone into the kitchen to help out. The room extended from the back to the front of the house, with the dining table at one end and the three-piece suite at the other. This was his parents' last house, and the first they had been able to furnish to their own taste. All about were objects collected from many postings, things put away in boxes and stored for years till "we have our own house" — a phrase he remembered from his earliest childhood. The ashtray with the leather thongs was in place, and the silhouetted palm trees and the North African brass pots. On the sideboard was his mother's collection of crystal and cut-glass animals, cutely represented, spiky and heavy to hold. He balanced on his palm a mouse with bead eyes and nylon whiskers.

On the dining table were wine glasses with long, green-tinted stems. He used to think of them as ladies with long-sleeved gloves. The placemats bore the RAF insignia, the coffee spoons the crests of towns Stephen had visited — Vancouver, Ankara, Warsaw. It was odd, the ease with which a whole past could be fitted into one room, placed out of time and bound by a blend of familiar smells that had no date — lavender polish, cigarettes, scented soap, roasting meat. These objects, this particular perfume — already his resolutions, the precise importance of his inquiries, was beginning to elude him. He had some questions, some topics he wanted to raise, but he was comfortably vague from three cans of beer, and hungry too, and now his mother was passing the covered bowls of vegetables through the serving hatch and they were to be placed on the hot plate; his father had brought in a bottle of his wine, homemade in four weeks from a special kit, and was filling the glasses, topping the meniscus as was his habit; the first course was in place, each melon slice with its lurid cherry. He sat down gratefully, and when his parents had settled too, the three raised their glasses and his mother said, "Welcome home, son!"

When Stephen looked at his parents' faces it was not the effects of age he saw so much as the devastation of Kate's disappearance. She was rarely mentioned now, which was why he had been surprised twenty minutes before. The loss of their only grandchild had whitened his father's hair in two months, and made his mother's eyes sink into wrinkled pits. They had built their retirement years around their granddaughter, for whom this room had been a paradise of forbidden objects. She could pass half an hour alone, her chin propped on the sideboard, meandering through obscure dialogues in which she did the voices of the glass menagerie in high squeaks. Beyond the physical signs, Stephen had seen nothing of his parents' sorrow. They had not wanted to add to his burden. It was typical of what bound the three of them that they had never been able to grieve Kate together, and that to say her name, as his father had done, was to break an unspoken rule.

It was not until the end of the meal that Stephen made the effort and raised the subject of the bicycles. He had this memory, he told them, which he could not quite place. He described the child's seat, the track towards the sea, the shingle bank and the thunderous noise behind it. His father was shaking his head defiantly, as he often did when faced with the irretrievable past. But Mrs. Lewis was quick.

"That was Old Romney, in Kent. We had a week there once." She touched her husband's forearm. "Don't you remember, we borrowed the bikes back off Stan. Those old things. We stayed a week, and not a day it didn't rain."

"Never been to Old Romney in my life," Stephen's father said, but he was hesitant now, waiting to be convinced.

"Something to do with a course you were on and you had a week's leave. We stayed in a bed-and-breakfast, I can't remember her name now, but quite nice, very clean."

"You borrowed the bikes back," Stephen said.

"That's right. We had them years, bought them new and gave them to your Uncle Stan when we got posted overseas."

This time his father was unequivocal. "We had all sorts of bikes but we never had new ones. Couldn't have afforded it. Not then."

"Well, I tell you we did, on hire-purchase, and we gave them to Stan and borrowed them back to go to Old Romney."

His certainty about the bikes had fortified his resistance to Old Romney. "Never been near the place. Not even near it."

To conceal her annoyance, Stephen's mother stood to gather in the plates. She lowered her voice in anger. "You forget what suits you."

Mr. Lewis was filling the glasses and giving Stephen a comical look that said, *Look what I've got myself into now.*

Good humor returned easily enough over coffee when the conversation turned to the funeral of an elderly relative who had been buried in Wimbledon cemetery the week before. Stephen's mother told the story, breaking off to wipe the tears from her eyes. A little boy, a great-grandchild of the deceased, had thrown a teddy bear into the grave during the service, and there it lay, on its back on the coffin, gazing up at the mourners with one eye missing. The kid set up a terrible commotion above the vicar's drone. There were snorts of laughter, and angry stares from the family's side. Nobody wanted to climb down and retrieve the thing and so it was buried with the dead.

"And more grieved for," added Stephen's father, who had heard the story through again with a huge grin.

When the three began to do the dishes, they followed the old routine. His mother made a start at the kitchen sink while Stephen and his father cleared away. When there were enough plates and dishes to be dried, Stephen went into the kitchen to begin. His father finished clearing the table and wiped it down. Then he joined the other two in the kitchen, where he dried and put away. Mrs. Lewis always dismissed the men in order to wash and dry the baking and roasting pans herself. This operation had about it elements of dance, ritual, and military maneuver. Now that Stephen's own arrangements were so chaotic, he found the process soothing where once it had filled him with despair. During the second stage, when his father was energetically buffing the dining room table and Stephen was alone in the kitchen with his mother, he asked about the bicycles again. When were they bought?

She was not curious why he wanted to know. Holding her gloved hands under the suds, she tilted her head and considered. "Before you were born. Before we were married, because we used to go courting on them. They were beauties, black with gold writing, weighed a ton."

"Do you know a pub called The Bell near Otford in Kent?"

She shook her head. "Is that near Old Romney?" she asked as Mr. Lewis entered the kitchen. With precisely the impulse he had intended to resist — the impulse to make the evening pass smoothly, not to provoke dissent, however minor — Stephen refrained from further questions.

When everything was washed and put away in its proper

place, they sat and chatted until it was time for him to set off for the last train. They gathered on the front doorstep in the warm air for farewells. A familiar sadness came over his parents; their voices were muted, though their words were cheerful enough. It was partly, he supposed, because he was leaving home again, as he had so many times in thirty years, each occasion an unrecognized enactment of the first; and partly because he was leaving alone, without wife or daughter, daughter-in-law or granddaughter. Whatever the cause, it would remain unspoken. As always, they stayed out on the front path waving at their son as he receded in the sodium dusk, waving, resting their hands, then waving again as they had on the desert airstrip, till a slight bend in the street lost him to their view. It was as if they wanted to see for themselves that he was not going to change his mind, turn round, and come back home.

❧ 5 ❧

"It was not always the case that a large minority comprising the weakest members of society wore special clothes, were freed from the routines of work and of many constraints on their behavior, and were able to devote much of their time to play. It should be remembered that childhood is not a natural occurrence. There was a time when children were treated like small adults. Childhood is an invention, a social construct, made possible by society as it increased in sophistication and resource. Above all, childhood is a privilege. No child as it grows older should be allowed to forget that its parents, as embodiments of society, are the ones who grant this privilege, and do so at their own expense."

— from *The Authorized Child-Care Handbook*, HMSO

STEPHEN WAS DRIVING a hired car along a deserted minor road, eastward towards central Suffolk. The sun roof was open wide. He had tired of searching for tolerable music on the radio and was content with the rush of warm air and the novelty of driving for the first time in over a year. A postcard he had written to Julie was in his back pocket. She seemed to want to be left alone. He was uncertain whether to post it.

The sun was high behind him, giving a visibility of luminous clarity. The road was flanked by concrete irrigation ditches and made wide curves through miles of conifer plantation set well back beyond a wide swath of tree stumps and dried-out bracken. He had slept well the night before, he remembered later. He was relaxed but reasonably alert. His speed was somewhere between seventy and seventy-five, which dropped only a little as he came up behind a large pink lorry.

In what followed, the rapidity of events was accommodated by the slowing of time. He was preparing to overtake when something happened — he did not quite see what — in the region of the lorry's wheels, a hiatus, a cloud of dust, and then something black and long snaked through a hundred feet towards him. It slapped the windshield, clung there a moment, and was whisked away before he had time to understand what it was. And then — or did this happen in the same moment? — the rear of the lorry made a complicated set of movements, a bouncing and swaying, and slewed in a wide spray of sparks, bright even in sunshine. Something curved and metallic flew off to one side. So far Stephen had had time to move his foot towards the brake, time to notice a padlock swinging on a loose flange and "Wash me please" scrawled in grime. There was a whinnying of scraped metal and new sparks, dense enough to form a white flame which seemed to propel the rear of the lorry into the air. He was applying first pressure to the brake as he saw the dusty, spinning wheels, the oily bulge of the differential, the camshaft, and now, at eye level, the base of the gearbox. The upended lorry bounced on its nose once, perhaps twice, then lazily, tentatively, began to complete the somersault, bringing Stephen the inverted radiator grill, the downward flash of windshield, and a deep boom as the roof hit the road, rose again several feet, fell back, and surged along before him on a bed of flame. Then it swung its length round to block the road, fell onto its side, and stopped abruptly as Stephen headed into it from a distance of less than a hundred feet and at a speed which he estimated, in a detached kind of way, to be forty-five miles an hour.

Now, in this slowing of time, there was a sense of a fresh beginning. He had entered a much later period in which all the terms and conditions had changed. So these were the new rules, and he experienced something like awe, as though he were walking alone into a great city on a newly discovered planet. There was space too for a little touch of regret, genuine nostalgia for the old days of spectacle, back then when a lorry used to catapult so impressively before the impassive witness. Now was a more demanding time of effort and concentration. He was pointing the car towards a six-foot gap formed between a road sign and the front bumper of the motionless lorry. He had removed his foot from the brakes, reasoning — and it was as if he had just completed a monograph on the subject — that they were pulling the car to one side, interfering with his aim. Instead he was changing down through the gears and steering with both hands firmly, but not too tightly, on the wheel, ready to bring them up to cover his head if he missed. He beamed messages, or rather messages sprang from him, to Julie and Kate, nothing more distinct than pulses of alarm and love. There were others he should send to, he knew, but time was short, less than half a second, and fortunately they did not come to mind to confuse him. As he shifted to second and the small car gave out a protesting roar, it was clear that he must not think too hard, that he had to trust to a relaxed and dissociated thinking, that he must imagine himself into the gap. On the sound of this very word, which he must have spoken aloud, there was a brisk crunch of metal and glass and he was through and coming to a halt, with his door handle and side mirror scattered across the road fifty feet behind.

Before the relief, before the shock, came an intense hope that the driver of the lorry had witnessed this feat of driving. Stephen sat motionless, still holding the steering wheel, watching himself through the eyes of the man in the vehicle behind. If not the driver, then a passerby would do, some farmer perhaps, someone who understood driving and would have the full measure of his accomplishment. He wanted applause, he wanted a passenger in the front seat turning to him now with shining eyes. In fact, he wanted Julie. He began to laugh and shout, "Did you see that? Did you see that?" And then, "You did it! You did it!" The whole experience had lasted no longer than five seconds. Julie would have appreciated what had happened to time, how duration shaped itself round the intensity of the event. They would be talking about it now, thrilled to be alive, curious to understand what it must mean, what significance it had for their future. He laughed again louder, and whooped. They would be kissing, taking one of the bottles of champagne from the back seat, beginning to undress each other, celebrating their survival in the settling dust. What a time they were having! He put his hands over his face and cried briefly and messily. Then he blew his nose hard on a yellow duster supplied by the hire firm, and got out of the car.

To have been watching Stephen, the driver would have needed to cut a hole in the roof of his cabin. Stephen was not immediately aware of this as he walked back up the road towards the lorry. The front end was so badly battered and wrenched that it was difficult at first to decide which way it would have been facing if it had been unscathed. Diligently, he kicked his ruined handle and side mirror to the edge of the road. The air ahead was warped by evaporating diesel fuel. Glass rasped unpleasantly underfoot. It occurred to him that the driver might be dead. He approached the cab warily, trying to make out where the door, or any other kind of opening, might be. But the structure had folded in on itself; it resembled a tightly closed fist, or a toothless mouth held shut. He put one foot on the wreckage and hoisted himself up till his face was level with the windshield. It had shattered into a milky, opaque surface. When he climbed further and found a side window, he saw only the padding of the cab's ceiling pressed tight against the pane. The road was of such a tidy construction that he had to jump over the irrigation ditch and search about in the bracken before he could find a large rock. He returned with it and banged the wreckage.

He cleared his throat and called out absurdly into the silence, "Hello? Can you hear me?" And then louder, "Hello!"

There was a stirring deep within the cab, then a short silence, then a man's voice close by spoke two words, two muffled monosyllables. It was a deadened acoustic, the murmur of a voice in a heavily furnished room. He called again, and broke off immediately. He had shouted over the voice as it repeated the words. He waited several seconds this time, and peered into the mess of chrome and metal, looking for a chink. When he called, the voice answered, two words of equal length. In here? Help me? He circled the cab, trying to keep the agitation out of his voice. "I can't make out what you're saying. I'm trying to find you."

He had returned to his original position. There was a pause in which, Stephen imagined, the man was gathering his strength.

He heard a sharp intake of breath and then a voice saying plainly, "Look down."

At Stephen's feet was a head. It protruded from a vertical

gash in the steel. There was a bare arm too, wedged under the head, pressing tight into the face and obscuring the mouth. Stephen knelt down. He had no reservations about touching the stranger's head. The hair was dark brown and thick. At the crown there was a bald patch the size of a large coin. The man was face down in the road, but Stephen could see that one eye at least was shut.

The gash was in fact a gap between two crumpled sections of tin plate. He could make out the top of the man's shoulder in the gloom, the red-and-black check of his workshirt. He slapped the man's face gently and the eyes opened.

"Are you in pain?" Stephen said. "Can you wait while I get help?"

The man was attempting to speak, but the forearm trapped under his jaw was obscuring his words. Stephen lifted the head with two hands and used his foot to shove the arm clear.

The man grunted and closed his eyes. When he opened them he said, "Have you got pencil and paper there, mate? I want you to take something down for me." It was a London accent, husky and friendly.

Stephen had a notebook and pencil in his pocket but he did not reach for them. "We've got to get you out of there. You might be losing blood. There's fuel everywhere."

The man spoke reasonably. "I don't think I'm going to make it. Do me a favor and take a couple of messages. Then if you rescue me after that there'll be nothing lost, will there?"

Stephen was as amenable as any man to the necessity of final messages.

"This one's for Jane Field, Tebbit House, number two three one six, Anzio Road, southwest nine."

"That's not far from me."

" 'Darling Jane, I love you . . .' " He closed his eyes and

considered. " 'I saw you in this dream I had last night. I was always going to come back. You know that, don't you. I knew something like this was going to happen. Yours, Joey.' Oh yeah, and put, 'Love to the kids.' The next one's to Pete Tapp, three hundred and nine, Brixton Road, southwest two. 'Dear Pete, Well old mate, it happened to me first. I won't be able to make Saturday.' Put a couple of, you know, exclamation marks. 'I still owe you that hundred quid. Get it off Jane. I want you to have Bessie. It's one whole tin a day, round about six, mixed in with some rusks and a cup of milk. And no chocolate. Cheerio, Joe.' Oh yeah, and put on the first one, 'P.S. I owe Pete a hundred quid.' "

Stephen turned the page of his notebook and waited.

The man was staring into the road surface. At last he said dreamily, "This one's for Mr. Corner, care of Stockwell Manor School, southwest nine. 'Dear Mr. Corner, I don't suppose you'll remember me. I left about fourteen years ago. You chucked me out of your class and said I'd never do nothing. Well I got my own business now, with my own lorry that's almost paid off, a pink twenty-ton Fahrschnell. I often think about what you said, and I wanted you to know. Yours faithfully, Joseph Fergusson, aged twenty-eight.' The next one's to Wendy McGuire, thirteen, Fox's Road, Ipswich. 'Sweetheart —' "

Stephen snapped the notebook shut and stood. "That's it," he called as he walked quickly to the car. He opened the trunk and rummaged irritably till he found the jack, which was held in an obscure place by a magnetic device.

"I tell you," the man said when Stephen returned and tried to wedge the jack sideways into the gap, "I can't feel a thing below my neck. I don't want to see it."

It looked as though there was no purchase along the crumpled sides of the opening. However, the thought of taking more dictation drove Stephen on, and at last the jack was in place and he began to work the ratchet.

He was kneeling on the ground with the head between his knees. The man was resting his cheek against the road. The jack was positioned about eighteen inches above his neck, and wedged at an angle. As it took hold, the lower end began to ease the tin plate aside, opening the gap a fraction with each hard turn of the ratchet. The upper end was against something too firm to shift and this provided a useful purchase. When the gap had opened up by three or four inches Stephen was able to reposition the jack, vertically this time, with the base close to the man's throat. With a penetrating squeaking sound, like that of a fingernail being run across a blackboard, a torn section of the lorry began to lift clear. It moved six inches before it jammed against something heavy. Stephen peered into a dark chamber where the man's body could be seen curled. There was no blood, or any evidence of damage. Careful not to disturb the jack, he took hold of the man's shoulder with one hand, cupped the other under his face, and pulled. The man groaned.

"You're going to have to help," Stephen said. "Raise your head so I can get my hand under your chin." This time there was movement, almost an inch. When this had been repeated several times, the man was able to use his free arm to push himself, and Stephen could grip him under both arms and pull him clear.

The man was nursing his wrist as they walked back to the car. "I think it's broken," he said sadly. "I was due to play in a snooker tournament on Saturday."

Stephen, who himself was shaking now and felt weak in the legs, decided that the man was in a state of shock. He helped him into the passenger seat and tucked a blanket round him. But the driver's door wouldn't open without its handle, and Stephen had to get the man out of his seat while he climbed across and squeezed behind the wheel. When at last they were settled they sat for a minute or two. The rituals of inserting the ignition key, of jiggling the gearstick, and of gripping the steering wheel calmed Stephen. He looked at the man, who stared through the windshield and trembled.

"Listen, Joe, it's a miracle you're alive."

Joe ran his tongue over his lips and said, "I'm thirsty."

Stephen reached for a bottle from the back seat. "Champagne is all we've got."

The exploding cork bounced off the dashboard and struck Joe hard on the ear. He grinned as he took the bottle. He closed his mouth over the foaming neck and sucked, and closed his eyes. They passed the bottle between them and did not speak until it was empty. When it was, Joe belched and asked Stephen his name. "You were brilliant, Stephen. Fucking brilliant. I wouldn't've thought of the jack." He looked at his wrist and said wonderingly, "I'm alive. I'm not even a cripple."

They laughed, and Stephen excitedly told the story of the six-foot gap he had driven through, how time had slowed, and how the road sign had sheared off the side mirror and door handle. "Brilliant," Joe murmured repeatedly, and "Fucking brilliant" when Stephen reached for the second bottle of champagne. They set about reconstructing the accident from their separate points of view. Joe said it felt as though a giant had picked his lorry up and tossed it in the air. He remembered the road surface coming towards him, then the upside-down glimpse of the car behind and of everything folding in around him. It was a miracle, they kept saying, a bloody miracle. Some time towards the end of the second bottle they cheered and roared for the hell of it, and for lack of anything else sang "For He's a Jolly Good Fellow," each man gesturing towards the other on the *he*.

As they drove away, Stephen remembered the jack and thought he would leave it where it was. They headed for the nearest town and discussed whether Joe should be taken to the hospital or the police station first.

He insisted on the latter. "Want it all aboveboard for the insurance man."

They were traveling at over ninety miles an hour when Stephen remembered that he was almost drunk and slowed down. Joe was silent for a while, murmuring only as they came into the outskirts of the town, "Used to know a nice girl lived round here." When they were in the center looking for the police station he said, "How long was I in there? Two hours? Three?"

"Ten minutes. Or less."

Joe was still muttering how incredible that was when Stephen found the police station and stopped. "What do you make of it, that thing about time?" he asked.

Joe stared through his window at three armed policemen getting into a patrol car. "I dunno. I was inside once for almost two years. Nothing to do, nothing happening, every fucking day the same. And you know what? It went in a flash, my time. It was all over before I knew I was there. So it stands to reason. If a lot happens quickly it's going to seem like a long time."

They got out of the car and stood about on the pavement. The celebration was at an end.

"You're alive," Stephen said for perhaps the tenth time that hour. "What do you think it means? What difference does it make?"

Joe had been thinking, he had his answers ready. "It means

I'm going back to Jane and the kids and bugger Wendy McGuire.
It means I'll buy two secondhand rigs with the insurance money."

Reminded by this of the important business in hand, he
turned and walked towards the police station, still too dazed,
Stephen supposed, to remember the formalities of thanks and
goodbyes. As Joe stood aside to let two policewomen pass
before disappearing through a set of swing doors, Stephen
thought of the messages in his notebook and felt encumbered
by them. He tore the pages out and then, taking the postcard
from his back pocket, he leaned over the gutter and posted
them all down a drain.

Perhaps the influence of the junior minister had kept the fir
plantations and the hedge-ripping machinery from the immediate vicinity of Ogbourne St. Felix. The five-hundred-acre
wood, coppiced since before Norman times and mentioned in
the Domesday Book, was set in a pocket of land visited by
commercial photographers and film makers because of its resemblance to what was generally accepted as the English countryside. The wood belonged nominally to an ossified charity.
In effect it was in the possession of the owner of the only house
on the property, who was obliged to pay for its maintenance.
A row of three woodcutters' cottages had been knocked together to form the house, which stood in a small clearing on
the southern side of the coppice. The approach was by a minor
road and then a potholed track lined with rowans and limes.
Only the experienced visitor knew that a spread of thickened
undergrowth was the Darkes' wild hedge, and that in summer
you had to search hard in a tangle of shrubbery to find the
wicket gate which opened the way to a green tunnel and out
through a rose arch into Thelma's cottage garden.

Stephen had stopped in the nearby market town to replace
the champagne. He had been feeling heavy-limbed as he crossed

a small square with his purchases towards the town's principal hotel. He wanted to wash and drink a large Scotch. He was not prepared for the group of beggars gathered by the entrance. They looked less beaten-down than the usual London types, healthier, more confident. There was laughter as he approached and a muscular old man in a string vest spat onto the pavement and rubbed his hands. None of the usual regulations seemed to apply here. By law, beggars were not even permitted to work in pairs. They were supposed to be on the move all the time, down certain authorized thoroughfares. They were certainly not supposed to be crowding round entrances like this, waiting to pester the public. Here, even badges were not correctly worn. They were strapped round tanned, sinewy forearms, or, on a couple of girls, sewn into colorful headbands. There was a giant wearing one as an eyepatch. A young man with a shaved, tattooed head had attached his to an earring.

As Stephen came closer, he was aware of his bag of clinking bottles and the provocative way the gold-foil tops protruded into the sunlight. The beggars were all watching him now and it was impossible to turn back. It was the government and its vile legislation, he thought. All the same, such a situation would not be tolerated for a moment in London, and he was on the lookout for a policeman. He had slowed his pace, and then he was among them. He stared ahead, seeing no one. He heard a voice say, "How about a tenner, then?" and he kept on. He glimpsed a pocket edition of Shelley in a girl's hand. Someone plucked at his bag, and Stephen pulled it towards him roughly. Another voice parodied a cultivated accent: "Hmm, Bollinger. What a frightfully good idea!" There was laughter as he shouldered his way through the grassy smell of sweat and the scent of patchouli.

It was this little confrontation rather than the crash that

preoccupied him as he turned the car down the Darkes' bumpy avenue. He felt guilty of a betrayal. Here was a pale man in a white silk shirt with his bottles of champagne, here were the gypsies at the gate. For years he had convinced himself he belonged at heart with the rootless, that having money was a merry accident, that he could be back on the road any day with all his stuff in one bag. But time had fixed him in his place. He had become the sort who casts about for a policeman at the sight of the scruffy poor. He was on the other side now. If not, why had he tried to pretend they were not there? Why not accept that he was outnumbered and look them in the eye as he might have once, and hand over some of the merrily accidental cash? He had stopped the car and was following an overgrown footpath to the wicket gate. The patchouli had jolted him. It was the scent of a dreamily self-destructive girl he had known in Kandihar, of chaotic shared flats in west London, of an open-air concert in Montana. He had been shaken by the commonplace of irreversible time. He had once felt light on the ground. He used to think his life was an open-ended adventure, he used to give things away, it amused him when the unexpected happened, benevolent coincidences used to bear him along. When had all that stopped? When, for example, had he started to think that the things he owned were really his, inalienably his? He could not remember.

He stopped in the gloomy tunnel of summer shrubs, set down his overnight case and the champagne, and prepared to meet his friends. His hands glowed white in the obscurity. He covered his eyes with them. He was so unhealthily stuffed up with his recent past, like a man with a cold. If he could only live in the present he might breathe freely. But I don't like the present, he thought, and picked up his things. As he straightened, he saw a silhouetted figure against the sky, framed by overhanging roses. Thelma had been watching him.

"How long were you hiding in there?" she asked as they kissed.

He failed to sound lighthearted as he said, "Years." In compensation he showed her the bottles, which were already cold, and suggested they open one immediately — the last thing he felt like doing.

Thelma led him towards the house. The door and all the windows were open wide to the evening sunshine. They entered by way of a small dining room whose stone floor gave off a watery coolness. Stephen waited here while Thelma went in search of the right kind of glasses. On the bookshelves were stuffed birds in domed cases, posing in their habitats. A tawny owl had its claws deep into a stuffed mouse. In a square tank an otter was closing its jaws round a decomposing fish. Stephen sat and rested his elbows on an unsteady round table and cheered up. By his arm was a bottle of Burgundy and its freshly pulled cork. The smell of roast meat and garlic mingled with that of the honeysuckle that trailed along the window ledge behind him. In the kitchen Thelma was filling an ice bucket, and from the garden came a cacophony of birdsong.

They sat beneath a pear tree at a rusting wrought-iron table which stood in a patch of unmown grass, surrounded by giant poppies, snapdragons, and what Stephen thought were lupins until he heard Thelma call them delphiniums.

She set down two glasses by the ice bucket and poured. "Charles is in the woods somewhere. You'll have to go and find him later."

Stephen shuddered at the acidity of the drink and thought of the red wine indoors. Another Scotch would do equally well.

Because there was rather too much to talk about, they talked about the garden. Or rather, Thelma explained, and Stephen nodded intelligently. Only when he pointed at a mass of cornflowers and asked what they were did she grasp the full extent of his ignorance. She told him how the outer edges of the garden were designed to merge with the wild growth of the wood so that there was no visible barrier between the two, and how she had been growing wildflowers for their seeds, which she planned to preserve for what she called the gene pool.

"Even the primroses have all but gone. It'll be the buttercups next."

"Everything's getting worse," Stephen said. "Isn't anything getting better?"

"You're out in the big world. You tell me."

He thought hard. "They're planting the Sussex downs with conifers. We'll be self-sufficient in wood in less than twenty years."

They drank to that, and then Stephen asked about the book. They were avoiding talking about Charles. The work was going well, Thelma said. The book was a quarter written, and another had been commissioned. She asked for the latest on the committee, and this led Stephen to report his conversation with the prime minister.

Thelma showed no surprise. "No question, Charles was favored. It was kept a secret, although I was never quite certain why. Perhaps to prevent jealousies. There was a touch of fondness and desire in there somewhere too."

"Desire?" The prime minister was said to be without it.

"Stranger things happen. In politics Charles could pass as a young man, a boy."

"Was that why you wanted him out here?"

Thelma shook her head. "I'm not saying anything till you've seen him."

"But he's happy?"

"Go and see for yourself. Follow the path from the kitchen. Where it joins the main track, turn left. You'll bump into him sooner or later."

Twenty minutes later he set off. A wide grassy track ran just within the perimeters of the wood, making an irregular oval which, according to Thelma, took an hour to walk round. There were stretches where it was possible on one side to see open fields through the trees. In other places the way veered deeper into the wood and narrowed to little more than a footpath. Here there was little light, and the grass gave way to an ivy which Stephen was reluctant to tread on because the leaves collapsed underfoot with an unpleasant popping sound. The last time he had walked in these woods, when Charles was still a government minister, everything had been skeletal and pure. Seasonal changes were just slow enough for the transformations to remain a surprise. For this hardly seemed the same place. The drought had not penetrated here. His ignorance of the names of trees and plants heightened his impression of their profusion. The wood had detonated; it was engulfed in such a chaos of vegetation it was in danger of choking on abundance.

Where the path crossed a brook, a slab of rock, the remains of an old wall, was host to a miniature Amazon, a jungle of moss, fluorescent lichen, and microscopic trees. And overhead were creepers, thick as rope, filtering the light. Down on the ground there were giant cabbages and rhubarbs, palm fronds, grasses bent double by the weight of their heads. In one place open to the sky there was an extravagant crop of purple flowers; in another, darker spot, the whiff of garlic, a reminder of dinner.

It needed a child, Stephen thought, succumbing to the inevitable. Kate would not be aware of the car half a mile behind, or of the wood's perimeters and all that lay beyond them — roads, opinions, government. The wood, this spider rotating on its thread, this beetle lumbering over blades of grass, would be all, the moment would be everything. He needed her good influence, her lessons in celebrating the specific, how to fill the present and be filled by it to the point where identity faded to nothing. He was always partly somewhere else, never quite paying attention, never wholly serious. Wasn't that Nietzsche's idea of true maturity, to attain the seriousness of a child at play?

He and Julie had once taken Kate to Cornwall. It was a short holiday to celebrate the string quartet's first public concert. Their beach was reached by way of a two-mile footpath. Late in the afternoon they started to build a sand castle near the water's edge. Kate was excited. She was at that age when everything had to be just so. The walls had to be squared off, there had to be windows, shells had to be embedded at regular intervals, and the area inside the keep had to be made comfortable with dry seaweed. Stephen and Julie had set out to amuse their daughter until it was time to leave. They had had their swim and eaten the picnic. But soon, and without quite realizing it was happening, they became engrossed, filled with the little girl's urgency, working with no awareness of time beyond the imperative of the approaching tide. The three worked in noisy harmony, sharing the bucket and two spades, ordering each other about remorselessly, applauding or pouring scorn on each other's choice of shells or window design, running — never walking — back up the beach for fresh materials.

When everything was completed and they had walked round their achievement several times, they squeezed inside the walls and sat down to wait for the tide. Kate was convinced that their castle was so well built it could resist the sea. Stephen and Julie went along with this, deriding the water when it simply lapped around the sides, booing it when it sucked away a piece of wall. While they were waiting for the final destruction Kate, who was wedged between them, pleaded to remain in the castle. She wanted them to make it their home. They would abandon their London lives, they would live on the beach forever and play this game. And it was about this time that the grown-ups cast off the spell and began to glance at their watches and talk about supper and their many other arrangements. They pointed out to Kate that they all needed to go home to collect their pajamas and toothbrushes. This seemed to her a delightful and sensible idea, and she let herself be coaxed back along the path to the car. For days afterwards, until the matter was finally forgotten, she wanted to know when they would be returning to their new lives in the sand castle. She had been serious. Stephen thought that if he could do everything with the intensity and abandonment with which he had once helped Kate build her castle, he would be a happy man of extraordinary powers.

He reached a point where the track made a right-angled turn towards the center of the wood and began a gentle descent into a hollow. The trees branched over the path to form a canopy through which the evening sun cast orange shapes onto the darkening grass. Where the track leveled out there was a dead oak, nothing more than a pillar of rotten wood. Stephen was thirty feet away from this tree when a boy stepped out from behind it and stood and stared. Stephen stopped too. The patchy light stirred when the wind blew. It was hard to see clearly, but he knew that this was just the kind of boy who used to fascinate and terrify him at school. The face was pale and fringed with sandy hair. The look was far too confident, cocky in that familiar way. He had an old-fashioned appearance — a gray flannel shirt with rolled-up sleeves and loosened tails, baggy gray shorts supported by a striped elastic belt with a silver snake clasp, bulging pockets from which a handle protruded, and scabby, blood-streaked knees. Stephen was reminded of photographs of World War II evacuees lining up with their teachers on a London railway platform.

"Hullo," Stephen said in a friendly way as he went forward. "What are you up to?"

The boy steadied himself against the tree while he lifted a leg and scratched above his ankle with the tip of his scuffed shoe. "I dunno. Jus' waiting."

"What for?"

"For you, idiot."

"Charles!" As Stephen closed the gap and extended his hand he was not certain whether it was going to be taken. It was, then Charles put his arms around Stephen's neck and embraced him. There was a smell of licorice and beyond that, of damp earth.

Charles sprang away and was crossing the track. "Want to see my place?" he said simply, and led the way down a path lined with tall ferns. Stephen followed closely, his attention fixed on the slingshot that stuck out of his friend's pocket. The leather pouch swung dangerously on rubber thongs. They crossed a clearing where wild corn grew among the tree stumps, and re-entered the wood where the trees were all mature giants. They went quickly, and occasionally Stephen broke into a run to catch up. Charles spoke in breathy, disjointed sentences, without turning his head. Stephen did not catch them all. Charles seemed to be talking to himself.

"It's really good . . . been building it all summer . . . by myself . . . my place . . ."

Stephen had time to notice that his friend had not, as he had first thought, actually shrunk. He was slighter and suppler in his movements. He had grown his hair across his forehead and cut it short behind the ears. It was his wide-open manner, the rapid speech and intent look, his unfettered, impulsive lurching, the way his feet and elbows flew out as they swung round a corner to take a second, even narrower path, the abandonment of the ritual and formality of adult greetings, that suggested the ten-year-old.

They had arrived at another, smaller clearing, in the center of which stood a tree of tremendous girth.

Charles rummaged about in the grass and picked up a rock. "See this? See this?" He would not proceed till Stephen had said yes. "This is what I used to bang these in with." He pointed to a six-inch nail driven into the tree two feet above the ground, and then to another, two feet above that. There were a dozen or so making a curving line in the trunk and reaching up to the first branch, thirty feet above the grass. He pulled Stephen by the elbow to a worn patch of ground at the foot of the tree. "Up there!" he shouted. "Look, look!" Stephen tilted his head back and saw nothing but a dizzying maze of branches dividing and subdividing. The top of the tree was not visible. "No, no," Charles said. He took Stephen's head in both hands and bent it back farther. In among the topmost branches was a black speck.

"What is it?" Stephen said. "A nest?"

It was the right thing to say. Charles jumped in the air. "It's not a nest, stupid. It's my place. My own place!"

"Amazing," Stephen said.

Charles pushed his slingshot deeper into his pocket. "Ready?"

He placed his left foot on the first nail, swung his right onto the second, and stood poised, his left hand holding the third nail, the right gesturing freely towards Stephen. "It's easy. Just do what I do."

Stephen ran his hand along the tree's bark. He stalled. "What . . . er . . . kind of tree is it, do you think?"

"A beech, of course. Didn't you know that? It's a whopper, a hundred and sixty feet, I'd say." He scrambled up till he was ten feet above the ground, then looked down. "I've been wanting to show you." Once a businessman and politician, now he was a successful prepubescent.

Stephen tested his weight against the first nail. He wanted to ask his friend what had happened to him, but Charles was too immersed in this new self, he was far beyond any appearance of pretense, or awareness of the absurdity of his transformation, and Stephen was uncertain how to approach the matter. Perhaps Charles was in an advanced state of psychosis and had to be handled with care. On the other hand, Stephen could not fail to be affected by the excitement, the challenge in the air, and the importance his old friend seemed to attach to this moment. He did not wish to appear stuffy. He had never been much good at climbing trees, but then he had never really given it a try. He pushed upwards and found himself standing with both feet squashed together on the second nail. That was easy enough, but when he looked down he was alarmed to find that he was already rather high up.

"I'm not sure this is for me," he started to say, but Charles, who by now was standing on the first branch with his hands deep in his pockets, was calling out instructions. "Put your hand on the nail just above your head, and bring your foot up, and get the next nail with your other hand . . ."

Stephen slid his hand upwards till he found the nail. Five feet might not be far to fall, but people broke their necks falling half that distance off chairs.

Minutes later he was lying face down on the first branch. It was almost as solid as the ground itself and he pressed his body to it. Inches away a woodlouse was going about its business. This was its place. Charles was trying to point out to him the route ahead, but Stephen dared not look up, nor did he want to look down. He kept his eyes on the louse. "I think I'll take it bit by bit" was all he could say. Charles offered him a sweet, threw one up in the air for himself and caught it in his mouth, then set off.

The difficult bit now was standing up, relinquishing the branch. Stephen pushed himself against the trunk as he straightened. The next task was to lift one leg high enough so that he could place his foot in the crook formed by the branch above. But once that was done, things became easier. There were so many branches shooting out from the trunk now that it was like ascending a spiral staircase. He had to do nothing more than proceed cautiously and not look down. A satisfying fifteen minutes passed. This was something he could do, something he had missed out on in childhood, and he fully understood why other boys bothered with it. He stopped for a rest and looked towards the horizon. He was way above the tops of the coppiced trees. In the distance was a church spire, and closer in, perhaps a mile away, part of the red-tiled roof of the Darkes' house. He took a tighter grip of the trunk and glanced straight down. There was a lurch in his stomach, but it was nothing too bad. He had seen the ground through a gaping arc of space and had not panicked. Emboldened, he took a deep breath, tightened his hold, and angled his head back. He was hoping to see the base of the treehouse not far ahead. His field of vision rotated about a central point, and something hot and cold plummeted from his stomach to his bowels. He rested his cheek against the trunk and closed his eyes. No, that would not do either. He opened them and stared into the bark. He had seen — and he dared not recall the image — the same endless, vertiginous branching he had seen from the ground, and way, way above just a flash of Charles's bare knees, and beyond them leaves and branches into obscurity, with no sight of the platform.

He passed a minute calming himself. He decided it would be better to return to the ground. He wanted to please his friend, but it was pointless, after all, risking his life. Here was another problem. To find the foothold below, he had to look down, and his nerve had gone for that. "Oh God," he whispered to the tree, "what am I going to do?" He did nothing. He strained to hear a comforting sound from the ground. Even birdsong would have done. But up here there was nothing, not even the wind. It occurred to him fleetingly that he was engrossed, fully in the moment. Quite simply, if he allowed another thought to distract him, he would fall out of the tree. Then he thought, I don't want to be doing this anymore. I want to do something else. Take me out, make this stop.

There was a sound above him, but he did not look up. Charles had climbed down to find him. "Come on, Stephen," he called, "the view's even better from the top."

Stephen spoke with restraint in case the force of his words propelled him backwards out of the tree. "I'm stuck," he said through his teeth into the bark.

"Oh Christ," Charles said as he appeared at his side, "You are pathetic."

"Don't move about so quickly," Stephen whispered.

"It's perfectly safe, this tree. I've been up and down it dozens of times, carrying planks and things and even a couple of chairs." Stephen lurched and Charles caught his arm. The smell of licorice was not reassuring.

"Look, see this branch. Put your hand here and pull yourself up till you can move your foot out, then put your weight on your knee and get onto this bit here . . ." The instructions continued. Stephen knew he had no choice but to obey to the letter. Useless to say he wanted to go down, for a dispute of any kind would be the end of him. He needed to trust. So he edged his way up, putting his hands and feet in exactly the places he was told, straining his attention to detect any dangerous ambiguities. A few times he interrupted. "Charles, do you mean my left hand or my right?"

"Your right, stupid!"

He kept his vision reined in on hand- and footholds. He was never sure where Charles was, and he did not want to look. There was always a disembodied voice somewhere above his head, issuing its scornful directions. "Oh God! Not your hand, your foot, you clod!"

There were times during the climb when Stephen thought to himself, I won't always be doing this. One day I'll be doing something else. But he was not entirely sure. He knew that for now all he had to do was climb and let circumstances look after themselves. One day he might, or might not, return to the old life. There was another thing, so appalling and large that he could not grasp it. The time came when at last he climbed up through a circular hole onto a ramshackle wooden platform. It was about twelve feet square and had no sides. At first he could only lie face down on it and suppress the sob rising in his throat.

"Well, what do you think?" Charles kept asking, and also, "Do you want some lemonade?"

When he had recovered, Stephen raised his head slowly, so as not to jolt the platform out of the tree, and looked about him. He kept his palms pressed flat against the boards. The whole wood was spread below them, and beyond it, five miles away across the fields, the town where he had stopped. To the west the sun was setting magnificently, the swirl of color prettified by the dust of the Thames Valley seventy miles away. Charles was sprawled on a kitchen chair, watching proudly as Stephen took in the view. The bottle of lemonade which he swung between finger and thumb was nearly empty. At his side was an orange crate on which stood a pair of binoculars, a candle in a holder, and a box of matches. Inside the case was a row of books: two on bird recognition, various boys' adventures, some William books, and, Stephen noted with no particular pleasure, his own first novel. Charles gestured towards a second chair, but Stephen did not wish to add to his height. Instead he made himself comfortable by edging away from the hole in the floor through which they had climbed.

Because his friend was looking at him expectantly, Stephen said at last, "It's very good. Well done." Charles passed the bottle and Stephen, who was prepared to show himself a willing sort of guest, took a deep swig. His mouth filled with a salty, flat liquid, something like the taste of blood, only colder and thicker. Common sense told him he should spit it out. He forced it down, however, careful not to retch, for he had noticed a loose plank by his foot.

Charles finished off the last two inches. "Made it myself," he said as he stowed the bottle among the books. "Do you want to know what's in it?"

The thought that had intimidated Stephen on the climb up now returned. It was the climb down. "Tell me," he said quickly, his words pitched higher by nausea and fear, "why are you behaving like a kid? What are we doing up here?"

For a moment Charles remained bent over the orange crate, straightening the books perhaps. Stephen could not quite see.

Had he said exactly the wrong thing? He was dependent on Charles's help and it was important that he say nothing to offend him, at least not until they were down.

Charles came and knelt beside him. He was smiling. "Do you want to see what I've got in my pockets?" The slingshot came first. He pushed it into Stephen's hands. "It's walnut. The best." There followed a magnifying glass, a sheep's vertebra, and a penknife with a dozen or so attachments. As Charles opened each one out and explained its purpose, Stephen watched his friend closely for evidence of humor, self-consciousness, for traces of the adult. But the voice was level, the face intent on every detail. There were old-fashioned peppermints stuck to the bottom of a paper bag, a larger-than-usual snail shell, a dried newt, and marbles. The one Charles put into Stephen's hand was big and milky.

To show interest, Stephen asked, "And where did you get it?"

The reply was defiant and quick — "I won it" — and he did not like to ask where. There was a ball bearing, a toy compass, a piece of rope and two empty cartridge cases, a fishhook embedded in a cork, a feather, two oval pebbles.

Looking down at these items spread before him on the planks, uncertain what to say next, Stephen was impressed by what appeared to be very thorough research. It was as if his friend had combed libraries, diligently consulted the appropriate authorities to discover just what it was a certain kind of boy was likely to have in his pockets. It was too correct to be convincing, not quite sufficiently idiosyncratic, perhaps even fraudulent. Momentarily, embarrassment overcame vertigo.

Besides, what small boy ever offered to turn out his pockets? Stephen glanced away to the west. The brilliance was fading from the display and the light was thickening. The leaves in

the few branches above their heads stirred. He was stuck for
something to say. He could no longer bear to humor the forty-
nine-year-old schoolboy, nor did he dare to upset him. Finally
he said, "Are you happy, Charles?"

Charles was stuffing his possessions back in his pocket in
roughly the order in which they had been presented. He finished, stood up quickly, and made a wide sweep with his arm.
Stephen cowered on the boards, trying to steady them with
his hands. "Look! It's fantastic. You don't understand it, it's
fantastic!"

"You mean the view?"

"No, stupid. Look . . ." He had taken his slingshot from
his pocket and was fitting a pebble into the pouch. "Watch."
He faced the sunset and drew the pouch back way behind his
head, till the rubber thongs were stretched out over two arm's
lengths. He held this position for several seconds, possibly for
effect. The air around them grew tight, and Stephen found it
difficult to breathe. Then, with the whack of rubber against
wood and a brief, high-pitched whine, the stone soared away
from the platform and rose high as it receded from them, for
an instant a precise black shape against the red sky. Even before
it began to drop, it had vanished from sight. Stephen guessed
it had cleared the wood and landed in the first field, a quarter
of a mile away.

"Good shot," he said enthusiastically. He wondered if he
should mention that it was getting dark.

Charles had his hands on his hips and was still gazing in the
direction of the stone's path when there rose towards them
through the trees the faint sound of a handbell being rung.
"Dinner," he said, and walked towards the hole and let himself
down. When he spoke again only his head showed above the
level of the platform. It was hard to tell whether the inarticulacy

was laboriously faked or was now simply a habit. "It's jus' . . . well, it's a matter of letting go . . ."

Stephen was so distracted, so sickened by fear as he crawled towards the hole, that he assumed his friend was talking about slingshot technique. He reached the edge and crouched there unhappily. His hands were shaking, and the lemonade was rising in his throat.

Charles lowered himself another couple of feet and stopped. He was almost out of control with laughter. At last he steadied himself, wiped his eyes, peered up at Stephen, and laughed again. "Now, do exactly as I tell you, or else you'll die!"

At the end of a day in which he had come close to smashing a car, seeing a man crushed to death, being set upon by beggars, and falling out of a tree, Stephen felt in need of a hot bath. Thelma said she had some reading to do and did not mind delaying the meal. He soaked in a long Victorian tub which was wedged in tight against the sloping roof of the guest bathroom. He was empty of speculation or memories. He thought only of the ripples pushed out across the water, the shock waves of his heartbeat. His kneecaps rose before him like promontories in a sea mist. The skin puckered on his fingerips. He closed his eyes and half dozed, rousing himself from time to time to turn the hot-water tap with his foot.

When at last he appeared downstairs, Thelma was reading a physics journal. Her elbows were propped on the dining table, where only two places were set. The door and windows were still open, now to thick darkness and the sound of crickets. As she fetched their meal from the kitchen she explained that Charles had already eaten and gone to bed, and that he was usually asleep by nine. "He stayed up late for you." This should have been Stephen's cue for a set of questions, and for a conversation about Charles's regression. He was glad, however, that Thelma passed him the carving knife and asked him to slice the roast. They talked about the best ways of cooking lamb. Thelma was in good humor. Weeks of country air, long afternoons tending her garden, and the chance to work at what she wanted had made her euphoric. Her bare feet made a pleasant scuffing sound on the stone floor as she moved between the kitchen and the dining room with salad and potatoes and glass bottles of vinegar and olive oil. She was wearing a collarless man's shirt tucked into a loose skirt. Round her neck was a set of painted wooden beads which might have come from a toy shop. She still kept the physicist's tight bun above the nape of her neck. There was a hint of the old conspiratorial spirit between them. It was good to live in the remote country and be visited by a friend. More than that, they were touched, liberated by Charles's behavior. Thelma no longer had to live with the secret all by herself. She splashed Burgundy into the glasses. There was a wild generosity in the air, and as Stephen took a long pull of the wine, which was warm from standing out so long, he regretted his suspicious attitudes. If only he knew what he himself wanted, what he wanted to be, he could be free to carry it through.

Fifteen minutes into the meal Stephen fulfilled a resolution he had made many weeks before and described his experience in the Kent countryside. Towards the end of his account he had himself coming round in an armchair by the fire in Julie's cottage. Thelma had been irritated by their separation; she wanted to bang their heads together, she said. He did not want to incite her with a description of a temporary, irresponsible intimacy. Otherwise, he remained faithful to the details, to the sense of another day intruding, the familiarity of the place, the bicycles leaning together outside the pub — and he went on

at length about the kind of old-fashioned machines they were —
his recognition of the young couple at their table, his father's
familiar gestures, the way his mother had looked towards and
beyond him as though he were not there, and the falling sen-
sation as he came back up the road, of tumbling through a
kind of sluice.

Thelma ate steadily as she listened, and when he had finished
went on to clear her plate before asking what had happened
before and after the experience, what had been on his mind.
He described the train journey, which he recalled with difficulty, and said he thought he had been thinking about the
committee. And afterwards? But what had happened then was
not Thelma's business. He and Julie had talked desultorily, he
said, and drunk two pots of tea and eaten the cake Julie had
made. Then he had walked back to the station, caught the train
home, and eaten supper with friends.

"And what do you make of it?" Thelma said as she poured
the wine.

He shrugged, and told her that he had learned that his parents
had once possessed new bikes.

"Do they remember the pub?"

"My mother doesn't. My father doesn't even remember the
bikes."

"You didn't describe this thing to them."

"No. I didn't want to. It was as if I'd been spying on a very
important conversation."

"Perhaps they were talking about you."

"Perhaps."

"But you still haven't told me what you make of it," Thelma
said.

"I don't know. It's got something to do with time, obviously, with seeing something out of time. And since you've
got all these theories . . ."

She clapped her hands. "You go out in the countryside and have a vision, a hallucination or whatever, and what do you do? Consult an expert, of course! A scientist, no less. You come cap in hand to the oracle you quietly despise. Why don't you go and ask a modernist?"

But Stephen was used to this. "Come off it, Thelma. Admit you're bursting to lecture me. You miss your students, even the stupid ones. Let's hear it. What's the state of the art on time?"

Despite her good mood, Thelma did not seem eager to offer the usual tutorial. Perhaps she suspected him of mental laziness; perhaps she was saving her ideas for her book. Initially, at least, her tone was dismissive and she spoke rapidly. It was only later that she warmed up.

"There's a whole supermarket of theories these days. You can take your pick. They're all written up for the layman in books of the 'fancy that' variety. One offering has the world dividing every infinitesimal fraction of a second into an infinite number of possible versions, constantly branching and proliferating, with consciousness neatly picking its way through to create the illusion of a stable reality."

"You've told me that one before," Stephen said. "I think about it a lot."

"In my view you might just as well go for a bearded old man in the sky. Then there are physicists who find it convenient to describe time as a kind of substance, an efflorescence of undetectable particles. There are dozens of other theories, equally potty. They set out to smooth a few wrinkles in one corner of quantum theory. The mathematics are reasonable enough in a local sort of way, but the rest, the grand theorizing, is whistling in the dark. What comes out is inelegant and perverse. But whatever time is, the common-sense, everyday version of it as linear, regular, absolute, marching from left to right, from the past through the present to the future, is either nonsense or a tiny fraction of the truth. We know this from our own experience. An hour can seem like five minutes or a week. Time is variable. We know it from Einstein, who is still our bedrock here. In relativity theory, time is dependent on the speed of the observer. What are simultaneous events to one person can appear in sequence to another. There's no absolute, generally recognized 'now' — but you know all this."

"It gets clearer each time around."

"In dense bodies with colossal gravitational fields — black holes — time can grind to a halt altogether. The brief appearance of certain particles in the cloud chamber can only be explained by the backward movement of time. In the big-bang theory, time is thought to have been created in the same moment as matter, it's inseparable from it. And that's part of the problem — to consider time as an entity, we have to wrench it apart from space and matter, we have to distort it to look at it. I've heard it argued that the very way our brains are wired up limits our understanding of time, just as it holds our perceptions to only three dimensions. That sounds like pretty dim materialism to me. And pessimistic too. But we do have to tie ourselves to models — time as liquid, time as a complex envelope with points of contact between all moments."

Stephen remembered from his last year in school:

"Time present and time past
Are both perhaps present in time future,
And time future contained in time past."

"There, you see, your modernists have their uses after all. I can't help you with your hallucination, Stephen. Physics certainly can't. It's still a divided subject. The twin pillars are relativity and quantum theories. One describes a causal and continuous world, the other a noncausal, discontinuous world. Is it possible to reconcile them? Einstein failed with his unified field theory. I side with the optimists like my colleague David Bohm, who anticipates a higher order of theory."

It was at this point that Thelma livened up and Stephen began to understand less. The prospect was always so tantalizing: a lucid account of what some of the best minds of the day were thinking about the elusive, everyday matter of time, what they were demonstrating in laboratories and giant accelerators. It was the promise of teasing paradox, and of personal intuitions confirmed, made official. What betrayed the promise was sheer difficulty, the indignity of coming up against the limitations of one's intellectual reach.

At first she was patient with him, and he struggled hard. Then, slowly, she began to leave him behind and speak of Green's function, Clifford and fermionic algebras, matrices and quaternions. Soon she abandoned all pretense of communication. She was addressing a fellow physicist, a soulmate who did not exist. Her eyes moved away from his and fixed on a point a few feet to his left, and her words became an uninterruptable torrent. She was talking for her own benefit, she was possessed. She spoke of eigenfunctions and Hermitian operators, Brownian motion, quantum potential, the Poisson bracket and the Schwarz inequality. Had she gone the same way as Charles? He watched her with alarm, uncertain whether he should reach across and touch her, try to bring her back. But he reasoned that she needed to get it out, tell her story of fermions, disorder, and flux. In fact she returned within fifteen minutes and seemed to become aware of him again. Her voice lost its monotonous intensity, and soon she was dealing once more in generalities he could understand.

She wanted him to share her excitement as she anticipated that in fifty or a hundred years' time, or even less, there might evolve a theory, or a set of theories, of which relativity and quantum theories would be special, limiting cases. The new theory would refer to a higher order of reality, a higher ground, the ground of all that is, an undivided whole of which matter, space, time, even consciousness itself, would be complicatedly related embodiments, intrusions that made up the reality we understood. It was not entirely fanciful to imagine that one day there could be mathematical and physical descriptions of the type of experience Stephen had recounted. Different kinds of time, not simply the linear, sequential time of common sense, could be projected through consciousness from the higher common ground, of which consciousness itself would be a function, a limiting case which in turn would be inseparable from the matter which was its subject, or the space within which it occurred.

Thelma was pouring the last of the wine into Stephen's glass. When science could begin to abandon the illusions of objectivity by taking seriously, and finding a mathematical language for, the indivisibility of the entire universe, and when it could begin to take subjective experience into account, then the clever boy was on his way to becoming the wise woman.

"Think how humanized and approachable scientists would be if they could join in the really important conversations about time, and without thinking they had the final word — the mystic's experience of timelessness, the chaotic unfolding of time in dreams, the Christian moment of fulfillment and redemption, the annihilated time of deep sleep, the elaborate time schemes of novelists, poets, daydreamers, the infinite, unchanging time of childhood."

He knew he was hearing a part of her book. "The slow time

of panic," he added to her list, and told the story of his near collision with the lorry and how he had freed the driver. From there on the conversation meandered tiredly, and it was not until the evening was almost at an end that Thelma returned to Stephen's hallucination, as they had now agreed to call it.

"You have to forgive my ranting. It's what comes of living alone in the country with only ideas for company. You don't need physics to explain what happened to you. Niels Bohr was probably right all along when he said that scientists should have nothing to do with reality. Their business is to construct models that account for their observations."

She was going round the room turning out lamps, pulling the windows to. Stephen watched her closely. The word *alone* took a long time to subside. The harsher overhead lights came on. She seemed tired and a little stooped.

"But don't we all do that?" Stephen said as they went up the stairs. "Isn't that what reality is anyway?"

She kissed him lightly. Her lips were dry against his cheek. He felt the heat from her face. She turned her back and went along the creaky corridor to her room, which, Stephen noted as he remained by his door, was separate from her husband's.

The next morning he slept late and woke to the unusual din of birdsong. He lay on his back for half an hour and decided to return to London. Two and a half years on, it still made him uneasy to be away when Kate, or someone who knew where she was, might come to the flat. Nor was he looking forward to spending a day in the woods with Charles. Enough had happened for one day. Now he wanted to be on the couch in front of the TV, surrounded by familiar mess.

He went downstairs and out into the glare of the garden. Thelma was sitting in the shade reading a book. Charles had left early for the woods and would see him there, near the treehouse. When he explained his plans, she did not try to press him to stay. They drank a cup of coffee together, and afterwards Thelma led the way through the green tunnel and spent a minute admiring the shorn-off door handle and side mirror. Stephen opened the passenger door, but did not get in. Around them in the nettles was an angry buzz of insects.

Thelma had gone round to the driver's side. She smiled across the dazzling roof. "It's all right, you can say it. He's completely mad."

"Well, you tell me."

"It would have been worse if we had stayed, you know. This isn't exactly a sudden thing. It's been coming for years. Why do you think he was so crazy about your first book?"

Stephen shrugged. He was wearing a recently cleaned linen suit and a fresh white shirt. The car keys were in his hand, his wallet was snug in his inside pocket — the equipment of adulthood. The prospect of a solitary drive pleased him. What had seemed wild and liberating about Charles's fantasies the night before now seemed merely silly, something he should snap out of. The metal strap of Stephen's wristwatch was snagging the hairs of his wrist. He made an adjustment, and was about to climb into the car.

She raised a forefinger in warning. "Now don't get all urbane with me."

He slid across the passenger seat and put the key in the ignition.

She spoke through the open window. "He's happy."

"I can see that. And you?"

"I'm working."

"And all alone."

Thelma pursed her lips and glanced away.

Stephen was annoyed with his friends. They had always managed to be both exciting and firmly rooted. Now they seemed to be making rather a hash of things.

Thelma put her hand into the car and touched his arm. "Stephen, be soft . . ."

He nodded briskly and started the car.

❧ 6 ❧

"Those who find it naturally hard to wield authority over their children should seriously consider the systematic use of treats and rewards. The promise of chocolate in return for, say, good bedtime behavior is, on balance, worth the minor damage to teeth which will in any case soon replace themselves. In the past, too much has been demanded of parents, who have been exhorted to inculcate altruism in their children at all costs. Incentives, after all, form the basis of our economic structure and necessarily shape our morality; there is no reason on earth why a well-behaved child should not have an ulterior motive."

— from *The Authorized Child-Care Handbook*, HMSO

THE RAINS CAME at last in late September, delivered by gales that stripped most trees bare in less than a week. Leaves clogged the drains, certain streets became navigable rivers, old couples were helped out of basement flats by policemen in waders, and there was a general feeling of crisis and excitement, at least on television. Weather experts were in demand to explain why there was no autumn, why it was summer last week, winter this. There was no shortage of comforting theories — the encroaching ice age, the melting ice caps, the ozone layer depleted by fluorocarbons, the sun in its death throes. From urban barracks no one knew existed soldiers appeared with heavy-duty pumps. A military helicopter was televised lifting a stranded boy from a tree and on news programs chief police constables or army commanders pointed at maps with sticks. The home secretary, Charles's old boss, was seen visiting the worst-hit areas. The prime minister was said by the Cabinet press office to be personally concerned. Responsible opinion agreed that the weather was serving the government well, for while no one yet knew how to stop the rain, things were seen to be done. It rained every day for fifty days. Then it stopped, normal life resumed, and it was not long till Christmas.

The weather had little effect on Stephen's torpor. The Olympic Games had given him a taste for morning and afternoon television. A new all-day channel had opened, sponsored by the government and specializing in game and chat shows, commercials and phone-ins. Stephen, sprawled out with his Scotch on the couch in pajamas and thick cardigan, watched the game shows with an addict's glazed patience. In the corner of the room an ice bucket caught drips from the ceiling. The hosts on various programs resembled each other to such an extent that he had warmed to them. They were professionals, dedicated men clearly working to order within a convention whose formal limitations they occasionally pointed up with cynical asides. And he liked the sweetly vulnerable couples who were welcomed on stage and never let go of each other's hands, the extravagant trumpet fanfares which might greet the unveiling of a Deepfreeze, the almost naked assistants with the fixed, brave smiles.

The audiences, however, brought him to bouts of delirious misanthropy. It was the doggish eagerness to please the host and to be pleased by him, their readiness to applaud and cheer on command and wave plastic pennants bearing the show's slogan; it was the ease with which their moods were regulated, whipped into uproar one moment, then calmed and made serious the next — naughty, then a little bit sentimental and nostalgic; embarrassed, shamed by their haranguing host, then cheerful again. The faces tilted into the studio lights were those of adults, parents, workers, but the wide-open expressions were those of children watching a teatime party conjurer. They were held by what looked like religious awe when the host descended to walk among them, first-naming, chiding, flattering. *Is she giving you enough, Henry? To eat, I mean. Is she? Is she? Come on now. Are you getting enough?* And here was Henry, a white-haired man with bifocals, who in a better cut of suit could have passed for a head of state, giggling and looking meaningfully at his wife, then sinking his face into his hands while all around him roared and clapped. Was it any surprise the world was led by morons, with these enfeebled souls at the ballot box, these ordinary "folk" — a word much used by the hosts — these infants who longed for nothing more than to be told when to laugh? Stephen tilted his bottle and sucked and was ready to disenfranchise them all. More than that, he wanted them punished, soundly beaten, no, tortured. How dare they be children! He was prepared to listen, tolerant, reasonable man that he was, while it was explained just what purpose these people served, and why they should be permitted to go on living.

For Stephen, these bouts — a democrat's pornography — were as pleasurably degrading as anything he could remember. They peaked just before he chose to recall that his parents, along with his mother's sister, Phyllida, and her husband, Frank, and their grown-up daughter, Tracy, had once been a part of just such a studio audience and had had the time of their lives.

Each of them brought away a medallion showing a profile of their host, wreathed in laurel like an emperor, and on the obverse a pair of hands firmly clasped in friendship.

This might be the time to rise to empty the water from the ice bucket, fix a sandwich or another drink in the kitchen, or spend time gazing out of the open window at the flooded street below. He had a list of preoccupations to keep him there, and the television to return to when he was tired of running through it. The Parmenter Committee's long recess still had almost a month to run and he was annoyed to find that he missed the weekly meetings and the structure it allowed his thoughts. It bothered him that he had not heard from Julie, and that he could not bring himself to write to her without resentment. Although he fully intended to, he had not visited his parents again. He thought about Charles with nothing but irritation. More absorbing than any of these was Kate's birthday. Next week, wherever she was, she was going to be six.

For days now he had been wanting to visit a toy shop ten minutes' walk from the flat. The thought was laughable. It presented a parody of bereavement. The willful pathos of it made him groan out loud. It would be play-acting, a pretense to a madness he did not really feel. But the thought grew. He might stroll in that direction, imagine the sort of thing he would have bought. It was folly, it was weakness, it would cause him needless pain. But the thought went on growing, and one morning in the newsagent's he picked up a roll of colored wrapping paper and thrust it at the assistant before he had time to change his mind. To buy a toy would undo two years of adjustment, it would be irrational, indulgent, self-destructive; and weak, above all weak. It was the weak who failed to maintain the line between the world as it was and the world as they wanted it to be. Don't be weak, he told himself, try to survive. Throw away the paper, don't cave in to fantasy, don't go down that way. You might never come back. He did not go, but he could not stop himself wanting to go.

Solitude had encouraged in him small superstitions, a tendency to magical thought. The superstitions had attached themselves to daily rituals, and in the constant silence of his own company his adherence had become rigorous. He always shaved the left side of his face first, he never began brushing his teeth until he had replaced the top of the toothpaste tube, he flushed the lavatory with his left hand although it was inconvenient, and these days he was scrupulous in placing both feet at once on the floor when he got out of bed. Magical thinking found ways of rationalizing a trip to the toy shop.

Before all else, it would be an act of faith in his daughter's continued existence. Since she certainly would not be celebrating this day, it would be an assertion of her previous life and proper inheritance, of the truth about her birth — he had imagined the lies she would have been told about that. The observance of a mystery would release unknowable configurations of time and chance, the number magic of birthdates would be activated, events would be set in train that otherwise would not occur. To buy a present would demonstrate that he was not yet beaten, that he could do the surprising, lively thing. He would purchase his gift in joy rather than sorrow, in the spirit of loving extravagance, and in bringing it home and wrapping it up he would be making an offering to fate, or a challenge — *Look, I've brought the present, now you bring back the girl.* If the purchase cost him pain, then the pain would constitute a necessary sacrifice. Since he had exhausted all possibilities on the material plane by searching the streets, by placing ads in local newspapers offering a generous reward for information, by pasting enlarged photographs on bus shelters and walls, then it only made sense to deal on the level of the symbolic and the numinous, to conjoin with those unknowable forces that dealt in probability, that both distributed atoms to make solid objects solid and unfolded all physical events, ultimately all personal destinies. And what had he to lose?

The toy shop occupied a section of a converted warehouse and was in the style of a supermarket. Three spacious aisles under high fluorescent lights ran its length, and by the door was a row of checkout counters with carts and wire baskets heaped up nearby. The floor was in black springy rubber which gave off a sporty, efficient smell. On the wall was a sign in Day-Glo paint in imitation of a childish scrawl which warned that breakages would have to be paid for. From speakers hung high above the hooded lights came music suitable for children — a bouncy clariet, a glockenspiel, a snare drum. It was Kate's birthday. Because it was early on a Monday morning and raining steadily when Stephen arrived, the shop was empty of customers. By the only till open sat a young man with severely cropped hair and a black ear stud, writing in a notebook. Before entering by the rubber-laminated turnstile, Stephen paused to take off his coat and shake out his umbrella.

The layout was simple. One end of the store was dominated by the khaki of combat drill and vehicle camouflage and the riveted silver of heavily armed spaceships, the other by the pale pastels of baby wear and the shining white of miniature household appliances. With his wet coat folded over his arm, Stephen paced the length of the shop, from slaughter to drudgery, and discovered that the more interesting toys lay in between, where imitation of adults gave way to purer fun — a clockwork gorilla who climbed the side of a skyscraper to deliver a coin, a machine for squirting paint, a farting cushion, putty that glowed and squeaked then molded, a ball that bounced unpredictably.

Each of these he put tentatively into the hands of a six-year-old he knew as well as himself. He needed to test her reactions. She was a reticent girl, in company at least, with a straight back and dark bangs. She was a fantasist, a daydreamer, a lover of strange-sounding words, a keeper of secret diaries, a hoarder of inexplicable objects. His first choices were safe: a set of colored pens and a wooden box filled with minute farm animals. She preferred soft toys to dolls, and he dropped into his wire basket a lifelike gray cat. She was a giggler with a taste for practical jokes. He took the cushion and a flower that squirted water. She could torment her mother with these. He paused in front of a display of puzzles. He was not mad, he knew what was real. He knew what he was doing, he knew she was gone. He had thought all this out quite carefully, and he was not deceived. He was doing this for himself, without illusions. Then he continued. She had no great taste for the abstract, enclosed world of puzzles. Her intelligence thrived on human contact, on the warmer complexities of fantasy and pretense. She liked to dress up. He reached for a witch's hat, then he went back and changed the gray cat for a black one. Now he thought he had his theme. He was pulling stuff off the shelves at speed. He took magic pellets that turned into flowers on contact with water, a book of rhyming spells and caldron recipes, a bottle of invisible ink, a cup that caused water poured into it to disappear, a nail that looked as though it had been driven through its wearer's head.

He was straying into the boys' section. Beyond all question she was a graceful child, but she was hopeless with a ball and it was time she knew how to throw. He took from the shelves a plastic sock of tennis balls. He fingered a cricket bat, well made in a child's size, real willow. Was it too strenuously against the roles? He took it anyway — useful for the beach. Now he was deep into boys' territory, passing guns, knives, flame-throwers, death rays, and toy handcuffs, till he came to it at last, a matter of instant recognition: Kate's present. It was a battery-powered, two-station, short-wave and frequency-modulated walkie-talkie set. On the packet a boy and a girl communicated delightedly across a small mountain range on what looked like the surface of the moon. From the antennas of their handsets sprang white arcs of lightning, a representation of radio waves and excitement.

He took the box from a pile of fifty or so. There was no room for it in the basket. As he crossed to the checkout, he was suddenly impatient to be home with his choices, to set them out and rehearse once more the reason for each one. Even better if Julie could have gone through them with him; she would have had ideas of her own, producing a richer set of possibilities, a greater offering to fate . . . But he knew what was real, he thought, as he handed over a surprisingly large sum of money. He knew that Julie was in her damp cottage with her partitas, with her notebooks and sharpened pencils, writing him painstakingly out of her existence. In his haste he forgot his umbrella by the entrance, but he was confirmed in his bold impulses when it stopped raining as he crossed the empty car park outside the store.

At home he unpacked the walkie-talkie last. As he inserted the batteries, a rectangle of paper fell into his hand. "The maximum range of this device," it announced, "is in accordance with government legislation." He placed one set on the floor at the end of his long hallway, near the front door. He took several paces backwards, lifted the other set to his mouth, and pressed the transmitting button. He had intended to say,

"One, two, three," but because there was no one there to judge him, because he knew exactly what he was doing and that he was not mad, he began to sing "Happy Birthday" in a croaky baritone, all the while retreating up the hall. It was a crude representation of a voice he heard from the other end, tinny, crackling, with rustling consonants and muffled vowels. It could indeed have been a broadcast from the moon. But it worked, it would be fun. When he was a little more than a dozen paces away and on the penultimate line of his song, the transmission ceased. He took a step forward and it resumed, so he stood there, just within range, to finish the last line. This was a machine to encourage proximity. It belonged in the plan.

It was early in the afternoon, while he was wrapping the presents, that his jauntiness began to fade and he felt the first ache of pointlessness. He had been whistling and he stopped abruptly, a long nail smeared with fake blood in his hand. Meaning was draining fast. He did not wish to leave half the presents unwrapped. He pressed on with less care. The black cat's tail protruded from the paper and gave itself away. He went to the kitchen for a fresh bottle of Scotch and returned to the sitting room. More than fifteen misshapen packages in red paper were spread about the floor. What dismayed him was the quantity. He had intended one gift, one purely symbolic item with which to protest her absence, assert his playfulness, blackmail fate. Now this pile mocked him for weak-headedness. It was a pathetic abundance. He heaped the parcels onto the table, packing them close to make them seem fewer.

He found himself at his usual place by the open window. The logical thing to do on Kate's birthday was to visit Julie. He could stop by The Bell at the same time, see if anything happened. In order to keep busy, he spent a quarter of an hour on the phone checking train times, changing his shoes, bolting the door onto the fire escape. He put a notebook and pen into his coat pocket. Then he returned to the window. Traffic, steady drizzle, shoppers waiting patiently at the crossing — it was a wonder that there could be so much movement, so much purpose, all the time. He himself had none at all. He knew he wasn't going. He felt the air leaving him slowly, without a sound, and his chest and spine shrink. More than two years on and still stuck, still trapped in the dark, enfolded with his loss, shaped by it, lost to the ordinary currents of feeling that moved far above him and belonged exclusively to other people. He brought to mind the three-year-old, the springy touch of her, how she fit herself so comfortably round his body, the solemn purity of her voice, the wet red and white of tongue and lips and teeth, the unconditional trust. It was getting harder to recall. She was fading, and all the time his useless love was swelling, encumbering and disfiguring him like a goiter. He thought, I want you. I want you back. I want you brought back now. I don't want anything else. All I want to do is to want you to come back. It became an incantation whose rhythm narrowed to a throb, a physical pain, till all that went before was held in the words *It hurts*. Hunched by the window with his empty glass, Stephen let his thoughts wither to those two words.

He remained immobile, unaware of the passage of time. For a while it stopped raining, then it resumed, a heavier downpour. At last he heard from another flat the remote chime of a clock striking two, reminding him of something he did not want to miss. He came away from the window, averting his gaze from the pile on the table, and turned on the television. Fractionally before the vision came the sound, the energetic drone of a familiar host's voice. He settled back and reached for the bottle.

.   .   .

During this inert time, friends returning home from summer trips abroad phoned to find out how Stephen was and whether he would like to join them for lunch or dinner. He would stand by the phone in his pajamas and make himself sound wide-awake and friendly but firm. He had started a book, something of a departure from the usual thing, he was working night and day and determined not to break his stride. He told the lie half a dozen times in a fortnight and worked it up so convincingly that he began to long for it to be true. To be lost to a daily quota of typewritten words, to pass the evenings under his lamp scrawling over them in black ink, to retype and, next day, press on into the unravelling of something only half known — he could almost believe himself as he made his apologies down the phone. But he knew he did not have the stamina, the essential optimism that made the effort of writing possible. As for ideas, the very word made him weary. His friends were understanding and, touchingly, excited on his behalf, and it was at this point he would become a little ashamed of his fiction and try to wind up the conversation as rapidly as he could. This in itself was interpreted as an eagerness to be back at work. When he returned to his couch, his drink, and the TV, he would be distracted for an hour or so, unable to concentrate.

One call, however, was different. A cautiously enunciating voice asked if it was talking to Stephen Lewis, and then introduced itself by a lengthy title whose key words alone he managed to grasp — assistant secretary, Cabinet, department, protocol. Every three months, the assistant secretary explained, the prime minister gave a lunch at Downing Street for a few people, not politicians, who were distinguished in their fields. Such occasions were informal and intimate, and not widely publicized. What was said at them was considered off the record. Journalists were not often invited. Dress for men was dark suit and tie, nothing flamboyant. Steel-tipped shoes were not acceptable. Smoking would be permitted after lunch, but not before. Guests, of whom there were only four on each occasion, were to present themselves a full hour before the lunch began to the Cabinet Office in Whitehall and make themselves known to reception there. They should be understanding and patient while they allowed themselves to be thoroughly searched by two members of their own sex. Recording and photographic equipment would be confiscated and destroyed. Personal objects such as nail scissors and files, steel combs, metal pens, spectacle cases, and loose change would be confiscated and returned later. Guests should present to reception two recent, passport-sized color photographs of themselves signed on the back. One of these would be used in the laminated security clearance card, which was to be worn on the left lapel at all times. The second photograph was for office purposes and would not be returned. The lunches were relaxed affairs at which there was no set agenda for conversation, which was usually free-ranging and of mutual interest. The following topics, however, were not expected to be raised since they were covered quite adequately by the prime minister in the House and in various speeches and broadcasts: defense, unemployment, religion, the private conduct of any Cabinet minister, and the date of the next general election. The lunch would begin at one and end ten minutes after the serving of coffee.

The assistant secretary paused. Stephen had been preparing his excuse: the work he had started, the new ground he thought he was breaking, and so on. But as the limitations to the event proliferated, so, perversely, did his interest grow.

"I take it you're inviting me," he said at last.

"Well, not quite. I am phoning to discover what your attitude would be if, and I only say if, you were to receive an invitation."

Stephen sighed. From the living room came laughter and a sharp round of applause. A particularly helpless young couple were in separate soundproofed booths exposing each other's sexual quirks. He stretched the telephone lead into the room, but he had moved the set only the day before and it was just out of his sight.

The assistant secretary was not moved by Stephen's diffidence. He explained as though to a child. "The prime minister does not like to be refused and it is part of my job to make sure this never happens. Invitations are issued only to those likely to accept them. This conversation now, however, should not be treated as an invitation. I would simply like to know your attitude in the event of your receiving one."

"I'll come," Stephen said as he squinted past the doorjamb at a portion of the television screen. The couple were out of the booths. The man was sobbing into his hands and was trying to leave the stage. The host had him firmly by the elbow though.

"You mean you'd come if you were invited."

"Right."

"Then an invitation may or may not be on its way to you," the assistant secretary said, and rang off. Stephen hurried into the living room.

It was a pleasure when mid-October came at last and it was time to walk the noisy route to Whitehall once more, collar turned up, umbrella held high. The air was keen and dust-free; the rush-hour crowd pushed forward quickly, purposefully. The year was hurrying to its end faster than ever before, having skipped a season, and there was an anticipatory sense of fresh beginnings. Stephen strode out, stepping in the gutter where necessary to pass. To have a destination, a place where you were expected, a shred of identity, was such a relief after a month of game shows and Scotch. To show his pass to the familiar taciturn guard, to saunter across the marble hall among well-dressed, self-important people, to penetrate deep into the building, knowing without giving the matter a thought which staircases and corridors to take, to arrive at just the room and make small talk with colleagues, to sip coffee from the plastic cups bearing the ministry's stamp, bought from a machine in the corridor that dispensed onion soup down the same noz-zle — it was for little repetitions like these that people kept their jobs, however dull. It was all Stephen could do to refrain from bursting into song.

Instead he jingled his house keys in his pockets. Here was Emma Carew, who laughed at everything he said and whose neck tendons were ready to snap in merriment, and Colonel Tackle, who gave Stephen's hand a manly squeeze and talked about tomato-growing in a rainless summer. Hermione Sleep, who wore a silk scarf wound round her head and who still remembered his audience with the prime minister, sounded him out about dinner. He met a questioning glance from Ra-chael Murray, who kept to the far side of the room, well away from the chatter. They had exchanged phone numbers at the end of the last session before the break and neither one had called. In his happiness Stephen regretted this and resolved to see her. By the tall windows the three academics and several others were starting up a loud seminar of their own. Then Lord Parmenter arrived in a gray pinstripe on whose lapel was a miniature red rose. As though snatching a moment of private prayer, he stood by the door and lowered his head, which was resplendently bronzed. Then he gargled the room to order.

There were opening formalities. Eventually Canham cleared his throat loudly and stood to read out some draft proposals for their final report. There followed twenty minutes of rambling, muted dissent, until Parmenter intervened. These matters could be discussed later, for it was time to take further evidence and visitors should not be kept waiting. So the committee took evidence, dull depositions from two experts, and Stephen gave himself over once more to the luxury of structured daydreaming.

The disintegration of contemporary marriage had been the subject of dozens of novels he had read in the past twenty years, of films he could no longer remember, of easy gossip or earnest debate among concerned friends; he had gone drinking with the protagonists, or held their hands and listened, or given them house room. On one occasion, when he was barely twenty, he had become involved to the extent of breaking into his lover's husband's house and stealing, or retrieving, the washing machine — a foolish act of devotion. He had half-read long articles in magazines and newspapers: marriage was a dying institution because more people got divorced than ever before; or it was thriving because more people got married more often than ever before — they had higher expectations, they were trying to get it right. Now that Stephen had joined the throng he expected, with so much reading and talking and listening behind him, to be an expert, like everybody else. But it was as if he were trying to write afresh a book that had already been written. The ground was so well prepared, planted up with myth and cliché, and the tradition so firmly established, that he could no more think clearly about his own situation than a medieval painter could, by taking thought, invent perspective.

For example, he made long and eloquent speeches in his mind to Julie, which he revised and extended over the months. These were founded upon the unhelpful idea of a final truth, an irrefutable overview amounting to a verdict, whose clarity and force — if only she could be exposed to it — would not fail to convince Julie that her understanding of their situation and her behavior in response to it were deeply flawed. He must have picked up that habit of mind by spending so long listening to the protestations of injured parties. In any other matter he accepted, with resignation, the fact that the way people understood things had a lot to do with the way people were, how they had been shaped, what they wanted; tricks of rhetoric would not shift them.

Equally there were ready-made roles he could adopt for both of them, many of them contradictory, mutually exclusive. There were times, for example, when he thought that Julie's problem was weakness — she simply did not have the force of character to see out a difficult time with him. In which case it was just as well she had gone. She had been tested, she had failed. But this was not quite enough; he wanted to tell her she was weak; more than that, he wanted her to know it, the way he did. Otherwise she would go on behaving as if she were strong. And there were other times, when his spirits were low, when he thought of himself as the innocent victim (he did not like to use the word *weak* here). Then he was displeased by the way his own life had shriveled to nothing while hers was so contentedly self-sufficient. This was because she had used him, stolen from him. He had gone out searching for their daughter while she sat at home. When he had failed to find her, Julie had blamed him and left, her head full of cant about the proper way to mourn. The proper way! Who was she to lay down rules about that? Had he found Kate, then his methods would never have been in doubt, though Julie would surely have found a way to claim credit. *By my inaction*, he heard her announce, *I moved you to strenuous efforts*.

This was a short distance from another well-prepared channel, the argument from malice. Julie had been waiting for an excuse to leave the marriage, being too great a moral coward to do so on the basis of her own grievances. She had used Kate's disappearance to effect her own. Or, more elaborately, she had wanted him out of her way, Kate was living with her in secret, the abduction in the supermarket had been carefully and cynically planned, probably with the help of some old lover. Or a new one. While he believed none of this, thinking it gave him a certain self-destructive and sentimental pleasure, it helped work up the rage to move him to unfold one of his set speeches, one of the final verdicts which, it would be suddenly apparent, needed adjustment, stronger words, harsher truths.

There was no succor to be had from the legends and symbology, the great, enveloping tradition of marital breakdown, for like many before him, he thought his own case was unique. His difficulties were not bred from within, like other people's, they did not grow out of anything so banal as sexual boredom or financial pressure. There had been a malevolent intervention and — he kept coming back to this — Julie had left. He was still there, in the same old flat, and Julie had gone.

Much later he was to realize that he never really thought about his situation at all, for thought implied something active and controlled; instead images and arguments paraded in front of him, a mocking, malicious, paranoid, contradictory, self-pitying crowd. He had no clarity, no distance, he was never looking for a way through. There was no purpose to his brooding. He was the victim, not the progenitor, of his thoughts.

They washed over him most effectively when he offered them
a drink, or when he was tired, or waking from deep sleep.
There were times when they left him in peace for days on end,
and when they resumed he was too immediately immersed to
propose the simple question, What did this preoccupation
amount to? Any drunk in a bar could have told Stephen that
he was still in love with his wife, but Stephen was a little too
clever for that, too in love with thought.

While a man with a trim black toothbrush mustache explained why children's books should not be illustrated, Stephen
gazed into his lap and drifted away. At some level desire pow-
ered his thoughts, but it was rarely a conscious element. When
he remembered his last visit to Julie's house, what came to
mind was the stifling awkwardness towards the end, and the
sense of everything having been played out. He did not dwell
on the intimacy and pleasure because they did not match the
self-protective mesh of his preoccupations. Today he was hap-
pier, however superficially. There had been just a touch of
tension, the briefest moment, in the glance he had exchanged
with Rachael Murray. Today he was disposed to gentler currents of vague longing and remorse. He heard Julie's voice,
not speaking words and sentences, but her voice in abstract —
its pitch, which was low, its rhythms, the melody of her phrases.
When she was insistent or excited, she broke register in a sweet
way. He tried to make this voice say something to him, but
none of the words sounded like hers. Then it was all the more
intimate for being wordless, a purer expression of character.
It murmured; he heard it as though through a thick wall. The
tone was neither loving nor aggressive. It was Julie in her
speculative mood, describing a course of action they might
take, something they might achieve together. A holiday, a
new set of colors for a room, or a more ambitious project?

He strained to hear her. He saw her in a characteristic pose, in an armchair, one foot on the floor, her other knee raised to support her crossed arms, which in turn supported her chin. She was proposing a difficult undertaking. She appeared excited as she made her proposals, but her voice was level and certain. Now he had her with legs folded beneath her, hands folded across her belly. She stared at him, silent, contentedly secretive. She wore a patched-up pair of old corduroys and a loose shirt with billowing sleeves and many pleats. She was plump and comfortable, she looked pregnant. He thought of her buttocks, the smoothness of their concavities. He saw his hand resting there, and then, unaccountably, his thoughts slid away and he was thinking of her two brothers, both doctors, obsessed by their work and their large families. There came to mind the small army of her nephews and nieces, the presents he and Julie bought for them every Christmas; now he saw her tough, grizzled mother, who worked for a charity and kept a small flat crammed with photographs and mementos — old toys, cracked dolls, rock, stamp, egg, and feather collections, and, in thick albums numbered by years, pictures of Julie with an Alice band, displaying a pet rabbit in a passionate grip, with a foot on each brother's shoulder. And Julie's father, dead when his children were teenagers, kept alive in family mythology and still cried for occasionally by Julie and her mother.

An inventory proliferated outward to remoter stretches of Julie's family: an architect uncle who had been to prison, her women friends, her ex-lovers, one of whom he was fond of, her work, the French family that had adopted her in her teens and still invited her over to their dismal château; and inward, to the pomander she kept in her drawer full of sweaters, her taste for exotic underwear and brightly colored woolen socks, the callused skin on her heels and the pumice stone she used,

the puckered disk on her hand from an old dog bite, no sugar
in her coffee, honey in her tea, an aversion to beets, fish roe,
cigarettes, radio drama . . . His sorrow was in the uselessness
of all this knowledge. He had made himself an expert in a
subject that no longer existed; his skills were outdated.

He looked across the table at Rachael Murray. With one
hand she pinched her forehead with forefinger and thumb,
with the other she was taking notes. Now and then she pushed
her hair clear of her eyes with an abrupt, irritable movement.
He heard himself addressed in the kind of high style adopted
by newspaper editorialists when they pronounced on the subject of national decline, an airy harangue that had sounded all
his adult life. A new role in the world had yet to be found,
the challenge of the future would be the mastery of new forms
of expertise, old skills must be replaced by new skills. Was he
up to the task? Involuntarily he shook his head.

He saw his hand on Julie's thigh just before she rose from
the bed and, naked, crossed the room. The bare boards creaked.
It was cold, her breath was visible as she opened a drawer and
pulled on a shirt. She was standing at the foot of the bed,
looking at him as she wiggled into her underpants. She dropped
a thick winter skirt over her head and as she fastened it at the
waist she half smiled at him and spoke. It seemed important.

On a mild morning shortly before Christmas, Stephen stood
in his underwear and examined the selection of suits in his
wardrobe, and in a mood of political, or childish, defiance
chose the most worn and least clean. On the jacket black threads
hung where a button should have been, and there was a small
burn, a precise, brown-fringed hole inches above the knee. He
took out a white shirt with a faded, three-year-old, sickle-
shaped Bolognese sauce stain down the front. His overcoat,

which was expensive and relatively new, detracted from the effect, but that could be removed when he arrived. He sat in it in the kitchen drinking coffee and reading the paper till his doorbell rang. He went down and found a uniformed chauffeur, pallid and tubby, looking about him with distaste.

"This your place?" the man asked, incredulous. Stephen made no reply, and they set out across the mud and round the litter-crammed puddles to where the car was parked, four wheels up on the pavement and all indicators flashing. It was the same beat-up model that used to call at Eaton Square for Charles.

In retaliation, Stephen called across the roof to the chauffeur, who was fiddling with the door key, "This can't be it, surely." He got in the front. With his heavy overcoat and the man's girth it was a squeeze and their shoulders were rammed tight together.

The chauffeur breathed heavily as he fumbled for the ignition. Now his tone was almost apologetic. "It's all allocated, see? Nothing to do with me. One day it's a Rolls, the next it's rubbish like this." The engine started and he added, "It all depends who you're picking up, see?"

They lurched out into the stream of traffic, which was moving a little faster than walking pace. A jet of very hot air was blowing against Stephen's trouser leg, releasing a blend of odors. He reached forward in the confined space and pushed and pulled at the ventilation controls, which swung back and forth freely, attached to nothing. "Nah," said the chauffeur, shaking his head. He wound down his window. But by now the traffic had come to a halt and the temperature in the car was rising steadily. While Stephen grunted with the exertion of getting out of his coat, the chauffeur began an explanation involving split pins and wing nuts and dual connecting rods, and by the time Stephen, all irritable and hot, had thrown the coat over his shoulder onto the back seat, the account had widened to embrace deficiencies in the management of the car pool, the compulsory overtime, the victimization of certain drivers like himself who did not falsify their fuel receipts or make out fake job claims or sell whatever they happened to hear to the newspapers.

Stephen wound his window down and leaned out with both elbows on the sill.

The chauffeur was relaxing into his monologue. "Take the case of one Mr. Symes," he said, and drummed on the steering wheel with extended forefingers. The traffic was starting up again. They moved slowly across the lights and then, where two streams of cars merged, they stopped again. They were taking Stephen's morning route to Whitehall. He should have walked. They edged forward a little further and began to draw level with the local elementary school. "Do you know when he last drove a car out? Can you make a guess?" Because Stephen's head was half out the window, his negative was lost, but the fat chauffeur did not mind. It was late-morning break, the playground swarmed. They came alongside a soccer game, roughly twenty-five to a side. Seven- and eight-year-olds were playing with violent competence. Passing movements swept one way and then the other across the asphalt; to the sound of first names and obscenities shouted in urgent falsetto, high balls were fought for in the air; midfield players fed the attackers and then hung back. "Nineteen eighty-five. That's when. Hasn't been out on a job since then. Nineteen eighty-five. And do you know who he took then, who he was driving, because this is the point?"

"No," Stephen said into the cooler air. By the entrance where they had stopped was a group of girls with a long jumprope, which swung to a rhythmic chant in powerful arcs above the heads of two girls who danced through it in quick sideways movements, lifting their feet as late and as little as possible to clear the rope as it cut down beneath them. The two were joined by a third, then a fourth, the chant became more insistent, then the rope snagged and there was a moan of good-natured disappointment. Between these two boisterous groups, the soccer players and the jumpers, were solitary figures — a girl tracing a line with the tip of her shoe and, further off, a ginger-haired boy with something moving inside a brown paper bag.

"The foreign secretary," said the chauffeur. "That's who. Not even our department. Symes was lent out. And the Foreign Office with almost as many drivers as we got." They had stopped right by the school entrance. An argument had broken out among the children. It had something to do with which couple was to turn the rope, for one girl had it pulled from her hands. Eventually her partner at the other end left her station to console her. They had been replaced by bigger girls. "Do you know where he took him? It's God's truth." Stephen shook his head. "Out to a brothel near Northolt airport. It's a place they got out there for diplomats."

"Is that so?" The rope was turning again, the chant was starting up. An impatient line had formed and now the girl at the front was pushed forward. She took up a position just a couple of feet from where the rope smacked the ground, nodding her head to the beat of the song, working the rhythm of it into her feet. The girls sang in unison, but a few were off pitch and the dense disharmonies jarred. The stresses were crudely emphatic on the downbeat: *Daddy, Daddy, I feel sick, Send for the doctor, quick, quick, quick!* "You can imagine it. Something happened. In return for a favor, something not mentioned perhaps, a word to the car-pool super, and Symes never does a day's work again. On full pay. For life."

Stephen watched the waiting girl. She fingered the hem of her skirt. She made a little feint, then she was in, bobbing like a Highland dancer, and the next girl was ready. *Doctor, doctor, shall I die? Yes my dear, and so shall I. How many carriages shall I have? One, two, three, four* . . . The two were face to face as they jumped. They clapped hands, left to right, right to right, both together, then left to right. The first girl was facing away from him. He was watching the blurred line of her moving shoulders, the tilt of her head, the pale crook of her knees. At the moment when the song came full circle, the two leaped higher, turned in the air, and landed back to back. The first girl's face was obscured by the crowd of chanting girls, who were pressing in closer. He half lifted himself out of his seat, straining to see. Ahead, the traffic was moving. They slipped forward ten feet or so before stopping, and suddenly he had a clearer view. There were five girls in the rope, a compacted line that rose and fell to the pulse of the chant. The first girl was closest to him. The thick bangs bobbed against her white forehead, her chin was raised, she had a dreamy appearance. He was looking at his daughter. He shook his head, he opened his mouth without making a sound. She was fifty feet away, unmistakable. The chauffeur roused himself from reveries of injustice and shoved the gearstick forward.

They were moving again, picking up speed. Stephen twisted around in his seat to look out of the rear window. The rope had snagged again, there was a lot of milling about, it was difficult to see faces. He had lost sight of Kate, then saw her briefly as she bent to retrieve something from the ground.

"Stop the car," he whispered, cleared his throat, and said it again louder. "Stop the car."

They were going at a steady thirty miles an hour. Ahead the lights were green, and the rush of cooler air into the dry heat was refreshing the chauffeur, generating a breezy optimism. "It's not all bad, though. You're your own boss, really. It's up to you to make what you can of it." The school was already half a mile behind them.

"Stop the car!"

"What's up?"

"Just do as I say."

"In this traffic?"

Stephen jerked the wheel, and as the car swerved to the left the chauffeur had no choice but to brake sharply. Moving at less than five miles an hour they scraped the length of a parked van. Behind them was a chorus of horns. "Now look," the chauffeur moaned, but Stephen was out on the pavement and starting to run.

By the time he was back, the playground was deserted. Its air of having been vacated of bodies and clamor only minutes before made its emptiness more complete, its walled boundaries more remote. A residual heat hung above the asphalt. The school buildings were of the late Victorian type, with high windows and steeply pitched roofs at many angles. From these buildings came not so much a sound as an emanation of children confined in classrooms. Stephen stood still by the entrance, all senses focused. Time itself had a closed-down, forbidden quality; he was experiencing the pleasurable transgression, the heightened significance that came with being out of school at the wrong moment. From across the playground a man with a zinc bucket was approaching, so Stephen strode purposefully towards a red door and opened it. He had no particular plan, though it was clear that if his daughter was here, it would be easy enough to find her. He felt no excitement now, only peaceful resolve.

He was standing by a fire hose mounted on a red drum on the wall at the beginning of a corridor which ended some sixty feet away with a set of swing doors. It looked familiar to him from schooldays; the floor was red-tiled, the walls were a creamy gloss for easy cleaning. He set off down the corridor slowly. He would search the whole building methodically, regard it not as a school so much as a set of hiding places. The first door that gave onto the corridor was locked, the second opened a broom closet, the third a boiler room where tea things were set out on an upturned crate. Another two doors were locked and by this time he had reached the swing doors. As he pushed them open he glanced over his shoulder to see the man with the bucket enter the corridor and turn to lock the red door behind him. Stephen hurried on.

He arrived at a well-lit reception area where two other corridors, wider and without connecting doors, converged. There were potted plants on shelves and child art on the walls. A sign that announced SCHOOL FEES AND INQUIRIES hung on a door which stood ajar. Beyond it someone was typing slowly. He smelled coffee and cigarettes, and as he passed, preferring not to be heard or seen, a male voice exclaimed, "But newts are not extinct!" and a woman murmured reassuringly, "Well, almost."

Stephen continued along one of the wider corridors, drawn by the sound of a rhythmic and resonant boom. At his feet the linoleum tiles had been worn through to the concrete beneath, making a fissure that ran ahead of him. He stopped at a door in which was set a semicircular window with wired glass. Glancing in and seeing nothing but an expanse of wooden floor, he pushed the door open and entered a gymnasium, on the far side of which thirty children lined up in silence to run at a springboard and launch themselves over a wooden horse. Standing on a rubber mat to steady them as they landed was a compact elderly man with his glasses swinging from his neck by a silver chain. As each child bounced off the board he emitted a staccato "Hup!" He glanced without interest at Stephen, who took up a position at the far end of the mat to watch the children come over.

Soon the bobbing faces had abstracted themselves into little moons, disks with a comic-book range of expressions — terrified, indifferent, determined. He had watched half the class before he became aware of the ideal form of the exercise. It was intended that the children should land on the mat with their feet together, perfectly still, at attention for a second or so before running off to rejoin the queue. Since no one could achieve this, the teacher appeared to have settled for the next best thing — each child sprang to attention, military style, after stumbling across the mat. At no time did the teacher, who was a kind of circus ringmaster, offer encouragement or instruction. His *hups* never varied in tone. It did not look as though he planned to do anything else, for there was no other apparatus in sight. The children ran straight from the mat to the end of the queue without talking or touching. It was difficult to imagine the process being brought to a halt. Stephen left when he started seeing faces for the second time. In recollection, the entire period of his search through the school took place against the background of the thwack and boom of the springboard, and the regular, strangled cry of the gym teacher.

Minutes later he was standing at the rear of a crowded classroom, watching a matronly teacher at the blackboard put the finishing touches to her picture of a medieval village. The roads converged to form the triangular green, round which were grouped primitive huts. There was a village pump out of proportion, and in the distance, drawn with some care, the manor house. With a low buzz, the children took their crayons and started out on their own versions. The teacher waved Stephen into a vacant seat halfway down the classroom, and it was from here, squeezed tight against his desk, that he surveyed the faces as they bent over their work.

The teacher appeared at his side and whispered exaggeratedly. "I'm so happy you can take part in the scheme. If you're unsure what to do, just raise your hand and ask." Solicitously, she spread paper before him and offered him a fistful of crayons. Stephen began to draw his village. He remembered this arrangement from thirty years ago. This was perhaps the fourth time he had represented a medieval village in his life, and he was able to work quickly, imparting to his row of huts a degree of perspective they had never had in previous attempts, and managing a lifelike pump on the edge of the green no larger than half the size of the nearest hut. The manor house, which he imagined to be at least half a mile away, gave him more trouble, and he began to slow down and raise his eyes to the blackboard, finding there some useful architectural hints. To render these features, however, meant drawing out of scale, and his picture began to acquire the primitivist qualities of all his previous attempts.

As he drew he looked about him. Fortunately, all the girls were on one side of the room, but only the faces of those behind him and immediately to his left were visible. As he shifted to improve his point of view, the tiny wooden seat beneath him squeaked loudly. The teacher called threateningly without looking up from her book, "Someone has the fidgets." He ducked down and resumed his drawing. The door opened and the man with the bucket popped his head round, smiled apologetically at the teacher, glanced round the class, and disappeared. There were three dark-haired girls to Stephen's left. It was difficult to see them because they held their faces so close to their work. He turned to watch them, careful not to move too quickly in his seat. The nearest girl became aware of this, tilted her head, and smiled furtively and prettily through the pencil she was biting. There was a movement up front, the harsh scrape of a chair. The teacher spoke to the class as a whole.

"There's no need to copy your neighbor. It's all up there on the blackboard."

She strolled the aisles with leisurely authority, pausing to murmur criticism or encouragement. She was still twenty feet or so behind Stephen; nevertheless, the whole of the back of his head registered her approach. He straightened the sheet of paper on his desk and tried to see his picture through her eyes. Would she be impressed by the detail on his pump, the artful, irregular spacing between his huts, the innovative horse he had set up by his manor house? He smelled her perfume moments before she was at his side. The painted fingernails of one hand rested momentarily on the village green, and then she had passed on, without comment. The brief disappointment was familiar to him. He took advantage of her retreating back to rise out of his seat and survey girls' faces. Indeed, there was a general relaxation now, a stirring of confined young limbs, a mutter that gained in volume. The teacher was on the far side of the class, engrossed in the work of one of the boys. Emboldened, Stephen darted out to the front. The girls were oblivious of his close scrutiny. The chatter was now almost a din, approaching cocktail-party level, but no one else had stood up. So far the teacher had pretended not to hear.

Now she straightened, and sternly pronounced the old formula. "Did I give anyone permission to speak?" The silence was immediate, resentful. No one had an answer. Stephen remained out in front, by the teacher's desk, checking all the faces one last time.

The teacher met his eye and spoke without a hint of humor. "And did I say you could leave your seat?"

There were titters from the back. These were moments of intense pleasure, the time it took Stephen to walk to the classroom door; to step out of the fantasy, to cease colluding in the teacher's authority, simply to turn his back and come away at his own pace, confident of immunity — this was his schoolboy daydream, nurtured through many dull hours, enacted at last, thirty years late.

At the door he turned and said civilly, "I'm sorry to have troubled you," and went out into the corridor.

Approaching him, with a thunderous drumming of shoes on a hard surface and with the pent energy of a tidal bore wave, was a classful, or perhaps two, of children who dared not run but could not quite restrain themselves to walk. They half skipped, half sprinted, pulling each other back as they pushed forward. Faces strained ahead in the anticipation of some pleasure. From out of sight a man called furiously, "Walk, I said walk!" They came on in a surge, stumbling, rolling, elbowing, and when they reached Stephen, who for his own reasons held his ground in the center of the corridor, they parted and converged around him as though he were a mere physical obstacle, a rock, a tree, a grown-up. His view was of bobbing heads, mostly dark brown to mousy, whorls of hair, and glimpses of features, and of couples barely conscious as they let go of each other's hands to pass on either side of him. They gave off a not-unpleasant baked smell from their exertions. Every single child was a fluting monologist, for there seemed to be no listeners here. However close they passed by him, he could not discern in the babble one intelligible phrase. There were the children who glanced up, as one might while passing under an arch of little architectural interest, and then there flashed upward, all the more vivid amid the dullness of the hair, a clear green, a speckled brown, a milky blue. The colors of the marbles they roll, he thought. Had he included marbles in the presents he had bought? And it was in clear vindication of those mad and trusting impulses that as the question shaped itself, he found he was staring into familiar dark eyes below thick bangs, and he was dropping down to her level, on both knees, placing his hands gently on her shoulders, repeating her name while the children wheeled about them to form a tight and curious wall that was never quite still or silent.

Inside the enclosure it was warm and moist and a little gloomy. He seemed to have arrived among a new species of intelligent, inquisitive animal. They were not unfriendly; there was a hand resting on his shoulder and someone touched his hair. He heard them panting and murmuring, he felt their breath as he asked, "Do you know who I am? Have you seen my face before, do you think?"

The girl's gaze was intent, her eyes moved across his face cautiously. Her voice, in contrast, was pert, not at all hostile. "No, I haven't. Anyway, my name's not Kate, it's Ruth."

He tried to take her hands, but this was a presumption. She clasped them behind her back.

"You used to know me very well," he said quietly, wishing they were alone. "But it was two years ago. You've forgotten, but it will come back."

She was thinking hard, or making a show of it, keen to collaborate. "Did you come to my house once for lunch and bring a big red dog?"

He shook his head. He was studying Kate's face, trying to estimate the kind of life she had led. There were no signs of maltreatment. What was most strikingly new was a brown mole high on her right cheekbone. Her teeth were a little crooked; she ought to have been wearing braces, he would make an appointment with the dentist before it was too late. There was much to be sorted out. Was this shabby ex-state school the right place for her, for example? Was she getting the guitar lessons they had always promised?

Kate was pondering and biting on the nail of her thumb. In fact, all her nails were chewed down to the quick. "You're not my uncle Pete," she said at last. "The one who broke his back?"

Stephen wanted to bellow down the corridor for all the children to hear, *I'm your father, your real father. You're my daughter, you're mine, I've come to take you home!* The situation was delicate, however, he had to stay in control. So he simply murmured, "You've forgotten who I am. But it doesn't matter."

It was as well he did. There was a commotion at the outer edge of the crowd, then a round and bristling adult head was peering over the wall into the obscurity.

"Can I help you?" Suspicion all but strangled the words.

"Don't go away," Stephen whispered confidentially. Kate nodded. She had always been one for secrets. He pushed his way gently through the children towards the teacher, who had retreated a few paces. Still in his earnest and confiding frame of mind, Stephen wanted to take the man's elbow and steer him further away from the children, but the teacher put his hands on his hips and refused to move.

"Are you a parent or guardian here?" he demanded. He was a stubby, muscle-impacted little man who kept his back straight to assert what height he had.

"Well, that's just the point, you see," Stephen began, and then faltered as he heard the cranky vigor of his own voice. He tried again, and kept it simple. "Our daughter was stolen from us, abducted, two years ago. And I think I've found her. That girl there who calls herself Ruth is my daughter. She doesn't recognize me, of course."

The man was speaking wearily over Stephen's last words. "We're meant to be leaving on a school trip. But I'll take you to the headmaster. He can sort it out. It's really not my sort of thing at all."

While the rest of the children were sent on to wait in the playground, the teacher, Stephen, and Kate went back along the corridor to where the pot plants and paintings were. She kept her distance from Stephen. Perhaps she feared he might try to hold her hand again. But she was interested, excited even, and at one point as they walked in silence she gave a little hop and a skip, and looked up quickly to see if he had noticed. When he smiled she turned away. They stopped outside the door with the crooked sign and the teacher indicated they should wait while he went inside. Before he pushed open the door he paused and let some air out of his lungs, reducing his height by an inch. Stephen thought he might have a minute or two alone with his daughter, and turned to her, but the teacher was out almost immediately, jerking his head to usher them in and hurrying off down the corridor without acknowledging Stephen's thanks.

One whole wall of the headmaster's office was a sheet of plate glass streaked by mud and rain, through which could be seen a portion of playground and a swath of turbulent gray sky. The effect was a harsh, flat light that denied volume or full color to objects and made the headmaster, a lean military type behind his desk, appear to have been cut out of thick cardboard. Contributing to this impression was the fact that he did not stir when Stephen and the girl came in, nor did he blink or speak or do anything at all other than stare across the room. Stephen was about to introduce himself, but Kate restrained him by placing her hand on his forearm.

They waited twenty seconds or so before the headmaster relaxed his features and said briskly, "Excuse me. Just running through some things there. Now . . . ."

Stephen introduced himself and apologized for intruding upon the headmaster's valuable time. He was halfway through his little speech when he realized he did not wish to explain himself further with Kate in the room. When he revealed his identity, he wanted to be able to speak freely and console her without the presence of a stranger. It was certain to be a delicate moment. He broke off and asked if she would mind waiting outside a minute or two. He held the door open for her and watched her settle in a chair across the corridor.

The headmaster was querulous. "I don't quite see why you had to bring her in here in the first place."

Stephen explained that he was feeling distraught. "But at least you'll know the girl I'm talking about," he said, and delivered the short and simple account he had given before.

The headmaster rose from his chair, stood by the window, and crossed his arms. He was a grave, slow-moving figure who appeared as though he might recently have come through a serious illness. He was looking critically at Stephen's suit, at the missing buttons, the burn hole, the unpolished shoes, the stained shirt. He was a believer in the outer man.

"In a supermarket, you say." He made the word resound with all that was civilian and dishonest. "I suppose you reported the matter to the police."

Stephen kept the anger out of his voice as he explained how a search had been conducted, how the case had been in the newspapers and on television.

The headmaster returned behind his desk, and leaned for-

ward on his knuckles. "Mr. Lewis," he said, stressing the title
to draw attention to Stephen's lack of rank, "I have known
Ruth Lyle since she was a baby. I have been acquainted with
her father, Jason Lyle, for many years, and for a short while
we were business associates. He was one of a group of prom-
inent local businessmen that bought this school from the education authority. He and his wife have five children altogether,
and not one of them have they stolen, I assure you."

Stephen badly wanted to sit down, but this was a time to
be standing up. "I know my daughter. That girl out there is
my daughter."

In response to Stephen's quiet monotone the headmaster's
voice softened. "Two years is a long time. Children change,
you know. On top of that, you must be wanting it to be her.
The mind plays its tricks, after all."

Stephen was shaking his head. "I'd know her anywhere. Her
name is Kate."

The headmaster reverted to his former manner. He stood at
attention by his desk with one hand resting on the back of his
chair as though posing for the kind of portrait that might hang
in an officers' mess. Stephen noted with relief the grease stains
on the regimental tie. "Look here, Mr. Lewis. Two possibilities come to mind. Either you are making an unfortunate
mistake, or you're one of these journalists wanting to make
trouble for the school again."

Stephen glanced around for something to lean on. Had he
been alone he might have stretched out on the floor for a minute
or two. He spoke with a reasonableness he did not feel. "I
don't think it will be difficult to sort this out. The police have
her fingerprints, and there are blood tests, chromosomes and
so on —"

"Two years, you said. Right." He snapped his fingers at the

door. "Let's have her in, for goodness' sake. I've got other things to do this morning."

Stephen went to the door and opened it. She was sitting where he had left her, writing in green ink on the back of her hand. He wanted to speak to her and establish some kind of bond before they went back inside. He needed something with which to counter the headmaster's abrasive self-confidence. She stood and came towards him. His weak performance in the face of the other man's certainty, the enormity of his claims and lack of immediate proof, the fact that he regretted dressing badly — all these were working towards a physical effect, weakening his legs, permeating to the very surface of the retina, right to the rods and cones, for the girl crossing the reception area was taller, more angular, especially about the shoulders, and sharper in her features. She looked up at him neutrally. These were the same eyes below the bangs, the same pallor. He clung to these details, concentrating so fully on them that he was not able to speak to her at all. They were back in the headmaster's office, and the investigation was resuming.

"Ruth," said the headmaster, "tell me your full name and your age."

"Ruth Elspeth Lyle, aged nine and a half."

"Sir."

"Sir."

"And how long have you been at the school?"

"Counting nursery, since I was four, sir."

"How long is that exactly?"

"Five years."

"Sir."

"Sir."

Stephen was shaking his head. The girl was betraying him. Her bold, overeager manner, her desire to please, was beginning to irritate him. She held nothing back, there wasn't a secret in her. From where he stood he could see her nose in profile and that was way off, a gross inaccuracy. She was going from him, she was letting him down.

The headmaster looked past Stephen to the end of the room. "Mrs. Briggs, take out, would you, the school register for five years ago and bring me the nursery section."

For the first time Stephen saw that behind him was a smaller desk in a recess, and by it a woman in a floral print dress, an odd thing for a cold day, who now stood to slide open a drawer in a tin cabinet. The headmaster took the folder and opened it in front of Stephen, who was neither looking nor listening as the headmaster spread out a typewritten sheet of names and ran his finger down them. "Lyle, Ruth Elspeth, admitted for the summer term, just after her fourth birthday . . ."

Stephen was thinking about Kate's spirit, how it might hover high above London, how it might resemble some kind of brilliantly colored dragonfly, capable of unimaginable speeds and yet remaining perfectly still as it waited to descend to a playground or street corner to inhabit the body of a young girl, infuse it with its own particular essence to demonstrate to him its enduring existence before moving on, leaving the empty shell, the host, behind.

The headmaster was turning pages, adducing fresh evidence. The girl was looking on, immensely pleased with herself. Stephen's concerns narrowed to practical matters: how soon he could leave the school, how he had left his coat in the car, how he had missed the prime minister's lunch.

Minutes later, as he came away from the office, he heard the headmaster tell the girl in a loud voice, no doubt for Stephen's benefit, that she should report back immediately if that fellow spoke to her again. The girl gave her enthusiastic assent.

It was the man with the zinc bucket who escorted him off the premises. Stephen glanced in it as they crossed the playground. It was empty. "Just why do you carry that around with you?"

The man, who was ushering Stephen through the school entrance, shook his head, and forced a smile to suggest that this was indeed a very stupid question, one that he certainly would not be bothering to answer.

By dementedly living through the very reunion that preoccupied him constantly, Stephen came to feel that if he had not exorcised his obsession, he had blunted it. He was beginning to face the difficult truth that Kate was no longer a living presence, she was not an invisible girl at his side whom he knew intimately; remembering how Ruth Lyle did and did not resemble his daughter, he understood how there were many paths Kate might have gone down, countless ways in which she might have changed in two and a half years, and that he knew nothing about any of them. He had been mad, now he felt purged.

He had returned home and slept till the early evening, a deep and dreamless sleep. Then he had set about reorganizing his flat. He had moved his couch back against the wall and the television back into an obscure corner. He had taken a long bath. Afterwards, he did not resist pouring himself a large drink. But this time he took it to his desk, which he tidied, and where he sat answering letters. He wrote an affectionate, undemanding postcard to Julie, telling her that he had thought about her on Kate's birthday and that, if and when she thought the time was right, she should get in touch. He took out a notebook and scribbled down a few ideas and then, encouraged, removed the dustcover from his typewriter and typed for two hours. Late at night he lay in bed in the dark and made elaborate resolutions before succumbing to a second untroubled sleep.

When, the following morning, the phone rang and the assistant secretary came on the line, Stephen listened patiently, but he had already made up his mind. The man began by expressing regret that Stephen had jumped out of the car that had been sent for him. Stephen explained that he had gone off in pursuit of what he thought was his long-lost daughter.

"Did that chauffeur hand in my overcoat, by the way?"

"No. If you left it, he would have reported it, I'm certain." No one, it seemed, had ever failed to turn up at a lunch without giving good reason. It was an unpardonable rudeness, but for some extraordinary reason — and the assistant secretary made it clear he disapproved — Stephen was being offered a second chance, another invitation was being offered.

"Ah well," Stephen said, "that's too bad. I don't want another invitation."

The assistant secretary was affable in his contempt. "What nonsense! Why ever not?"

"In the first place, I'm busy. I've started a piece of work, something of a departure for me —"

"That doesn't stop you eating lunch."

"In the second, and nothing personal in this, I resent what the prime minister's been doing in this country all these years. It's a mess, a disgrace."

"Then why did you accept the first time?"

"I was a mess too. Depressed. Now I'm not."

There was a pause while the assistant secretary adjusted his approach. He spoke in sorrow, as though lamenting an irrefutable physical law. "I'm afraid, Mr. Lewis, there's not much I can do. The P.M. absolutely insists on seeing you."

"Oh well," Stephen said, "you know where I live," and replaced the receiver.

He went to the kitchen to make coffee, and ten minutes later, as he was carrying his cup through the hallway, the phone rang again. It was a very peevish assistant secretary.

"As it happens, we seem to have lost your address."

Stephen gave it, then hung up and hurried with his coffee to his desk.

❧ 7 ❧

"Child-care writers of the postwar era sentimentally ignored the fact that children are at heart selfish, and reasonably so, for they are programmed for survival."

— from the introduction to
The Authorized Child-Care Handbook, HMSO

THROUGHOUT THE EARLY MONTHS of the following year, the Parmenter Committee edged towards agreement on the final draft of its report. Attrition, weariness, vague wording where there were insurmountable differences smoothed the way. Helpful reversals of position, or the sudden abandonment of eccentric views without too much loss of face, were made possible by Canham's suggestion that they meet only twice monthly, and by pleasant lunches given for individual members by Lord Parmenter. It was also suggested to the committee that, while it might not be possible to be the first of the sub-committees to deliver a finished report to the commission, however desirable that might be, it would not do at all to be last.

Stephen made his contribution. He put forward what he thought was a balanced case, arguing on the one hand for a degree of discipline and the instillation of certain ground rules

— writing was a social act, a public medium — and on the other for the imagination — writing extended the private life; idiosyncrasies should not be discouraged at its expense. This harmless argument was easily assimilable, or the first half of it was, and he was not invited to eat lunch with the chairman. On the morning Stephen spoke the committee was more interested in deleting all references to the phonetic alphabet and in preventing one of the academics from reading a late paper, "Class Ascendancy and Prescriptive Grammar." By mid-March the report of the Parmenter Committee on Reading and Writing was submitted to the Commission on Child Care. Most members felt that they had fulfilled their mandate in producing a document that was judicious in tone and authoritarian in stance. The chairman was congratulated in the press on the absence of a minority report. A farewell sherry party was held in a remote and rarely used annex of the ministerial building where the thirty-year-old floral carpet was still queasily vivid, still capable of delivering an invigorating electric shock to those who touched the door or window fittings.

Stephen came late to this gathering and left early. Since Christmas the committee meetings had ceased to represent a refuge of organized time in a chaos of wasted days. The sessions now bored him and threatened his fragile routine of work, study, and physical exercise. He was learning classical Arabic from Mr. Cromarty, a retired don who lived alone on the floor below. Four mornings a week he went downstairs for his tutorials in Mr. Cromarty's cold, sparse study, where the only source of heat was an old gas heater whose weak yellow flames seemed to exhale the very narcotic fumes referred to in the poems the old man translated for him.

Stephen was not interested in the language itself or its literature. If Mr. Cromarty had offered Greek or Tagalog, Stephen would have been equally satisfied. The idea was to shake himself awake by learning something difficult, he wanted rules and their exceptions and the grim absorption of learning by heart. As it turned out, he was immediately enchanted by the alphabet. He bought a bottle of ink and a special pen with which to practice his calligraphy. Within a month he was intrigued by the grammar, by its proud dissimilarity from English and by the strange predominance of verbs, the forms of which yielded with minimal strokes subtle gradations of meaning: regret *(nadam)* became a drinking partner *(nadim)*; a pomegranate, a hand grenade; old age, freedom.

His teacher was quiet and stern in manner, and gave the impression that he would be genuinely annoyed if his pupil was ever late or failed to fulfill the daily assignments. For the tutorials Mr. Cromarty wore a dark suit, from the waistcoat of which he would draw a silver pocket watch and address his closing remarks to its face. His apartment had an air of dour, old-fashioned poverty — bare boards, yellowing walls with oily patches of damp, doors and baseboards caked in flaky brown paint, a smoky kerosene heater under a bare light bulb in the hall. There were no ornaments, pictures, or soft chairs, no evidence of a past. His luxuries were all in the formal, sensuous verse he loved and from which he quoted at length, first in Arabic, then in Scots English, with his eyes closed and his head lifted as though recalling another life: "Slender-waisted she was, and tenderly plump her ankles, shapely taut her belly, not the least flabby." Mr. Cromarty avoided Stephen in the street and discouraged small talk of any kind before or after the hour-long sessions. Stephen never learned his Christian name.

Stephen's other new commitment was tennis three times a week on an indoor court. He had played a mediocre game for more than twenty years, a slow decline from his late teens, when he had represented his school without distinction. For the first hour he took instruction from and in the second he played a game with his coach, a beefy, balding American who had given him a frank summary of the task ahead after the first session. His forehand and backhand strokes would have to be scrapped and rebuilt from the start. Similarly, the footwork needed fundamental rethinking. His service could be forgotten altogether for the moment. None of these items, however, was in such urgent need of attention as Stephen's attitude. At the time they were standing close together on either side of the net. Stephen was uncertain what expression to adopt as he listened to this brisk slander from a man whose considerable fee he was paying.

"You're passive. You're mentally enfeebled. You wait for things to happen, you stand there hoping they're going to go your way. You take no responsibility for the ball, you're making no active calculations about the next move. You're inert, spineless, you're half asleep, you don't like yourself. Your racket has to be going back sooner, you've got to be moving into the stroke, going in low, enjoying the movement. You're not all here. Even as I'm speaking to you now you're not all here. You think you're too good for this game? Wake up!"

As well as his Arabic and tennis, Stephen had his work, and when he was not doing that he read indiscriminately, brick-shaped novels, international best sellers, the kind of book whose real purpose was to explain the workings of a submarine, an orchestra, or a hotel. He was beginning to feel capable of a limited social life in the evenings, but he made a point of confining himself to his well-established, undemanding friendships with other men. Before Christmas his mother had succumbed to a long illness. He made frequent visits, first to the hospital, then home, and though she was in no danger, she was too weak for any but the briefest conversation. If he was not exactly happy during these months, nor was he catatonic. He sometimes felt himself to be in training for an undisclosed event; he expected change — he had no clear idea of what kind — or perhaps even upheaval, and he was on the lookout for the first signs, the first small indication that his life was about to be transformed. The long books he was reading made him think in terms of useful formulas, of tides turning, fresh winds, shadows lifting. He had no doubt, though, that he was still in the shadows; after all, he paid cash for his most regular weekly human contacts.

The changes came, but there were no early warnings, no emerging details to prefigure a larger scheme. Instead there was a series of sudden and seemingly unrelated developments, the first of which began starkly one evening with two short rings at his front door. He had finished supper and was about to start copying in ink part of a poem that he would be reading out to Mr. Cromarty the following morning. It had been snowing lightly all day, and on returning from tennis Stephen had lit a fire which was now well in. The thick velvet curtains were drawn, he had poured himself a small glass of Armagnac — he was down to a single shot of spirits a day — and stately orchestral music was processing quietly from the radio. He had already sketched out the characters in pencil and was enjoying the prospect of forming the first character, a curved line below a triangle of dots, by wiping the gold nib with a cotton rag. When the doorbell rang he clicked his tongue in irritation, and, as he stood, took time to replace the top of his ink bottle. As he did so he wondered whether he was beginning to resemble, in his unhurried movements, his annoyance at disturbance, Mr. Cromarty himself.

What he saw first was blood, almost black in the dim stair-well light, completely obscuring the face of a man who held a brown paper bag against his chest. The source of the blood was not evident. It seemed to have oozed through the pores, obliterating the features so entirely that only the ears showed white. Drips were forming at the point of the chin and falling onto the package.

Into his brief, shocked silence, the man spoke quickly with cultivated hesitancy. "I'm awfully sorry to be bothering you at this late hour. I — I should have phoned first . . ." The voice, which was familiar to Stephen, expressed no pain. The man was extending a smeared hand. "Harold Morley, you know, from the committee."

"Ah yes," Stephen said, opening the door wider and step-ping aside. "You'd better come in." It was only when he had closed the door that he placed Morley as the man with the phonetic alphabet, the briefest reference to which had been deleted from the final report.

Morley was staring at his hand, touching his chin gently and examining the ends of his fingers. "I tripped on your stairs."

Stephen was leading the way into the bathroom. "You're not the first."

Morley steadied himself in the doorway while Stephen filled the basin and rolled up his sleeves. "Do you know, I think I might have knocked myself out for a moment or two."

"You're a mess," Stephen said. "You better let me take a look."

Morley spoke wonderingly. "I remember going down, and I remember picking myself up, but there was some time in between, I'm sure of it."

Stephen was emptying antiseptic fluid into the water. The

smell heightened his awareness of his own efficiency. Morley removed his shirt. The cut was high on the forehead, barely an inch long and already beginning to congeal. As Stephen sponged down his head and face, Morley was talking disjointedly into the reddening water, repeating his account of the fall. By the time Stephen was finished, the man's narrow, pimply back was beginning to tremble. When he straightened he immediately lost his balance. Stephen made him sit on the edge of the bath, gave him a towel, and devised a makeshift compress. By now Morley was shaking badly. Stephen gave him a thick sweater, wrapped a blanket round him, led him into the study, and sat him in an armchair close to the fire. He poured out a cup of strong coffee into which he heaped a half-dozen spoonfuls of sugar. But Morley was incapable of holding the cup himself. Stephen took it for him and heard his teeth clink against the rim. Ten minutes later Morley had calmed down and was beginning an elaborate apology. Stephen told him to rest. Five minutes after that his visitor had fallen asleep.

Stephen downed his Armagnac in one, refilled the glass, and was surprised to find that he was able to continue with his preparation for the next day's tutorial. From time to time he glanced across at Morley. The ragged compress sat comically on his head, held in place by congealed blood alone. "She shows me a waist slender and slight as a camel's nose rein, and a smooth shank like the reed of a watered, bent papyrus . . ." Later he stared at his finished work and longed to know if anyone other than Mr. Cromarty would be able to make sense of the miniature circles, dashes, and curlicues that floated freely above the lines with their sudden cruel hooks. Could they possibly be a private code, an intricate game devised by the old man to pass the years?

After a quarter of an hour's doze, Harold Morley began to stir. Suddenly he jerked to attention in his chair, his face taut with accusation. "Where is it?" he demanded, then, in an unfaltering transformation, closed his eyes and struck his face with an open hand. "Oh God! The taxi. I left it on the seat."

Stephen went to the bathroom and retrieved the brown paper bag from the floor. Then he went to the kitchen for the pot of coffee. By the time he returned to the study, Morley's memory had been restored. He was standing by the fireplace examining the mess of bandages which he had pulled clear of the wound. "Quite a whack," he said, impressed.

"You might need stitches," Stephen said. "You should do something about that tonight, really." He gave Morley his paper parcel.

His guest was looking in the direction of the drinks tray. "Open it and have a look. I'd like a Scotch, if you wouldn't mind."

Stephen poured drinks for them both. Watched closely by Morley, he sat down to examine the book he had taken from the bloodied paper bag. The plain flimsy cover bore the word *Proof,* and below that a white label stuck on at a careless angle announced RESTRICTED READING CODE E-8. COPY NO. 5. The front pages were blank. Stephen arrived at the introduction and read "Child-care writers of the postwar era sentimentally ignored the fact that children are at heart selfish, and reasonably so, for they are programmed for survival." He flipped through the book backwards and read a few chapter headings — "The Disciplined Mind," "Adolescence Overcome," "Security in Obedience," "Boys and Girls — Vive la Difference," "A Sound Smack Saves Nine." In this last chapter he read, "Those who argue dogmatically against all forms of corporal punishment find themselves urging a variety of psychological reprisals against

the child — withdrawal of approval or privileges, the humil-
iation of an early bedtime, and so on. There is no evidence to
suggest that these more protracted forms of punishment, which
can waste a good deal of a busy parent's time, cause less long-
term damage than a swift clip across the ear or a few smart
slaps to the backside. Common sense suggests the contrary.
Raise your hand once and show you mean business! It is likely
you will never have to raise it again."

Morley waited, rising from his chair at one point to refill
his glass. Stephen turned more pages. A cartoon showed two
little girls at play. Underneath, a caption read, "There's nothing wrong with this miniature ironing set. Let the girls assert
their femininity!" At last Stephen returned the book to its bag
and tossed it onto the table. The commission was still collecting
reports from its fourteen subcommittees and was not due to
complete its work for another four months. His one wish was
to phone his father and congratulate him on his judgment. But
he could do that when he saw him later in the week.

Morley said, "I ought to tell you how it came my way." A
middle-level civil servant, whose name was not known to
Morley, had phoned him at work and asked to meet in a nearby
workmen's café. The man turned out to have responsibilities
in government publications. He belonged to a long line of
disaffected civil servants; every year two or three were tried
in the courts for treason or the like. But that was not his
primary reason for wanting to hand over the book; it was
because he was able to do so with impunity. There had been
a break-in the night before at the offices where he worked.
The thieves had been interested mostly in heavy-duty office
equipment. They had taken the coffee- and soup-making machine. Morley's man had been one of the first on the scene the
following morning. He had slipped the book into his briefcase

and reported it as one of the items inside a small safe that the thieves had somehow carried away.

The book had come to the government press three months previously and there were now ten bound copies circulating among the civil service elite and three or four Cabinet ministers. Each copy was accounted for and tracked with the diligence usually associated with defense papers. In fact, it was only because of a forgotten clerical error that this particular copy was not inside the stolen safe. Morley's civil servant believed that the intention was to publish a month or two after the commission had completed its own report, and to claim that the handbook drew from the commission's work. Quite why proof copies were circulating so early on was not clear.

"Perhaps," Morley said, "Downing Street needed to carry a few ministers along for political reasons."

Stephen said, "I don't see why they couldn't trust the commission to come up with the kind of book they wanted. They appointed its chairman, and all the chairmen to the subcommittees."

"They couldn't have it both ways," Morley said, "even though they tried. They couldn't leave it to the great and good, experts and celebrities gathered for public consumption to come up with exactly the right book. The grown-ups know best." Morley was probing his cut with his fingertips. He winced. "Anyway, this is how seriously they take it. You've heard it all, I'm sure — how the nation is to be regenerated by reformed child-care practice."

He said that his head was beginning to throb and that he wanted to go home. He explained that he had come in order to discuss what was to be done. He could not talk to his wife because she too worked in the civil service, as a medical officer, and he did not want to compromise her. "She'll fix my head when I get back."

Since they could do little more than create a degree of embarrassment, the matter was easily settled. It was agreed that after Stephen had made a copy for a newspaper, he should keep the book in his apartment, and that the identifying number should be scraped off to protect the civil servant. Stephen phoned for a taxi, and while they waited for it to arrive, Morley talked about his children. He had three boys. Loving them, he said, was not only a delight, it was a lesson in vulnerability. During the height of the Olympic Games crisis he and his wife had lain awake all night, speechless with fear for the boys, horrified by their own helplessness to keep them from harm. They lay side by side, unable to speak their thoughts, reluctant even to acknowledge that they were awake. At dawn the youngest had climbed into bed with them as usual, and it was then that his wife had started to cry, so hopelessly that in the end Morley had carried the boy back to his room and slept with him there. Later she told him that it was the child's absolute trust that had broken her up; the boy believed he was safe beneath the covers cuddling against his mother, and because he was not, because he could be destroyed in minutes, she felt she had betrayed him. Remembering his own savage insouciance at that time, Stephen shook his head and said nothing.

After Morley had left, he went into his daughter's bare room and turned on the light. There was still a garbage sack full of her stuff lying on the mattress of the single wooden bed. The room smelled damp. He knelt down and turned the valve on the radiator. He remained crouched for a moment on the floor, testing his feelings; it was not loss he confronted now, it was a fact, like a high wall. But inanimate, neutral. A fact. He said the word out loud, like a curse. Returning to the study, he took Morley's chair by the fire and thought about his story.

He saw them, man and wife, side by side on their backs like stone figures on a medieval tomb. Nuclear war. He was suddenly, childishly, afraid to undress and go to bed. The world outside the room, outside his clothes even, seemed bitter, harsh beyond reason. The frail sanity he had established was under threat. He had been still for twenty minutes, and he was sinking. The silence was gaining in volume. He made a great effort and leaned forward to build up the fire. He cleared his throat noisily to hear his own voice. As the flames took hold of the new coal, he settled back, and before he fell asleep he promised himself he would not let go. His tutorial was at ten the next morning, and he was due on court at three.

Stephen's mother had begun her convalescence in February. She was allowed out of bed for the afternoons and early evenings. As soon as it was warmer, she would be permitted to walk the four hundred yards to the post office. She had lost fifteen pounds during her illness, and most of the sight in one eye. Knitting, reading, or watching television gave her pains in her good eye, so the radio and conversation were her main pleasures now. Like many women of her generation, she did not like to mention discomfort. When his father had to spend half a day away from home visiting his sister, who was also ill, Stephen was asked if he would come and keep his mother company. He was happy to oblige. He liked seeing his parents singly; it was easier to break the habitual patterns, he felt less limited in his role as son. And there was the possibility of resuming the conversation they had begun in the kitchen half a year before.

He was surprised to be met at the front door by her, to see her once more in everyday clothes instead of the bedjacket in shocking pink. Losing weight had tightened her facial skin, giving her a superficially youthful appearance which was

heightened by a rakish eye patch. After they had embraced
fleetingly, and while he was complimenting her on her progress and making a cumbersome pirate joke, she led the way
into the living room.

She apologized for a chaos there visible only to herself. One
reason why she was keen to regain her strength, she said, was
because she wanted to start putting the house to rights. Though
not a single object seemed out of place, Stephen said it was
surely a good sign she felt that way. It was also an indication
of just how enfeebled she was that after only ritual protest,
she permitted him to make them a pot of tea in her own
kitchen. But she called out instructions through the open hatch,
and while he was not looking pulled out the nest of coffee
tables and arranged them to receive the tray and their cups. In
the kitchen Stephen waited for the kettle to boil and examined
the contents of an array of pill bottles. The iridescent intensity
of the reds and yellows suggested powerful technology, deep
intervention in the system. Elsewhere, an innovation was the
large sign in his father's hand by the wall phone listing the
doctor's emergency numbers and those of a few private am-
bulance companies.

Mrs. Lewis presided over the pouring, though her hand
shook with the weight of the teapot. They pretended not to
see the splashes which drenched the tray. They talked about
the weather; it was forecast that before the first signs of spring,
they would have to endure heavy snowfalls. Mrs. Lewis skill-
fully evaded her son's questions about the doctor's most recent
visit. Instead they discussed Stephen's aunt's illness and whether
Mr. Lewis would be safe crossing west London by public
transport. They debated the suitability of large-print books.
Twenty minutes passed and Stephen began to worry that his
mother would tire before he could move the conversation in

the direction he wanted. So after the next short break in the talk he said, "Do you remember you were telling me about those new bikes?"

She seemed to have been waiting for this. She smiled immediately. "Your father has his own reasons for wanting to forget about those."

"You mean he's pretending to forget?"

"It's the air force training. If it's untidy or it doesn't fit, throw it out." She was speaking affectionately. She continued, "The day we bought those bikes was a difficult one, for both of us. He likes to think that everything that's happened since then was bound to happen, that there was never any choice. He says he doesn't remember, so we never talk about it." Though her tone was still reflective and unaccusing, a firmness in these last words seemed to be establishing a pretext for indiscretion. She was also being willfully obscure and a little self-dramatizing. She sat back in her chair with her teacup suspended an inch above its saucer, waiting to be prompted.

Stephen took care not to appear too interested; he knew her guilty loyalties could be easily aroused. He let a few seconds pass before saying, "I suppose forty years is a long time, after all."

She was shaking her head emphatically. "Memory's got nothing to do with years. You remember what you remember. The moment I first set eyes on your father is as clear to me now as it ever was." Stephen half knew the account of his parents' first meeting. But he was aware that what was being offered as evidence of the timelessness of memory was her way into the story she wanted to tell.

During the first three years after the war Stephen's mother, Claire Temperly, worked in a small department store in a market town in Kent. The full social impact of the war, in particular the disappearance of a whole class of domestic servants and with it the way of life of the less-than-wealthy middle classes, had yet to make itself fully felt, and the store — a kind of local Harrods on two floors — still managed to keep up some prewar pretensions.

"It wasn't the sort of place my mum would feel happy doing her shopping in. She'd be made to feel out of place." Boys in dark blue uniforms with silver braid and caps bearing the store's insignia waited by the revolving doors to conduct the lady shoppers across the plum-colored carpet to the appropriate department. If the assistants there were busy, the ladies would be shown to comfortable chairs. The boys said "ma'am" and touched their caps frequently, but they were never tipped.

The assistants, who were all girls, wore uniforms too, for which they were personally responsible. Each morning before the store opened they lined up for dress inspection in front of Miss Bart, the elderly head of personnel. She liked to pay special attention to the arrangement of the starched white bows "her girls" tied behind their backs. Girls who were not born to it had to concentrate on saying "think," not "fink," and remembering to pronounce their aitches and to tighten the muscles round their lips as they spoke. When they were not serving customers they had to remain behind the mahogany counters without slouching or talking to one another unnecessarily; they were required to look alert and friendly, but not "forward" — "which meant not looking at a customer until the customer had looked at you. It took a month or two to learn how to do that."

Claire was twenty-five and still living at home when she began at the store. She was an odd mixture of shyness and independence. "I wriggled out of two offers of marriage, but

I had to get my mum to do the talking for me." Still, family
and friends were growing concerned about her age and telling
her she only had a year or two left in her. She was pretty in
a bright, birdlike way. It was not ambition but nervous energy
and dread of criticism that made her work so diligently. Even
Miss Bart, whom everyone feared, came to like her for her
punctuality, and said her bows were the cleanest and the most
neatly tied. She learned to speak the shop girls' posh ("If modom
would care to step this way . . .") and was one of the few
assistants to be transferred to a new department every six months,
"probably because the powers that be were thinking of pro-
moting me."

It was for this reason she found herself starting in the clock
department, having come from haberdashery, where the su-
pervisor had been a second mother to her and had made her
feel less anxious about not being married. Now her boss was
Mr. Middlebrook, a tall, thin man who intimidated both un-
derlings and customers with his clipped, sarcastic manner. He
had a striking purple birthmark on his forehead and the story
among the girls was that "if you let your eyes rest on it even
for a second you'd be fired on the spot." Mr. Middlebrook
was not unreasonable, but he was cool towards the girls and
had a knack of making them feel stupid.

Men were not often seen among the customers in the department store. It was a quiet, scented, womanly place. Occasionally an elderly gent might come, looking well out of his
depth as he bought an anniversary present for his wife, and
loving it when a girl took him in hand and made respectful
suggestions. And there were young couples, married or engaged, "furnishing their nests," and much gossiped about by
the assistants during their half-hour lunch break. But a young
man alone in the shop, and a handsome man with a black

mustache, a man in the cool blue-gray of the RAF uniform, was bound to cause a stir. News of his approach was telegraphed through the ground floor. Girls looked up from their counters, alert and friendly. Followed, not preceded, by a pageboy, he strode across the tranquil expanse of plum carpet towards Claire's department, a cap under one arm, under the other a clock, and demanded to see Mr. Middlebrook. While someone went to fetch him from his office, the man set down the clock and his cap side by side on the glass counter, stood himself at ease, hands behind back, and stared fixedly ahead. He was a strong-looking man with an impressively straight back. He had the bony, flinty handsomeness much in fashion at the time. His wavy black hair was thickly Brylcreemed, and his miniature black mustache was waxed right to its tiny tips. The clock was a mantelpiece chimer in a rosewood case. Claire was twelve feet away, dusting, which was the nearest Mr. Middlebrook would allow his girls to doing nothing. Trained in the impropriety of initiating an insubordinate eye contact, she kept herself busy with the glass faces of the grandfather clocks, every one of which showed a waiting man in uniform. "But you know, without turning, I could feel something like a warmth coming off him. A sort of glow."

It did not help matters off to a good start that Mr. Middlebrook was slow in coming, and that even when he did at last appear behind the counter and, presumably, register the presence of a man with a complaint, he first took down a brown envelope, removed a sheet of paper and unfolded it, wrote out a list of numbers, then refolded the sheet and returned it to the envelope and the envelope to its proper position on its shelf. Only then did he mount the barely credible drama of becoming aware of a customer in need of attention. Drawing up to his full height and inclining forward, with his weight supported by splayed fingers against the glass counter, he said, "What seems to be the problem?"

Throughout this the man in uniform had not stirred from his position, nor did his gaze wander until he was spoken to. Then he took half a pace forward, picked up his cap, and used it to point to the clock. He said simply, "It's broken. Again." Claire's dusting was taking her nearer the scene.

Mr. Middlebrook was brisk. "Then there's no problem at all, sir. The guarantee still has seven months to run." His hand was resting on the clock, and he was about to gather it up for processing. But the man put out his own hand and set it firmly on top of Mr. Middlebrook's, trapping it there while he spoke. Claire noticed the stubby fingers of this second hand, and the black, matted hair along the knuckles. The physical contact violated all the unspoken rules governing confrontations with customers. Mr. Middlebrook had gone rigid. To struggle would have intensified the contact, so he had no choice but to listen to the man's short speech. "I loved his way of talking. Straight to the point. Not rough, or rude, but not la-di-da either."

The man said, "You told me it was a reliable clock. Worth paying the extra money for. Either you were lying, or you were mistaken. That's not for me to judge. I want my money back now."

Here, at least, Mr. Middlebrook knew himself to be on familiar ground. "I'm afraid we cannot authorize refunds on goods purchased five months ago."

Reassured by a statement of company policy, Mr. Middlebrook attempted to pull his hand clear. But the man's larger hand encircled his wrist and the grip was tightening.

He spoke again, as if for the first time. "I want my money back now." And then came the surprise. The man turned to Claire. "And what's your opinion? This is the third time it's broken down." Until he asked her, she didn't *have* an opinion. "I was just watching to see what was going to happen. But before I could stop myself, I was saying bold as you like, 'I think you should have your money back, sir.' "

The man nodded at the till and kept a good hold of Mr. Middlebrook. "Come on then, girl. Seven pounds thirteen and six." Claire opened the till, thus initiating a lifetime of domestic obedience. Mr. Middlebrook made no attempt to prevent her. He was, after all, being extricated from a most unpleasant situation without having to back down. Douglas Lewis took the money, turned on his heel, and walked smartly away, leaving the broken clock behind him on the counter. "I'll always remember, the hands stood at a quarter to three."

Claire was sacked at lunchtime, not by Mr. Middlebrook, who was at the doctor's having his wrist bandaged, but by the disapproving Miss Bart. Claire was surprised to find her man waiting for her as she stepped out onto the pavement. He bought her a slap-up lunch at the George Hotel.

"There was no question," said Mrs. Lewis as she extended her cup and saucer for a refill. "He was a catch. When he came to tea he did all the right things. Arrived in his best uniform and brought flowers, said nice things about the garden to my dad, thrilled my mum by eating three helpings of cake. After that, everyone started treating me with respect."

Three months later, when news came through of Douglas's posting to north Germany, the couple were engaged. Claire had been just a little disappointed when she discovered during their lunch at the George that he was not a fighter pilot. He had never even been in an airplane. He was on the admin. side, a filing clerk in charge of all the other filing clerks. Now she was greatly relieved that he would be doing nothing more dangerous in Germany than collecting the squadron's wages from the bank each week. She went to Harwich to wave his ship goodbye, and sobbed in the train on the way home. They wrote regularly, sometimes every day for weeks on end. Though Douglas found it easier to describe bomb craters in ruined towns and food queues than his tenderest feelings, he was able to take a lead from his fiancée, and between them they managed a growing intimacy by post. When he came home on leave at Christmas, they were a little shame-faced, shy of holding hands even, for the postal affair with its extravagant declarations had run on ahead of them. But by Boxing Day they had caught up, and traveling in the train to Worthing to his parents, Douglas made a short murmured speech, almost lost to the iron clatter of wheels, in which he told Claire how in love he was with her.

Conditions in Germany were still far too unsettled for wives to be permitted to accompany serving men, so they agreed not to get married until Douglas was posted back to the U.K. He was not home again on leave until spring, and then only for a long weekend. The weather was warm, and since there was nowhere they could be alone indoors, they passed the days walking on the North Downs, making their plans. They strolled carefree along the very path used by Chaucer's pilgrims. The tranquil Weald was spread out before them, there were wild-flowers, larks, and abundant solitude. They were deliriously happy, it was a delirious weekend; and by the repetition of the word Stephen took his mother to be absolving them of a degree of carelessness.

Sure enough, when Douglas returned on more extended leave in July, Claire had momentous news for him. She had already decided to choose her moment, to wait until they were back up on the hills among the wildflowers with the easy, joyful intimacy re-established. When she anticipated that moment, she could almost hear a film score and see the midsummer sun illuminate the scene — Douglas struck dumb with pride, his features softened by reverence, and admiration, and a new kind of tenderness. "But it didn't occur to me that it would be cold and windy." Even worse, Douglas seemed different. He was edgy, abstracted, difficult to get close to. Sometimes he seemed bored. Whenever Claire asked him if there was anything the matter, he would take her hand and squeeze ferociously. If she asked him too frequently he became irritable.

At the end of his previous visit, they had decided to buy bicycles in order to free themselves from the erratic local buses, and since this was to be their first joint purchase, the first acquisitions for the little empire they were about to build, it seemed appropriate to buy new ones. They had already made their choices and a down payment and now, on the third day of Douglas's July leave, they set out with a picnic already packed to collect their bikes and brave the weather. Claire had made up her mind to tell her news that day, even though it was raining and Douglas was more silent than ever. He cheered up once they were on their bikes, however, and began to sing, which was something he had never done in her presence before. So Claire seized her opportunity and blurted out her secret as they wobbled down the busy high street.

It was difficult to talk. Not until they were on a country lane and had dismounted to push their heavy machines over a railroad crossing and up a steep hill were they able to discuss the matter. It was raining steadily now and they were struggling into a headwind. It was all so very different from Claire's imagined scene and quite unfair, for it had not seemed so improbable that the spirit of their delirious weekend should continue into the summer. Douglas was looking troubled. How long had she known? How did she know? How could she be so sure?

"But aren't you excited?" said Claire, whose tears were lost to the rain. "Aren't you happy?"

"Of course I am," Douglas said quickly. "I'm just trying to get things straight. That's all I'm trying to do."

At the top of the hill, where the rain eased off a little and the wind dropped quite suddenly, Douglas mopped his face with a handkerchief. "This is all a bit sudden, you know."

Claire nodded. She felt she owed an apology, but she was too choked up.

"And it'll mean changing all our plans."

She had taken that for granted. And the minor scandal of a child born, say, six months after they were married would be nothing against their happiness. She nodded grimly.

The road swept down invitingly towards the woods, but it did not seem right to get back on their bikes and coast at such a serious time, so they walked them down the hill in silence with their hands on the brakes. During the descent, Claire began to feel she was about to confront something quite un-speakable, something it had not occurred to her to take into account. "It was his silence. It was as if I could taste it, taste the things he was not saying. I began to feel sick. You know how bad smells affect you when you're pregnant."

They did in fact stop while Claire retched into the hedgerow. Douglas held her bike. When they continued she felt she had already heard the arguments and had suffered a miserable de-feat; Douglas was bored, he regretted the commitment, he had another woman in Germany. Whatever it was, he did not want the child. That was what was on his mind. It was abortion — "and the word in those days had a very different, very nasty ring to it" — it was abortion, the difficulty of raising the sub-ject, which was forcing his reticence.

Anger was clearing her mind. Now she felt lucid. If he did not want it, nor did she. The baby inside her was not yet an entity, not something to be defended at all costs. It was still an abstraction, one aspect of their love; if that was finished, then so was the baby. She would not submit to a lifetime's ignominy of unmarried motherhood. If Douglas was no more than a passing episode, she did not want to be reminded of him forever. She must be free, she must be rid of this idiot who had wasted her time. She must start again.

They entered the wood, where the light was a watery green and giant beeches dripped calmly onto the unfurled leaves of the abundant ferns. She was furious. She squeezed her brakes in her fury and had to push all the harder. She wanted it ended now, by the roadside, on the ground, in the dirt, under this tree, now and quickly. The pain would mean nothing, it would purify her, justify her. Then she would be on her bike, pedaling swiftly. The wind and rain would cool her face, freshen and heal her. She would not dismount for the uphill stretches. She would push on, leave far behind this weak man whose silence smelled and made her nauseous.

Yes, she had made her decision, it was already a fact. It was almost in the past. But just as at Christmas their intimacy had had to catch up with their letters, so now they still had to break into speech, raise the difficult subject, tortuously reason it through with lies and false emotion and pretensions to logic before they could attain the conclusion she had already accepted. They would have to go through all that before she could be free. Her impatience was so great she wanted to shout, she wanted to pick up her stupid bicycle and dash it against the road. Instead, she raised her hand to her face and bit her knuckle hard.

They walked on. Some intensification in the quality of Claire's silence made Douglas conscious of his own. He put his arm round her shoulders and asked if she was feeling better. She made no reply. He became solicitous, guiltily so when he noticed she had been crying. He apologized for his diffidence. It was wonderful she was pregnant, a cause for celebration. He remembered there was a pub a little way ahead. A glass of beer was called for, they could escape the fine, drenching rain, and above all, they would be able to sit at a table and think things out carefully. Claire knew then that the process had begun, for if the child was to be born, careful thought would have been less appropriate than indulgent feeling. She nodded bravely and got on her bike to lead the way. After turning right onto a slightly wider road they came to the pub. They left their bikes on the porch, out of the rain. It was barely twelve, and they were the first customers of the day. The bar was damp and gloomy, and Claire shivered as she sat waiting for Douglas to bring their beers. She rubbed her legs to make them stop trembling — she felt as if she were waiting in a hospital bed for an operation. She resented the cheerful, vacuous conversation her ex-fiancé was having with the landlord. Was he not remotely troubled? Her anger returned, and with it her resolve. The trembling stopped. She had to do nothing more than sip her beer while Douglas talked them round to the only correct decision. She would make him pay cash for his betrayal, and after that she would never see him again.

He lowered himself into the alcove seat beside her with a little well-here-we-are sigh. They raised their glasses and said "Cheers." There was a silence during which Claire tapped her foot rhythmically and Douglas ran his fingers through his wet, Brylcreemed hair. He cleared his throat and recalled for her the time he had last been in this pub, less than a week before war was declared. Another tense interlude, and then at last he began. It was wonderful she was pregnant, not least because they knew for sure now that they could start a family at any time. We *have* started a family, Claire thought, but she did not speak. She sat rigid, trying not to listen too closely. If she could just hold on, it would be over as soon as she had extracted his guilty commitment to pay and make the arrangements. Other couples, Douglas was saying, tried for months, years, sometimes without success. It was evidence of their love, of how right it all was, that they could have a baby with such ease. It made him love her all the more, he felt boundless confidence in her and in their future together. She had never heard him say so much in one go. He took her hand and squeezed it, and she returned the squeeze encouragingly. "I thought to myself, 'Get on with it, you oaf. I want to go home.' " Then he spoke about the difficulty of their position. He had heard nothing so far about his posting home, and in Germany they had only just started building the married quarters. His awkwardness was less noticeable when he left the more personal matters to deal with wider issues. He talked about the housing shortage in England, the international situation, the Berlin airlift, the new cold war, the nuclear bomb.

He had long finished his beer, hers was barely touched. She was growing impatient, she felt she should move things along. She interrupted. "If you're trying to say you think I shouldn't have it, let's start —"

Horrified, Douglas raised two hands to forestall her. "I wasn't saying that, sweetheart. I wasn't saying that at all. All I am saying is that we ought to take everything into account, look at all sides, and ask ourselves if this is really the best time, and if it is . . ."

She regretted her intervention. Douglas had been scared off his subject and was telling her all over again how lovely she was, how deep his feelings ran. If they could talk everything over now, then whatever they decided would strengthen them for the future. He went on in this way, timidly enlarging on his "whatever," edging his way back to his previous position.

It was during this speech that Claire, still just holding on, still distracted, glanced across the saloon bar towards the window by the door. "I can see it now as clearly as I can see you. There was a face at the window, the face of a child, sort of floating there. It was staring into the pub. It had a kind of pleading look, and it was so white, white as an aspirin. It was looking right at me. Thinking about it over the years, I realize it was probably the landlord's boy, or some kid off one of the local farms. But as far as I was concerned then, I was convinced, I just *knew* that I was looking at my own child. If you like, I was looking at you."

As Douglas talked on and the child at the window continued to stare in, a transformation was taking place in Claire. How extraordinary that she could think of destroying this child simply because she felt piqued by her fiancé. The baby, her baby, was suddenly flesh. It was holding her in its gaze, claiming her. It had acquired an independence of anything that might pass between this man and herself. For the first time she contemplated the idea of a separate individual, of a life that she must defend with her own. It was not an abstraction, it was not a bargaining point. It was at the window now, a complete self, begging her for its existence, and it was inside her, unfolding intricately, living off the pulse of her own blood. It wasn't a pregnancy they should be discussing; it was a person. She felt herself to be in love with it, whoever it was. A love affair had begun.

Then the child was gone. She did not see it move away. It simply faded into nothing. Now she turned again to Douglas, who was pressing on with his devious speech, and she felt protective of him. Benignly, she remembered her love and the adventure they were beginning together. It was not duplicity or cowardice she was witnessing here. This was a man summoning all his manly powers of reason and logic, all his considerable knowledge of current affairs, because he was in a deep panic. How was he to know what it was to have a baby? It was not inside him, it was not part of him in any way, and yet he sensed correctly it could change his life forever. Of course he must panic. How was he to know that he would not love the child till he saw it, till he could see who it was? Douglas was enumerating instances of something or other on the fingers of his left hand, unaware that his fate was being fixed. She recalled how magnificent he had been in the department store, how strong. It was her mistake to believe that he or any man could be strong in all circumstances. She had broken her news in a passive spirit, expecting him to react just as she had, to take the matter in hand for her. And then she had been sulky, masochistic, self-pitying. Where Douglas had been weak, she had made herself weaker. And yet the truth was she was one step ahead, for she already loved the child, she knew something Douglas could not. So this was her responsibility and this was her time. This was the moment for her to be decisive. She was having the baby, that was beyond question now, and she was having this husband. She placed her hand on his forearm and interrupted a second time.

Mrs. Lewis closed her eyes and tilted her head back against a cushion. They sat in silence in the darkening room. Her steady breathing suggested sleep, but finally she spoke in a murmur without opening her eyes or moving her head. "Now you tell me." Without hesitation he began his own story, omitting all references to Julie. He was walking in the country, he said; and at the end, after the experience of falling through the undergrowth, he had himself coming to by the roadside, a hundred yards from the pub. When he described the bicycles, which he did with great care, he watched his mother closely. She showed no response, nor did she when he recalled the gestures, the clothes, the hairclasp. She spoke only when he had finished, and then it was a brief sigh. "Ah well . . ." There was no need for discussion. After a minute's reflection, she said she was tired. Stephen helped her from her chair and up the stairs, and they said goodnight on the landing. "It almost connects up," she said. "Almost." She turned her back on him and went into the bedroom, her hand trailing the wall for support.

An hour later his father returned, so exhausted that he could barely sustain the weight of his own overcoat or bend his arms to unbutton it. Stephen helped him and guided him into the chair in which his mother had been sitting. Not until a beer had been brought and he had sipped quietly for a quarter of an hour was Mr. Lewis able to recount his ordeal. A day of anxious waiting, failed bus connections, jostle, and dependence on strangers had demanded all his reserves. The unaccustomed squalor of public places, the aggressiveness of the beggars, had shocked him.

"The filth on the streets, the dirty messages on the walls, the poverty — son, it's all changed in ten years. That's the last time I visited Pauline, ten years ago. It's a new country. More like the Far East at its worst. I haven't got the strength for it, or the stomach."

He drank his beer. Stephen saw the glass tremble. Thinking it might rally his father, he told him how he had been right all along, the child-care book had been written months before the commission had even gathered all its evidence. But Mr. Lewis merely shrugged. Why should he be pleased? He stood up creakily, refusing Stephen's help, and announced that he was going to bed. Mr. Lewis had never before missed out on an evening of beer and talk with his son, but now he clapped Stephen weakly on the shoulder and set off up the stairs, making impatient little gasps as he went. It was barely nine-thirty when Stephen, having cleared away the tea things and the beer glasses, turned off the lights and slipped quietly out of the house in which his parents were sleeping.

8

"On these occasions the hard-pressed parent may find some solace in the time-honored analogy between childhood and disease — a physically and mentally incapacitating condition, distorting emotions, perceptions, and reason, from which growing up is the slow and difficult recovery."

— from *The Authorized Child-Care Handbook,* HMSO

NEWS OF A child-care handbook secretly commissioned by the prime minister's office broke in a single column on the second page of the only newspaper that did not actively support the government. The story was sly in its reticence, referring to nothing more than rumors and usually reliable sources, encouraging perhaps the prime minister's brisk denial in parliamentary question time two days later that such a book existed. Then the story moved to the bottom of the front page and offered up tantalizing quotations, but still made no claim to physical possession of the book. Over the weekend a copy of a photocopy made its way to the leader of the opposition party, and on Monday the paper ran a headline that foretold the storm to come and underneath generously cited charges from the opposition headquarters of "gross and indecent cynicism" and "a disgusting charade" and "this vile betrayal of parents, Parliament, and principles." By midweek other papers were running the story. The government's back benches were "troubled" or "outraged." An emergency debate was demanded and granted, but delayed for a week.

Since Charles Darke's time in office, Stephen liked to think he had an insider's knowledge of how these things worked out, and so far it seemed to be going well. An enfeebled opposition was making an effort, there were no other stories likely to eclipse this one, and after all these years there still appeared to be a general requirement for a measure of probity in high office.

A week's delay was important. On the Wednesday, in the interests of open government and informed discussion, the prime minister ordered two thousand copies of the offending book to be printed and distributed to newspapers and other involved parties. The government presses ran all night, and the deliverymen were out at dawn. Journalists read all day and wrote through the evening to meet their late-night deadlines. The reviews the following morning were at least favorable, and otherwise ecstatic. One tabloid gave a front page to "Sit Down, Shut Up, and Listen!" Another said: "Kids, Get in Line!" In the quality press the book was "masterful and authoritative." It marked "the demise of confusion and moral turpitude in child-care writing," and, in the paper that had first carried the story, "with its honest quest for certainties it encapsulates the spirit of the age." However it had come about, the book was exemplary and should be made widely available. A handful of obscure civil servants working at high speed had set standards of which the official commission should take note. In its wisdom or carelessness, the government had come up with the kind of lead parents would respect.

Once the issue of the book itself was set aside, the remaining question was a simple one. Had the prime minister lied to

Parliament at question time? This simplicity was immediately muddied by rumors, whose source was difficult to locate, that the book had originated not in Downing Street at all but at an intermediate level within the Home Office. Two days before the emergency debate both the book and the lie faded from discussion. The issue now was presentation — whether the prime minister could rise to the moment and achieve the kind of performance in the House of Commons that would enthuse the back benches and restore confidence in the leadership. Whereas truthful explanations were desirable in some degree, convincing, heart-felt ones were vital.

Hunched by the radio with a can of beer, Stephen listened to the matter resolving itself over an unbroken background of cheers and groans. The familiar voice, pitched somewhere between a tenor's and an alto's, did not falter over a syllable as it set out to convince. Downing Street had known nothing of the existence of the book until the week before. The prime minister would not condemn the commissioning of the book, despite the existence of the official commission. It was an internal document, intended to focus the issues for the department concerned. Apparently there had been only three copies in existence, and they were not in circulation. Strictly speaking, the home secretary had acted improperly in not informing the Cabinet office, and that was regrettable, but no important principle had been violated. It was childish nonsense to suggest that the government had intended to publish the book in place of the official commission's report. What was to be gained from that? It was deeply regrettable if the commission's work had been made redundant by the necessity of publishing the book, but the blame for that lay with the irresponsible civil servant who had leaked the document to the press. This criminal would be pursued and punished. There would be no official inquiry, for the matter was too trivial. The names of the authors of the book would not be made public, nor would these civil servants be available to answer questions before any interested select committee.

It had been shown that there was deep concern among parents and educators about falling standards of behavior and lack of civic responsibility among many elements of society, particularly the young. Upbringing clearly played an important part in this, and there was no doubt that parents in the past had been led astray by foolish and fashionable theories about child care. There was a call for a return to common sense, and the government was being asked to take a lead. This it was doing, and would continue to do, undeterred by the pathetic slurs, the irresponsible calumnies, of its political opponents.

The tremulous voice of the leader of the opposition was failing to penetrate the loyal shouting and foot-stamping when Stephen snapped the set off. The home secretary, who had never been popular with the prime minister, would be writing his letter of resignation. The Official Commission on Child Care had received an encoded death sentence. It was tidy work, impressive. Stephen stared into the aluminum latticework of the speaker and marveled at his own innocence. This was one of those times when he felt he had not quite grown up, he knew so little about how things really worked; complicated channels ran between truth and lying; in public life, the adept survivors navigated with sure instincts while retaining a large measure of dignity. Only occasionally, as a consequence of tactical error, was it necessary to lie significantly or tell an important truth. Mostly it was sure-footed scampering between the two extremes. Wasn't the interior life much the same?

Stephen made a late lunch and brought it to his desk. In the gray air between his window and two nearby tower blocks, widely separated flakes were tossing on a bitter wind. The promised March snow was on its way. He had meddled inexpertly. It was not enough to send a book to a newspaper, to set something in motion and sit back. Political culture was theatrical, it required constant and active stage management of a kind he knew was beyond him. He hoped Morley did not phone. While he was constructing a version of the conversation they might have, the phone at his elbow did ring and made him start. It was Thelma.

Since his visit the summer before, they had maintained infrequent contact. She sent humorous, recriminatory postcards. She was amused, or made out she was, that he should be so alarmed by Charles's behavior, and took this as proof of incipient middle age. "You used to be an experimenter yourself," she wrote. "You championed Dada at our dinner table. Now Dada's warming his slippers by the fire." She pretended to believe that he was personally responsible for Charles, that it was all the fault of his first novel: "Dear Gerontophiliac, please write Charles a novel extolling the virtues and joys of senility. Or take some scissors to your longest pair of trousers and come and see us." She had enjoyed the story of his climb to the treehouse: "Charles is installing a fridge. Please come and help him carry it up." Behind this jokiness, which at times was very strained indeed, was an accusation that he had let them down. Whether Charles had undertaken a courageous journey into his past or had simply gone mad in a sweet and harmless way, then he, Stephen, should be on hand to lend his old benefactor support. He had proved himself to be rather too squeamish.

While his spirits had still been low, Stephen's feelings had been uncomplicated. Charles and Thelma had once seemed the

very embodiment of lively maturity. Their house exuded so-
lidity and excitement. Against the background of an expensive,
orderly hush, people talked competitively, extravagant or non-
sensical theories were expounded by physicists and politicians
who drank and laughed a lot and went home to rise the next
day to responsible jobs. In the early days, Stephen sometimes
thought that this was the kind of household he would have
liked to have been brought up in. As second best, he had his
breakdown in Thelma's tasteful guest bedroom, he sat at her
feet and listened, or pretended to, and took lessons in world-
liness from Charles.

Once they had gutted their lives and moved to Suffolk, and
after he had witnessed the lengths Charles needed to go, Stephen had felt that he was the one who had been betrayed. The
loss was all his. And he padded himself with sensible objections: Charles's fake boyhood, and Thelma's encouragement
of it, was a private, marital business. They needed Stephen
much as some couples need an observer to heighten their sexual
pleasure or dramatize and validate their arguments. He was
being used. Neither of them had wanted to explain to him
what they were doing, which made it impossible to know how
to behave. Besides, when Charles returned to his old life, which
he surely would one day, he would be saved embarrassment
if Stephen kept his distance. Their friendship could resume.

Now that he had his work, his Arabic and tennis, he was
less certain. He still winced in anticipation of meeting Charles
in short trousers again, talking his boned-up schoolboy English; but Stephen's curiosity and sense of duty were growing.
Previously, when he had been hanging on, groping from day
to day, he had needed to protect himself against other people's
madness. Now, he thought, he could risk more, be generous.
And yet he had done nothing. He was attached to his daily

routines, reluctant to disturb them even for a day or two. He was waiting for change, for developments like this, Thelma's phone call.

Her voice was strained and breathy. The telephone acoustics exaggerated the dry tick of her tongue against the roof of her mouth.

"Stephen. Can you come immediately? Can you get here today?"

"What's up?"

"I can't tell you now. Will you try to get here as soon as you can? Please." He squeezed the empty beer can in his hand. It made a cracking noise which caused Thelma to say quickly, "My God! What's that? Stephen, are you there?"

"Look," he said, "I'll go to the station and get the first train out. I don't know when that will be."

Thelma seemed to have moved the receiver away from her mouth. "I won't be able to meet you. You'll have to find a taxi." She hung up.

He took the remains of his lunch to the kitchen, washed the plate, and set about locking up the flat. As he was bolting the windows he noticed how the snowflakes were thickening and becoming whiter against the darkening air. He went to his bedroom and packed enough clothes for a week. In his study he wrote a note to Mr. Cromarty which he intended to drop off on his way out, and a letter to the tennis coach which could be posted at the station.

He had his overcoat on and was fiddling with the switches on his answering machine when the phone rang again.

A woman's voice called out with military precision, "Movement here, wanting to talk to Mr. Lewis."

"Yes?"

"Are you alone in your house? Good. Please don't leave it

within the next ten minutes. And keep this line clear. You have a visitor."

The line snapped silent while Stephen was demanding an explanation. He went to a window and looked down onto the wide street engorged with lines of rush-hour traffic. Visible only where it tumbled through wedges of red and yellow light, the snow was dissolving as fast as it could fall in an alien environment of asphalt and hot metal. He was tempted to leave immediately for the station, but curiosity kept him pacing in the hall. More than ten minutes went by. His packed bag was by the front door and he was turning to walk towards it when he saw a shadow fall across the door's frosted glass an instant before the doorbell rang.

The four men outside could have passed for Jehovah's Witnesses. With brief, apologetic smiles they pushed past him, their gazes fixed ahead on details — the skylight in the hall, the box that housed the electricity meter, dado rails, baseboards, doors. Ignoring his "Now look here!" they dispersed through the apartment. He was about to go after them when more footsteps on the stairs made him step out onto the landing and look down the stairwell.

A young man in glasses, with an armful of telephones, was running up, followed by two women, one carrying a typewriter, the other a portable switchboard. There were more people farther down. He heard someone fall hard on the loose step and murmur the mildest of curses. The first three filed past hurriedly without acknowledging his presence, intent on their jobs as they disappeared into his flat. He waited for the rest to come up, but for the moment there was no sound. He leaned out over the banister rail and saw the polished tip of a black shoe twenty feet down. They were waiting.

The small dining room off his kitchen was being transformed

into an office. One red, one black, and two white telephones had been connected to the switchboard, on which pinprick lights pulsed. The man with glasses was speaking on the red phone, reciting a long code. A woman was already typing without looking at the keys and using all her fingers, a trick Stephen had long admired. One of the four security men stepped in from the fire escape. It was beginning to look homely. A secretary was arranging on the table in and out trays, a thick pile of stationery, and a shallow box that contained colored paper clips, pushpins, rubber bands, and a pencil sharpener in the shape of a tomato. Someone was bringing in an extra chair and asked Stephen to watch out. Once he had guessed what was happening, he adopted an air of face-saving bemusement. He crossed his arms and was leaning in the doorway watching the activity when he heard a movement behind him and a voice in his ear.

"We were driving out of town with a quite unprecedented gap between appointments and the P.M. insisted. They'll put everything back, I promise."

Stephen's elbow had been taken and he was being led along the hallway at a snail's pace by a bald gentleman with half-moon specs. From the living room came a hiss of short-wave radio interference.

"We thought you'd be most comfortable in the study." They stopped outside the door and the gentleman drew from his inside pocket a printed form and a fountain pen and handed both to Stephen. "Official Secrets Act. Sign between the penciled crosses, if you wouldn't mind."

"And if I don't?"

"We'll go away and leave you in peace."

Stephen wrote his name and handed back the paper and pen. The gentleman tapped softly on the study door, and at the sound of a voice held the door open for Stephen and closed it quietly behind him.

The prime minister, who was already installed in the arm-chair by the fire, nodded as Stephen, still in his overcoat, took a wooden chair and sat down. On a shelf two feet above the armchair, just within the line of shadow cast by a lampshade, was Morley's book. He tried not to look. He was being addressed.

"I hope you'll forgive this. As you see, I don't travel lightly." For a moment their eyes met, then both looked away. Stephen had not replied, and what followed was cool, without an interrogative tone. "Is this an inconvenient moment?"

"I was on my way to the station."

The prime minister, who was known to despise railways, appeared relieved. "Ah well. Movement will give you a lift, I'm sure."

Enough time passed to allow the blandness of formalities to die away. They cleared their throats in turn. Stephen hunched forward on his chair and stared into the fire as he prepared to listen, drawing his coat round him as though for protection.

The voice raised itself impersonally to deliver a set speech. "Mr. Lewis — Stephen, if I may — I wish to discuss a matter of great delicacy, a personal matter, with you. I know little enough about you, but you are recommended on two counts which make me hope we may be of like minds, that we share a certain way of looking at the world."

Stephen did not demur. He wanted to hear more.

"You worked on one of the subcommittees, and as far as I know you did not dissent from its conclusions. And you are a close friend of Charles Darke's. I've come here at some considerable risk of being embarrassed, of appearing ludicrous, to talk about Charles. I have to trust you. I'm rather putting myself in your hands. However, I ought to warn you that should you decide to report our conversation, or even my presence in your house, you will find it very difficult to make yourself believed. All that's been taken care of."

"Such is trust," Stephen said, but he was ignored.

"I have thought long and hard about what I should do. I have not come here on impulse. I thought we might meet naturally, formally, and that I would be able to give you at least a hint of what was on my mind. I was sorry you were unable to come to lunch."

The phone was ringing in the kitchen. From habit, Stephen stirred, then sank back into his coat.

"Before I go any further, I think I ought to explain to you, in case you've never thought it through, the unique constraints of my position. I want to communicate with Charles, in a personal way, that is. The clichés are true. Leadership is isolation. From the moment I am woken until late into the night, I am surrounded by civil servants, advisers, and colleagues. The cultivation and expression of feeling is an irrelevance in my profession and I can speak with none of these people in an intimate way. In the past this has presented no problem at all. Only now, when I have something to express, do I find myself confined, curiously incapable. Unbriefed. Others might set their thoughts down in a letter and trust it to the post. For obvious reasons that is out of the question. The telephone is so complicatedly controlled where I am, screened, filtered, monitored, that a personal conversation is unthinkable. I've tried communicating with Charles at an official level, of course, but he simply ignores that kind of thing. I think his wife gets there first. Recently, I have felt almost desperate."

"Your speech just now in the Commons didn't seem much impaired," Stephen said.

The prime minister resumed in a quieter voice. "Charles was introduced to me at a lunch I gave for a fresh intake of MPs, one October many years ago. His energy and wit — he seemed determined to make me laugh — his charm and his enthusiasm for everything the party stood for seemed quite implausible. I thought he was pulling my leg, parodying something I did not quite understand, and that made me think he was clever, but perhaps a little untrustworthy. Over the next few meetings that impression was dispelled and I became very fond of him. So youthful, cheerful, funny, and with useful experience behind him in a number of fields. Seeing him — and of course I never saw him alone — always bucked me up. I began to envisage a future for him. Something on the public relations side. I thought that one day he might make a very impressive party chairman.

"I brought him on, advised him to get his name about so it wouldn't be difficult to offer him something. He needed bulking out with experience, I thought. Then there would be no stopping him. When I initiated the child-care project, I made sure Charles had responsibility for some of the subcommittees. That gave us the opportunity to meet confidentially every now and then. He was full of ideas and I looked forward to these meetings. I began to call them a little more often than was necessary. You might think it extraordinary and perverse that I should form an attachment to a young man —"

"Oh no," Stephen said, "not at all. But he is someone's husband. And you are the upholder of family values."

"Oh that," said the prime minister. "He has no children and one would hardly describe what he has with his wife as a family. There's a lot of unhappiness there, you know."

"Really?"

"Even with Charles at the Home Office, the project under

way, and regular full Cabinet meetings, I still saw very little of him. So, after much reflection, I called in MI5 and had him, well, followed, on a daily, round-the-clock basis. I had no suspicions, of course. He was as loyal to his country and government as I am myself. I went to great lengths to make sure that no file was opened on him. You see, having him followed was a way of being with him all the time. Can you understand that?"

Stephen nodded.

"Seven o'clock every evening I received detailed, typed-up accounts of his movements and contacts during the preceding twenty-four hours. I read them late at night in bed, after the usual papers from the dispatch boxes and the Foreign Office telegrams. I imagined myself at his side. I got to know his habits, his favorite places, his friends. You yourself featured a fair amount. It was as though I were his guardian spirit.

"Over the months the reports accumulated and I read back through the pages, as one might a favorite romantic novel — not that I read such things. I noticed how rarely his wife accompanied him, how insistent she was on keeping her distance from his political career, at least outside the home."

"She had a job," Stephen said.

"So you say. Other disturbing patterns in Charles's behavior were emerging. There were visits to unlikely private addresses in Streatham, Shepherd's Bush, Northolt. It was concern, not jealousy, I assure you, that made me ask MI5 to investigate more thoroughly. You can imagine my shock when I learned that he was visiting prostitutes. Then it came out that these were places that catered for highly specialized tastes."

"What sort of tastes?"

"The clients did a great deal of dressing up. More than that I did not wish to know. What I did know was that this was clear evidence of deep unhappiness in his marriage. This was surely the behavior of a very lonely man. After all, he did not even remain faithful to one establishment. I thought I must help him, talk to him, reassure him. I was devising the pretext for a meeting when I received his letter of resignation. I was upset — more than that, angry. I wanted to have him watched in Suffolk, but MI5 were complaining about the allocation of manpower with no justifying results. To send people out there without convincing explanations would have aroused suspicions. So since that time I have been cut off entirely from Charles. I have nothing but the old reports and, of course, the minutes of our project meetings."

Stephen was careful to keep his tone neutral. "Why not take the day off and go down there yourself and see him?"

"I can't go anywhere alone. Bodyguards apart, I have to take the nuclear hotline, and that means at least three engineers. *And* an extra driver. *And* someone from Joint Staff."

"Disarm," Stephen said, "for the sake of the heart."

The prime minister had the knack of ignoring irrelevant remarks. "I'd like to know how he is, what he's doing. You were going to phone me, remember?"

"I only stayed for the evening, and saw more of his wife. I think he's well enough, taking things quietly, thinking of writing a book."

"Did he talk about his political career? Did he mention me at all?"

"No, I'm afraid not."

"No doubt you think this is all quite ludicrous since he's young enough to be my son."

"Of course I don't." Once more his phone was ringing.

The prime minister glanced at the clock at Stephen's desk. "What I would like you to do, Mr. Lewis, is to convey a simple message to Charles. I would like to talk to him, in person, not on the telephone. If he prefers to be left alone, then I shall respect his wishes after one last meeting. It is easier for him to contact me, and he knows how that's done. Will you be seeing him soon, do you think?"

Stephen nodded.

"Then I will be grateful to you."

Though neither of them rose, the interview was at an end. To be alone with the head of government was an opportunity to give voice to an interior monologue that had been running for years, to confront the very person responsible and question, for example, the instinctive siding in all matters with the strong, the exaltation of self-interest, the selling off of schools, the beggars, and so on; but these seemed secondary to what they had been discussing, little more than faded debating points to which there would no doubt be well-rehearsed responses.

Stephen thought of Thelma. "I'll be very happy to pass on your message."

The prime minister rose, releasing the scent of cologne, and smiled as they shook hands. "You signed the form?"

"Yes."

"Good. I know I can trust you completely."

The gentleman with the half-moon specs heard the scrape of the wooden chair; the door opened just before the prime minister reached it. Stephen watched the receding back, then, as soon as he was alone, set about making his final preparations to leave. He raked out the fire and bolted the study window. The snow was beginning to pile on the stone ledge. He opened a drawer in his desk and took from the leaves of a blank notebook six fifty-pound notes which he kept for emergencies.

He stepped out into the hall in time to see the man with the armful of telephones going out the front door. The others followed right behind. The last to leave was one of the security men, who, with a theatrical gesture of his hand, indicated that Stephen should inspect his dining room. Everything was back in place, even the dirty teacups and old magazines. Lying on the table was a Polaroid of the room just before it had been requisitioned. Stephen turned to congratulate the man on his colleagues' thoroughness, but he too was gone.

He turned out the lights, took his bag, and used three separate keys to lock his front door. On the next floor down, Mr. Cromarty's flat was in darkness. Stephen had to pause while he searched his bag for the note he had written, and it was while he was pushing it under the door that he heard his own phone ringing upstairs. He hesitated, calculating his chances. Perhaps, just, if he rushed and was competent with the keys. But there had been enough delay. He picked up his bag again and took the stairs three at a time. He ran out towards the roar of traffic, out onto the pavement, his arm already raised for the taxi he had not yet seen.

He had less than thirty minutes to wait for his train. He was too restless, too squeamishly intent on protecting the random movement of his thoughts to squeeze into the moist, breathy din of the station café. In the pub next to it serious drinkers were three deep at the bar and someone was shouting. So he bought an apple, posted his letter, and wandered up and down the platforms, stamping his feet against the chill of the glistening concrete. He got up close to a diesel that had just come in. In the cab the driver was snapping switches, shutting the monster down. Stephen still had an ambition to be asked up. As a boy he had never dared approach a train driver. Now it was even harder. He stood breathing clouds and eating his apple, trying not to look ridiculously hopeful and yet unable to move away in case the driver was inspired to invite him. But the man had put a folded newspaper under his arm and was climbing down. He passed Stephen without a glance.

Further back from the platforms, by the tall doors of the ticket hall, a crowd of beggars clustered round a kicked-in photograph machine. There were more than a hundred of them, driven in off the streets by the cold. Many were wearing army surplus greatcoats. Still with ten minutes to spare, he wandered in their direction. They were not on the job. It was not allowed in stations, and no one risked giving when there were so many of them about. But a few optimistic types on the edge of the crowd were calling to passersby without seeming to move their lips. The rest were silent. Only expectation could keep them placid, all in one corner of the station. There was a soup kitchen on its way perhaps, or a meal-ticket handout.

The sweet reek of unchanged clothes and methylated spirits was strong even in this frozen air. A thirty-foot ventilator grill had become a packed dormitory. Stephen walked its length. If they could hang on another two months for the warmer weather they had every chance of making it through to the following autumn, when the sifting would begin again. To-night the minority without greatcoats would have trouble. He had reached the end of the row of bodies and was looking down at a familiar face. It was hard, small-boned, for a moment ageless. It belonged to a figure curled up on the iron bars, knees drawn up to make space for a large old man. The dulled eyes were open and stared past him. It was an old friend, someone from his student days, Stephen was beginning to think, or someone from a dream. He had always known that sooner or later he would run into someone he knew with a badge. Then he saw her — the girl he had given money to the year before, ten months ago. He recognized the yellow frock, now gray, beneath the nylon anorak. The face, though unmistakable, was transformed. The mocking liveliness was gone. The skin was pockmarked and coarsened, pudgily slack around features that had edged closer together for safety. Her arms were crossed over her chest.

He had decided to give her his coat. It was old, and he was about to step into a warm train. He removed it, set down his bag, and, crouching down, shifted into her sight line, which she was too tired or indifferent to adjust. He tried to remember how he had seen Kate in this girl. He put his hand on her narrow shoulder. The man next to her had propped himself up on an elbow. For such a large body the voice was squeaky and depressingly cheery. "Oi, oi. Fancy that, do ya? She's not interested." He laughed.

Stephen spread his coat over the girl and touched her hand. It was as cold as the surrounding air. He touched her face and the eyes continued to stare, their indifference confirmed in absolute terms. He picked up his bag and straightened. To retrieve the coat now was impossible. He could not remember whether he had emptied the pockets. Behind him a whistle blew and a train creaked into motion. By the station clock he could see he had less than a minute and a half.

The man was watching him and the coat. "Go on," he said shrewdly, "or you'll miss it."

Stephen knew that if he reported the matter he would not be leaving London that night. He dithered a moment, backed off, turned and walked quickly, then broke into a run when he saw a guard on his platform walking the length of the train slamming the doors. He did not look back until his hand was resting safely on an icy door handle. Over a hundred yards away, obscured for a moment by a passing mail cart, the man was on his knees, holding the coat aloft and feeling through the pockets. A shudder ran through the train. Stephen jerked the handle and climbed on, and began his customary search for the loneliest seat.

Only four people got out at the unstaffed Suffolk station two hours later. While Stephen searched the length of the badly lit platform and then the front of the station for a phone box, his fellow passengers drew out of the car park in three cars. The snow had stopped falling and lay two inches deep, diffusing the smoky light of a moon wrapped in wispy cloud. The station was on the edge of town, virtually in the countryside, on a road marked by what looked like single domestic light bulbs strung high on poles. Stephen paused a moment, struck by the novelty of total silence. Then he turned up the collar of his jacket and set out for the hotel in the center. From the deserted bar he phoned for a taxi and sat drinking by an electric coal fire.

The driver was a friendly, motherly woman who insisted on fastening his seat belt for him. She had taken over the work from her husband, who had had his license revoked two Christmases before. Now he ran the house and, according to his wife, loved the work. And she had discovered a new life. She talked on and drove with exaggerated caution so that it took them forty-five minutes to cover the fifteen miles. Stephen basked in blasts of hot air on his legs and face. He slumped deeper into the nylon fur of the seat cover, mesmerized by the flow of undemanding talk and the swaying furry die that hung from the rearview mirror.

The driver agreed to take her car up the Darkes' rutted track. It was half past eight when she left him at the edge of the wood. Again he paused in the silence. He watched the taillights recede bumpily, and took in the stillness, the startling bareness of the trees. Thelma and Charles would have heard the car, and he was expecting a light through the trees, a voice calling. He waited, but there was nothing. He picked up his bag and walked towards the front gate, which was no longer concealed. The snow in front of it was undisturbed; nor were there footprints along the path that ran between the parallel lines of high, naked shrubs — the dark green tunnel in summer.

The cottage was in darkness but for a yellowish glow at a downstairs window. He knocked quietly and, hearing nothing, pushed the door open. Thelma was sitting facing him at the dining table in the light of two candles. Her face registered no shift in expression.

"I'm sorry I took so long." The room was cold. He sat down beside her. "What's wrong? Where's Charles?"

There was a wet sound, loud in the country silence, as Thelma sucked her lower lip. A minute passed, long enough for Stephen to regret giving his coat away. He was beginning to shiver, he needed something to happen, if only to keep him warm. He covered her hand with his own. It was as if he had touched a switch. She turned her head from side to side, quite wildly, then stopped and began to cry. The child in him was disturbed by an older woman in tears. She did not want comfort from him. She had pulled her hand free to cover her face, and she shrugged when he touched her shoulder.

He pulled a blanket off an armchair and put it round her. In the living room he found a heater and brought it in. While Thelma continued to sob, he set about lighting the woodstove, whose ashes were still hot. He found a bottle of Scotch and two glasses and fetched a jug of water from the kitchen. The room was warm by the time she had quieted down. She kept her hands over her face, however. Then she stood abruptly, and murmuring, "Sorry," hurried upstairs. He heard her in the bathroom. He poured a drink and sat down by the stove to prepare himself for the bad news.

She reappeared twenty minutes later with a thick cardigan over her arm and carrying a flashlight. She put these items down on the table and came and sat by Stephen's chair, taking his hand and pressing it between her own. She looked calm enough now, but weary, used up.

"I'm very glad you're here," she said.

He waited.

To say what she had to say, she rose and stood by the table, and half turned away from him. She pinched the woolen folds of the cardigan between her finger and thumb. She spoke in a rapid monotone, trying to outdistance the words. "Charles is dead. He's dead. He's out there in the woods. I've got to bring him in. I can't have him out there all night. I want you to help me carry him."

Stephen had stood up. "Where is he?"

"By his tree."

"Did he fall?"

She shook her head. The tightness of the movement suggested that if she was to remain in control of herself she could not speak.

"I'll need a coat," Stephen said, "and some boots."

For the next few minutes they were silent and practical. She showed him into the scullery, where an old jacket and a sweater hung on a nail. There was also a pair of gumboots heavy with dried mud. He found a length of rope on the floor and, with no clear plan for its use, stuffed it in his pocket. Before they left the house he built up the stove.

The moon had risen clear of the clouds and the flashlight was only necessary where the track curved into shadow. Stephen held back his questions. The only sound was the squeak of trodden snow and the rustle of their clothes.

Then Thelma said, "He went out this morning and didn't come back at lunchtime, which was unusual. I went looking for him and found him just as it was getting dark. I don't remember coming home. I think I must have run. Then I phoned you."

They walked on, and when it had become clear that Thelma was not going to volunteer more, Stephen asked cautiously. "How did he die?"

Her tone was uncertain. "I think he just sat down."

By a frozen brook they passed the slab of rock under whose covering of snow, deep in the fissures, were the ingredients of a miniature tropical forest. Even by moonlight it was possible to see fat and sticky buds and unassuming ground plants raising tiny spears through the snow. One season was piercing another. In the smoothed-out spaces between trees, profusion waited its turn. The track turned towards the center of the wood. They descended into the hollow towards the rotten oak, an unchanged feature from the summer before. They turned right onto the path that joined the track at this point. Thelma had slowed her pace by the time they reached the clearing. On the far side mature trees, indistinguishable in shadow, rose up like a vast mansion. She had pocketed the flashlight and was warming her gloveless hands on her breath and then crossing her arms into the folds of her coat. Stephen could think of nothing to say that was not another question. In the pocket of his jacket he had found a marble, which he rolled between his fingers, guessing absurdly at its color. It was comforting to remember that this was not a wilderness; the nearby town threw up brownish light all over one part of the sky; on the road a mile away two cars went by; the land they crossed was heavily tended, fenced, and coppiced. Only the temperature was as it would have been if no one had ever existed.

The high wall of trees that leaned over the clearing seemed aware of what it contained and why they had come. As they crossed into its shadow, Thelma gave Stephen the flashlight. She was hanging back. By the time he had drawn level with the first of the beeches, she was standing still, several yards behind him. She raised a hand to indicate that he would have to go in alone.

Like many of his generation, Stephen had had little experience of death. As he walked towards his second corpse of the day, he imagined a smell, tasted it in his throat, of damp parlors, black cloth, the trapped gas between organs seeping through the pores of larded skin. It was an impression with no basis in memory or fact, but it was hard to dispel. He breathed the odor out into the clean air. To persuade himself that he had simply come to do a job, carry a heavy weight for a friend, he took the rope from his pocket and attempted to coil it efficiently as he went along.

He arrived at the small clearing sooner than he wanted. The yellowing beam of the flashlight cut across something blue. He stood still and let the light travel back. His breath left him in clouds. There was a shirt, a midriff, the waistband of corduroy trousers which were, mercifully, long ones. He was not ready to point the torch upwards to the face, so he picked out the legs, then the bare feet whose toes were erect and splayed. To one side was a pile of clothes, a sweater on top of a coat, and, spilling off the pile, shoes and socks.

His dependency on a narrow cone of light made him uneasy. He switched the flashlight off and circled the clearing, keeping his back to the trees and his gaze on the vague form on the other side. Its stillness scared him, but so too did the idea that it might move. Charles was sitting with his back to the tree in which he had built his platform. A foot above his head was the smudged silhouette of the first nail. When he was less than three feet away Stephen switched on the light. A two-inch layer of unmelted snow sat on Charles's shoulders and in the folds of his shirt along the arms. It had drifted deep on his lap and it sat wedge-shaped on his head. It was on the line of his nose and lightly across his upper lip. The effect was comic, nastily so. Stephen swiped at the snow with a cupped hand, dusted the head and shoulders clear, and used his forefinger on the nose and lip.

It was the brief contact with this last, the lip, that made him draw back. It was too pliable, it slid across the gum, and he thought he had felt warmth. He stood in front of his friend, six feet away, and shone the light in his face. The eyes were closed. That was a relief. The head was resting against the tree and the expression, if there was anything there at all, was one of tiredness. Charles's legs were stretched out in front of him, and his arms hung straight down, the palms resting flat on the snow, the backs of the hands obscured by it. The top three buttons of the shirt were undone.

Stephen poked the pile of clothes with the flashlight. If there was a note, Thelma had found it. He stood about, delaying the moment when he would have to pick the body up. He took the rope out again but he could conceive of no use for it. At last he knelt down by his friend's feet, put his hands round the waist, and pulled forward. As he straightened he tipped Charles up, gripping his thighs to drape the body over his shoulder.

When he was standing erect and turning clumsily to find the path, he heard from behind him, where Charles's head nudged the small of his back, a long sigh of disappointment, whispered through the letter *o*. Stephen yelped and skipped sideways across the clearing as he dropped Charles in the snow. Now he had to drag the body back, prop it against the tree, and repeat the most difficult part, which was to put his face up close to his friend's. When he straightened with the weight the second time there was no sound.

If he changed direction too suddenly he staggered. Otherwise it was a manageable load because it was evenly spread. He was in decent shape from his tennis. He set off down the path, realizing as he left behind the relative brightness of the clearing that the flashlight was trapped in his pocket. But the moon was almost directly overhead, the shadows had shrunk. Initially, it was not the weight of the body that oppressed him so much as the chill it communicated through its bulk to the bones of his shoulder and down his back. It drew the heat from him greedily, as if they might soon change places and the corpse, warmed to life, would carry Stephen's cold body to the cottage.

He was shivering as he sweated. Ahead he could see through the trees the brightness of the larger clearing. Thelma was standing where he had left her. As he approached, he thought he would drop Charles at her feet. She could help lift him into position when he had had a rest. But she turned as soon as he was close, and began to walk back the way they had come. She did not look round as she hurried on. He had no choice but to go after her.

By the time they were among the coppiced trees and were climbing the slow incline of the hollow, the weight was causing Stephen severe pain, principally in his legs, across the neck, and in his arms where they were clasped behind Charles's knees. Thelma had paused only once, to pull the flashlight out from Stephen's pocket. So far they had not spoken.

As the pain intensified, he resolved not to put Charles down until they reached the cottage. He would atone for his poor showing as a friend. He had dropped his friend before; he would not drop him now. It was with heroic thoughts such as these that Stephen tolerated the pain. But when at last Thelma had led the way through the cottage garden and into the scullery, and had indicated that this was where she wanted the body set down, he could not activate the right muscles, they had hardened beyond his control. He stood swaying in the confined, brightly lit space, unable to shed his burden. "Pull," he cried. "For God's sake get him off me!"

It was less in the interests of hygiene, more in the way of re-establishing the line between the living and the dead, that Stephen went immediately to the kitchen sink to wash his hands. The kitchen was too warm now and closed in. He went through to the living room. Years ago a wall had been knocked down to form a long gallery. The furnishings were sparse, the air cool and unused. Thelma was there already, resting against a window ledge, still in her coat. He headed for a chair but found he could not sit. Though his hands looked steady, his whole being seemed to be vibrating at a high frequency. There was a keening in his ears, or in the room, at the limits of the audible range. He walked from the chair along the polished boards to the far wall and turned. He would have liked to run. He thought he might be formidable on a tennis court now. She crossed the room, reached the adjacent window, and walked back. He returned along the boards, making a loud noise with his heels. Thelma stood by the empty fireplace. He looked up when he thought he heard her whispering, but it was the sound of skin on skin as she rubbed her hands together. He fetched the Scotch and glasses from the kitchen. It was difficult to control the flow.

The drink tasted salty. "Do they put salt in this?" he asked.

She looked puzzled and he did not repeat the question. All the same, after a pause she nodded. Holding the glass in two hands, she went up the room along Stephen's route. She kept her back to him while she drank.

"You ought to know," she said at last, still without turning, "this isn't a surprise. He tried it in London, more than once. I thought coming here would be a reprieve. In fact it was a postponement."

"I thought I knew him well," Stephen said. "But obviously I was wrong."

"It's how it usually is. The manic side, the energetic, successful side, was public, and the rest, the mad lows, was all for me. Moving out here was supposed to reconcile the two . . ." She had walked back to where Stephen stood.

"Except," he said, "out here I was the only public."

She was looking at him, without accusation. "It's true, he was upset when you went off without warning that day, when he was waiting for you. He wasn't counting on your approval, although that would have been nice. What he wanted was for you not to mind."

Stephen felt winded; his arms were heavy. He glanced behind him and sat down. "I suppose I did mind," he said sadly.

Thelma sat on the arm of the chair. "Don't misunderstand me. It would have made no difference in the end. It certainly didn't hang on your attitude. I didn't mean to suggest that. I could have told you more, prepared you for what to expect. But Charles was against that. He didn't want us talking about him in that way, he didn't want to be a case." Then she added, "And at the time I thought he was right."

A clock at the end of the room set about striking eleven. The final reverberation had to fade into nothing before it was possible to resume.

Thelma had entered a state of emotional neutrality. "He

couldn't square it," she said in a matter-of-fact way. "He wanted to be famous, and have people tell him that one day he would be prime minister, and he wanted to be the little boy without a care in the world, with no responsibility, no knowledge of the world outside. It wasn't an eccentric whim. It was an overwhelming fantasy that dominated all his private moments. He thought about it, he wanted it in the way some people want sex. In fact, it had a sexual side. He wore his short trousers and had his bottom smacked by a prostitute pretending to be a governess. You might as well know that, it was one of the things he wanted to tell you about. It's a pretty standard minority taste among public-school boys.

"But it had a more important emotional side which he found harder to understand in himself or talk about. He wanted the security of childhood, the powerlessness, the obedience, and also the freedom that goes with it, freedom from money, decisions, plans, demands. He used to say he wanted to escape from time, from appointments, schedules, deadlines. Childhood to him was timelessness; he talked about it as though it were a mystical state. He longed for all this, talked to me about it endlessly, got depressed, and meanwhile he was out there making money, becoming known, creating hundreds of obligations for himself in the adult world, running away from his thoughts. Your book *Lemonade* was very important to him. He said it was one part of himself addressing the other. He said it made him realize that he had a responsibility to his desires, that he had to do something about them before time removed the opportunity. It was a warning of mortality. He had to do something quick or regret it forever."

She blew her nose. She maintained her detached, analytical style.

"But he did nothing. Conventional ambition is hard to break

with. There was a suicide attempt — pretty halfhearted, actually. He changed jobs and went on being more successful, as you know. The years raced by, just as he had feared. The pressure was building up. He went into politics, got his job in government. He started reading your book again. It was because of the child-care project. The prime minister invited him, which in that world means ordered him, to write a shadow child-care manual, the one there's been all this fuss about. Charles and the prime minister worked on it together. He was being fancied, I mean sexually fancied. He was repelled, but he couldn't help flirting. He wanted to get on, he couldn't stop himself wanting that. He wrote the manual under his leader's supervision, and he reread your book. Everything got stirred up again, and he wanted to make his plans. He was desperate, he said. He was running out of time. He had to have this, he was pleading with me to make it happen for him, to let him be a little boy. And in the end I agreed, I thought he should have it or he would go to pieces. Of course it suited me too, which was good, because the thing could not have worked if I had felt resentful. I wanted to get out of London, I was tired of teaching, I had my book to write, and I love this house and the land around it.

"We often talked about where this obsession came from, whether it was something in his past that had to be relived, or completed, or whether it was compensation for something he had missed out on. Charles never really wanted to delve. I think he was frightened of what he might find. Perhaps it was his mania protecting itself. You know his mother died when he was twelve, so you could say he associated prepubescence with her. And he had a photograph, a horrid little picture taken when he was eight. It shows him standing next to his father, who was fairly important in insurance — a dull man, I remember, but tyrannical. In the photograph Charles looks like a scaled-down version of his father — the same suit and tie, the same self-important posture and grown-up expression. So perhaps he was denied a childhood. But other people lose their mothers in childhood or have fathers with awful ambitions and manage to grow up without Charles's sexual and emotional cravings. In all the talking we did, I don't think we came anywhere near the root of the thing.

"Anyway, we dropped everything and came here. For a while, during the hot weather, it was fine — it was more than that, it was an idyll. What to an outsider would have seemed ridiculous and fantastical became quite ordinary between us. I was mother to a little boy who played in the woods all day and came home to eat and sleep. I've never known him so happy, so simple in his needs. He discovered he liked solitude. He learned the names of plants, though I never saw him with books. When he was back here he was quite simply merry, and affectionate. At night he slept ten hours straight through. Before, he used to make do on four or five. You came, and that was a disappointment, but not a serious setback.

"Then the weather turned, rather suddenly as it happened, and Charles began to fret about what was happening in London. He wanted us to take newspapers, and I refused. He tried to mend an old radio and got in a fury when he failed. Then he started on about how we were going to run out of money unless he went back to work, which was nonsense. Worst of all, he was getting letters from the prime minister inviting him to Downing Street, hinting that a place could be found for him in the Lords, a peerage that is, and a job in government, with even better jobs to come.

"He was sitting up all night agonizing, and he was still out in the woods during the day, trying to maintain his innocence.

But it was getting harder all the time. He was in his treehouse in his short trousers wondering whether he should style himself Lord Eaton and whether anyone else had taken the name. I'm sorry, I don't mean to laugh, Stephen. It was tragic, but it was also thoroughly absurd. I'm not crying. I'm not going to cry. We talked a lot, of course. I suggested psychoanalysis, among many other things, but he had the usual English aversion to that. When I told him I thought it was extraordinary for a man with such powerful conflicts as his to refuse any process of self-examination, he flew into a terrible rage, a grown-up tantrum. He actually lay on the floor and beat it with his fists.

"After that he became increasingly depressed. He was trapped. If he went back to London, to the old life, he knew from experience that the old longings, the compulsions, would start to drag him down and he would be craving the simple and secure life he had made for himself here. And if he stayed here he would be agonizing forever about his growing irrelevance in what he was beginning to call the real world. My patience was wearing out. My work was suffering, I was exhausted with the whole business. After a great deal of thought, I decided he should return to politics. He had survived out there for years, and if he was going to be unhappy, it would be no more than the unhappiness of the child who could not have everything.

"Once this was put to him and talked through, he sank even deeper, and then we had an argument. That was this morning. He accused me of putting him out in the cold, cutting him off from the thing he wanted to be. I'm afraid I lost my temper. I told him I had tried to help him in every way I could. Now he would have to take responsibility for his own life. And that is exactly what he did. He wanted to hurt me by hurting himself — thoroughly depressive reasoning. He went out into the woods and sat down. He put himself out in the cold. As suicides go, it was petulant and childish. And sorry as I'll always be, I don't think I'll ever quite forgive him for it."

Thelma's anger had caused her to stand. Stephen watched her walking up and down. Agitation had returned to the room.

"If Charles wrote that child-care book," he said at last, "why was it so harsh? From what I've seen, it doesn't look like the kind of thing someone who felt himself to be a child could write."

"I've read it right through," Thelma said. "It's a perfect illustration of Charles's problem. It was his fantasy life that drew him to the work, and it was his desire to please the boss that made him write it the way he did. That's what he couldn't square, and that's why he fell apart. He could never bring his qualities as a child — and really, Stephen, you should have seen him, so funny and direct and gentle — he couldn't bring any of this into his public life. Instead it was all frenetic compensation for what he took to be an excess of vulnerability. All this striving and shouting, cornering markets, winning arguments to keep his weakness at bay. And quite honestly, when I think of my colleagues at work and the scientific establishment and the men who run it, and I think of science itself, how it's been devised over the centuries, I have to say that Charles's case was just an extreme form of a general problem."

"I'm sure that's true," Stephen said.

Now her anger was turned on him. "That's what you say. But think back over the last year and all *your* unhappiness, all the floundering about, the catatonia, when right in front of you was — well, then you see the difference between saying a thing is true and knowing it to be so."

Stephen had risen from the chair. "What are you talking about?" he demanded. "What was right in front of me?"

She hesitated, and was about to answer when the brief silence disintegrated in the crashing ring of the telephone. Even before she had answered it, he realized that all evening he had been hearing unanswered telephones.

She said, "Yes? But he's here, with me. Good. Yes, trust me. I will . . ." She held the receiver towards him and cupped her free hand over the mouthpiece. She made it clear she was not diverted from answering his question. "Julie," she said. "Julie was in front of you. She wants to speak to you."

He took the phone and listened.

Thelma was smiling broadly, and all the time her eyes, narrowed and tearful, were on him.

❧ 9 ❧

"More than coal, more even than nuclear power, children are our greatest resource."

— from *The Authorized Child-Care Handbook*, HMSO

I<small>T</small> <small>HAPPENED</small> that a nightly train from Scotland swung eastward through Norfolk and Suffolk on its way to London and stopped briefly at the local station at twenty past one in the morning. Stephen borrowed Thelma's car, left the keys under the seat as arranged, and arrived on the platform a minute before the train was due in. He paid the guard for a sleeping compartment and arranged to be woken as soon as they arrived. He lay with his feet at the pillow end, and watched through the spyhole in the frosted glass the leading edge of the carriage's shadow cut across a blur of cinders. From the next compartment came the muffled thumps of lovemaking. For over twenty minutes he wondered at its unvarying persistence, the awesome single-mindedness of passion. Could he ever be driven quite that way again himself? When the train began to slow for the next station the rhythm slackened too; he had been listening to something loose swaying against the partition wall.

He fell asleep as they entered the outer suburbs and was woken abruptly by a loud knocking at his door. In his confusion he misinterpreted its urgency and hurried out too quickly with his bag onto the platform, the one he had left from the evening before. He stood swaying a little, remembering himself. But for porters loading mail and magazines onto a nearby train, the station was deserted. Still numb from his sleep, he set off to find a taxi. The rank was empty, and on the street outside the station there was no traffic at all. He walked towards St. Paul's with the collar of Charles's jacket turned up against a cold and gritty wind. He had been walking for half an hour before he was picked up by a taxi with its light out. The driver was going home across the river and agreed to take him to Victoria station.

Minutes later, Stephen slid back the glass panel and offered two hundred and fifty pounds to be taken to Kent.

The driver immediately shook his head. "Nah, stuff that. No disrespect, but I need my kip."

"Three hundred then."

"Sorry."

"Two and a half thousand?"

The cab came to a standstill and the driver turned in his seat. "I'd want to see it first."

Stephen showed him empty hands. "I wanted to know if you had a price."

The man laughed as he pulled away from the curb. He was still smiling to himself when he accepted Stephen's money at the end of the journey.

Partly because of the nearby soup kitchens, this station was busier than the last. By the closed ticket office there was a cider and sherry party in progress, a quiet affair in view of the number of unsteady figures in greatcoats. Three black women, each operating a giant suction machine, were working their way steadily towards the group from different directions. Down the platforms dozens of men were involved in the desultory loading of trains. Occasionally a shout echoed languidly from the distant roof. From the departures board Stephen learned that the next stopping train along the Dover line left in three hours' time, at six-forty-five.

He walked behind a clattering cart laden with bundles of semipornographic magazines. When it stopped he went forward to ask the driver if there was a mail train leaving for Dover. The man shrugged and rephrased the question for the benefit of the porters who were preparing to unload the cart. Two-twenty, they murmured in ragged sequence — an hour and a half ago. Stephen was about to walk away when one of the porters, a boy in his teens, spoke out with the intensity of a train enthusiast.

" 'S only maintenance going down there now."

"Where's that?"

"You won't get on him." All the same, he pointed to where the platform ramp sloped down into the night.

Stephen thanked him and walked on, ignoring a sharp call of "Oi!" at his back, which was followed, encouragingly, by loud laughter.

The platform dropped away from under the station roof past a warning sign to passengers not to advance further, and out among the mess of rails along a narrow cinder path. The lines were creamy in moonlight and gave off a bitter taste of cold. Two hundred yards ahead, in a siding lit by high arc lights, was a diesel engine with a single carriage behind, both vivid yellow. Stephen approached without any particular plan. He arrived below the cab and found himself looking up at a man of about his own age who wore a beret balanced on thick black curls. Stephen took the beret to be a good sign, evidence of a sense of humor.

He had to shout above the throb of the engine. "Are you the driver?"

The man nodded.

"I'd like a word."

"Come on then."

He swung himself up awkwardly with his bag. In the warm, narrow space there were fewer dials than he expected, and fewer controls. The floor vibrated pleasantly under his feet. He noticed two paperback thrillers, a Thermos flask, a tin of tobacco, a pair of binoculars, a pair of thick woolen socks folded into each other. It was dingy and intimate, like a rented room. The driver had moved towards the other door to make room. Stephen resisted an impulse to lower himself into one of the driver's seats. It would have been a presumption.

Instead he rested his hand on it and said, "I wondered if you could drop me off somewhere on the way to Dover." As he spoke he reached into his back pocket and brought out the fifty-pound notes. "I know it's strictly against the rules, so . . ."

He had extended his hand with the money. The driver sat down, put his elbow on the control panel, and propped his cheek against his knuckles. He looked past the money at Stephen's face.

"You on the run or something?"

Because he had not expected to explain himself, Stephen could think only of the truth. "I've had an urgent summons from my wife, my ex-wife." He sat down, feeling that he had earned the right.

"When did you last see her, then?" The driver stressed the pronoun, as if he knew the woman in question.

"Last June."

The man grimaced and said, "That figures."

Stephen waited for an explanation, or a decision, but the

driver, still leaning on his elbow, with his free hand playing over the controls, said nothing. Stephen transferred the notes to the other hand. He was reluctant to put them away in case it seemed he was withdrawing his offer. He was considering a new approach when he saw through the windshield lights sliding fractionally to one side. The train was easing forward at less than walking pace. On a gantry a quarter of a mile ahead, an arrangement of illuminated signals had shifted, though he could not remember which colors had been added or changed. The driver had straightened in his seat. They increased speed as they ground over a quick and complex set of points which swung them right across the belt of track to the far side.

Stephen waited until the noise of that had passed and said, "Thank you." The driver did not look in his direction, but the adjustment he made to his beret was a form of acknowledgment.

It was infinitely preferable to look forward rather than sideways, to see not embankments or back gardens but miles of metal ribbon spooling in, and railway furniture curving in on collision course to flip by with finely gauged accuracy. As they gathered pace through south London it began to snow, heightening for Stephen the pleasure of forward motion; they were hurtling into a vortex of snowflakes whose open end rotated about them, seeming to screw itself tighter round the train.

The driver clicked his tongue against his teeth and looked at his watch. "Where was it you wanted to go?"

Stephen named the stop.

"She lives there, does she?"

"About three miles south."

For the first time since they had started moving, the driver looked at Stephen. "We don't have to stop at stations, you know."

Stephen tried to describe the plantation, the bend in the road, then he remembered The Bell.

"I know it," the driver said. "I can set you down nicely."

They traveled out from under the orange glow of the suburbs into the darkened remnants of countryside between bedroom communities. The snow eased off, and then stopped completely. Their speed increased. Stephen was still holding the money tight. He offered it again, but the driver kept his eyes on the track ahead and had one hand on a crescent-shaped brass handle, the other deep in his pocket.

"Give it to your ex. She'll be needing it, I should think."

Stephen pocketed the money, and felt that the least he could do was offer his name.

"Edward," the driver replied, and explained that he was taking a mobile workshop and canteen to where a gang was due to start that morning. They would be working a tunnel, resetting the bed of the track, which had been damaged by water. It was a fine old tunnel, one of the best in the south. The week before they had admired by flashlight the brickwork of the roof and the buttresses at the mouth.

"It's a cathedral in there. You could call it fan vaulting, what they got up at the top, and no one ever sees it." In two years' time the line was due to be closed down. "They'll never get it back," Edward said after a pause. "They'll sell the land off and they'll never get it back."

"It's irrational," Stephen said.

Edward shook his head. "It's too rational, my friend. That's the problem. Here's a cathedral in the dark. What's the point of that? Close it down. Build a motorway. But there's no heart in motorways. You won't see kids on the bridges taking car numbers, will you?"

It took an hour to reach the little station. As soon as they were through it, Edward began to apply the brakes. "I'm going to put you down by a level crossing. You can't get lost. Go up the hill, down the other side, through a wood till you come to a junction. Take a right turn there and you'll see the pub on your right."

They stopped on the far side of the automatic crossing. Stephen shook Edward's hand. "You are very kind."

"Go on, off you go. I don't want the sack, and you've got business to do."

Stephen climbed onto the track and Edward threw the bag down. There followed the commotion of a celebration. The huge machine roared as it inched forward, and behind him the bells were ringing out and red lights were flashing as the gates restored the right of way to the road. Then, within a minute, there was silence.

Beyond the crossing, the hill rose steeply. No cars had been through since the last fall of snow, and the way ahead was a band of unbroken white between the hedgerows. The moon was in front of him, sinking at last. It was a haunted road. He walked silently on its edge, aware of the young couple at his side pushing their bikes into the wind and rain, lost to their unspoken, unharmonious thoughts. Where were those young people now? What separated them from him beyond the forty-three years? Their moment here was a tapering echo. He could hear the stern ticking of their back wheels, the different lengths of stride falling in and out of step. He reached the top with them, and paused as they had.

The brilliant road dropped and curved into the wood a mile away. He set his bag on the ground and fiddled with the straps, adjusting them to fit across his shoulder, and then he retied a shoelace with the nervous competence of a sprinter in the blocks. He straightened and took deep breaths. He felt the imperative of his summons as a tautness in his stomach wall, a cold thrill.

For one last moment he savored the pent energy of altitude before tilting forward and letting the hill draw him down and fix his pace, a near effortless sprint across the snow. In two hundred yards he had settled his breathing to the thump of each footfall. It seemed he might rise through the air if he threw off his bag. He pounded the earth to aid its rotation, so that things raced towards him as he did to them. He was down among the first trees and into the wood, where road broke through the snow. He decided on the tree where his mother had schemed his own termination. He increased his speed, though he was on level ground now and his breathing came harder. A quarter of a mile ahead was the junction, so he cut across open rough ground, stumbling on hillocks concealed in the snow.

The second road was wider, he remembered the look of it and the tall trees that crowded to its verge. Ahead was the telephone box, the rise, and the sharp bend in the road where the footpath led off to the prairie field, and nearer, on the right, was The Bell, in this light a bold pencil sketch. He drew level with the porch and glanced across. It was then that he understood that his experience there had not only been reciprocal with his parents', it had been a continuation, a kind of repetition. He had a premonition, followed instantly by a certainty, borne out by Thelma's smile and Edward's instant understanding of the months, that all the sorrow, all the empty waiting, had been enclosed within meaningful time, within the richest unfolding conceivable. Breathless as he was, he gave out a whoop of recognition, and ran on up the rise and along the path that led to Julie's cottage.

The front door was not locked. It gave straight onto the living room, whose warmth and faint aroma of bread and coffee suggested wakefulness. When he closed the door he smelled Julie's perfume on a coat and scarf that hung behind it. Light from a coal fire spilled across the floor; the rest of the room was in semidarkness. On the scrubbed work table, by the notebooks, was an earthenware vase with sprigs of holly and a violin resting on a yellow duster. On a chair was an orderly stack of ironed laundry. By it, on the floor, was a book about the night sky and a cup and saucer. He was halfway across the room when he heard from upstairs the familiar creak of the bed, then footsteps above his head.

He went to the foot of the stairs and called up, "It's me." The shadows of the balusters bowed and thickened on the wall. She was standing at the head of the stairs. He thought he saw the white of a nightdress, but all he could see clearly was her face by the candle she held out before her. He wondered if she had been abroad. She looked tanned.

"You were quick," she whispered. "Come up."

She was back in bed by the time he entered the room. His breathing had yet to return to normal, and he tried to conceal this. He did not want her to know he had been running. Besides the candle there was a lamp on the dresser and a fire in the grate. Surrounding her, all across the quilt, were books, newspapers, a magazine, and loose sheets of music. There were flowers by the bed, and a carton of fruit juice. Behind her were half a dozen plumped-out pillows. He stood at the foot of the bed and set down his bag. For the moment he did not want to go closer.

She drew the quilt towards her. Somewhere in the shadows something slid to the floor. "I think I had the beginnings of a contraction as soon as I came back from talking to you. But don't worry, they can go on for days. It's not due for a week or so."

Stephen said stupidly, "I didn't know."

She shook her head and smiled. The whites of her eyes were luminous in the soft light as she glanced up at him and away. She wore a cardigan draped across her shoulders, beneath that a cotton nightdress unbuttoned to the cleavage of her heavy breasts. Her skin was dark and looked hot. Her hands rested demurely where the swell of her belly began. Even the fingers, he thought, looked plumper. They parted and she patted the bed.

"Come and sit down."

But he still felt wild from his running. His drenched shirt clung to his spine. He needed time to adjust to the warm confines of the room before he could sit close in to her, to this potency. To soften his refusal he said the first thing that came to him. "I got here in a railway engine, I rode in the cab."

"Your boyhood dream."

"The driver dropped me off at the crossing. He seemed to know his way around here." He was about to describe Edward to her, tell her how much she would have liked him, then he decided it was too difficult, irrelevant. He said, "Julie, why didn't you tell me?"

"Come and sit here."

He hesitated, then he laid his jacket and sweater over a chair and put his shoes and socks to dry by the fire. As he walked round the bed, the feel of the warm boards under his feet brought to mind again the idea of home, and of barely imaginable pleasures. He sat on the edge of the bed, not quite where she had patted. But she was determined to draw him closer. She took both his hands in hers. He was unable to speak, he was charged with more love than he thought he could bear. Light and warmth radiated from his stomach. He felt weightless and mad. She was smiling at him, she was close to laughter. It was the triumphant good humor of one who has her best hopes confirmed. He had never seen her so beautiful. Her skin had a finer grain, like a child's. What had grown in her was not confined to the womb but was coiled in every cell. Her voice was melodious and grave as she answered his question.

"I had to wait, I had to have time. When I first found out, last July, I was furious with myself, and with you. I felt cheated. It seemed so unfair. I came out here for solitude, I wanted to make myself stronger. This seemed exactly the wrong time, and I was thinking seriously about an abortion. But all that was just a moment of adjustment, two or three weeks. Being alone by choice can make you very clear-headed. I knew I couldn't really face another loss. And the more I thought about it, it did seem extraordinary, the ease with which it happened. Remember how long it took us to have Kate? I realized that what I meant by the wrong time was really the inconvenient time. I began to think of this as a gift. There had to be a deeper patterning to time, its wrong and right moments can't be that limited.

"I could have written to you then. I knew you'd come. We would have been all right, we would have settled things and thought that the worst was behind us. But I knew that was dangerous for me. Important matters would have been buried if I'd called you then. I came out here to face up to losing Kate. It was my task, my work, if you like, more important to me than our marriage, or my music. It was more important than the new baby. If I didn't face it, I thought I could go under. There were some bad, bad days when I wanted to die. Each time that came back it was stronger and more attractive. I knew what I had to do. I had to stop running after her in my mind. I had to stop aching for her, expecting her at the front door, seeing her in the woods or hearing her voice whenever

I boiled the kettle. I had to go on loving her, but I had to stop desiring her. For that I needed time, and if it took longer than the pregnancy, that would have to be how it was. I haven't been completely successful . . ."

Her gaze shifted to a corner of the room. The old grief was constricting her voice. He felt it flare his nostrils. They waited for it to go. The curtains were drawn wide apart and in the uppermost panes was the whitish glow of the moon's approach down the side of the cottage. On the table under the window was a package of medical items ready for use by the midwife. By it, obscured by the shadow of a wardrobe, was a vase of daffodils.

"But I've made some progress. I tried not to shy away from the thought of her. I tried to meditate on her, on the loss, rather than brood on it. After six months I began to take comfort from the idea of the new baby. That grew, but it was so slow, Stephen. I still had days when it seemed I'd got no-where at all. One afternoon the quartet came out. They brought an old friend from college, a cellist, so we played, or tried to play, the Schubert C major quintet. When we got to the adagio, you know how lovely it is, I didn't cry. In fact, I was happy. That was an important step. I started playing again properly. I'd stopped because it had become an evasion. I was taking on these difficult pieces and working at them furiously — any-thing to stop thinking. Now I was playing for its own sake, I was looking forward to the baby coming, and I was beginning to think about you and remember, and really feel how much we loved each other. I felt it all come back. I'm sorry it had to be this way. But I know this was right. I'm ready to go on now. I had to trust that you were getting stronger too, going your own way. So at last I phoned you, all yesterday afternoon. I couldn't bear it when you weren't there . . ."

He wanted to show her how much stronger he was. In his

elation, he was ready to spring up from the bed and demonstrate his rebuilt backhand, or take up a pen and show off his calligraphy, compose a poem for her in classical Arabic. But he could not let go of her hands. The pure gray eyes shifted their attention from his left to his right eye, down to his mouth, then back. Her mouth was ripe with its held-in smile. She pushed the covers away and guided his hand. The head was engaged, the skin above the tangle of hair was hot and hard, almost like bone. Higher up, below her right breast, he felt a fluttering against his palm, the kicking of a foot.

He was about to speak and looked up at her. She whispered, "She was a lovely daughter, a lovely girl."

He nodded, stunned. It was then, three years late, that they began to cry together at last for the lost, irreplaceable child who would not grow older for them, whose characteristic look and movement could never be dispelled by time. They held onto each other, and as it became easier and less bitter, they started to talk through their crying as best they could, to promise their love through it, to the baby, to one another, to their parents, to Thelma. In the wild expansiveness of their sorrow they undertook to heal everyone and everything, the government, the country, the planet, but they would start with themselves; and while they could never redeem the loss of their daughter, they would love her through their new child, and never close their minds to the possibility of her return.

Throughout this they lay face to face on the bed. Now Julie kicked the bedclothes clear of her feet. She lifted her nightdress and turned and crouched on all fours. She spread her elbows till her face was pressed into the pillows. He murmured her name at the sight, in a body so dignified and potent, of the sweet helplessness of her raised buttocks, untidily framed by the embroidered hem of her nightie. The silence resounded after all their promises, and merged with the stirring of a billion needles in the plantation. He moved inside her gently. Something was gathering up around them, growing louder, tasting sweeter, getting warmer, brighter; all senses were synthesizing, condensing in the idea of increase. She called out quietly, over and again, drawn-out sounds of *oh,* each of which dipped and rose in pitch like a baffled question. Later, she shouted something joyful he could not make out, lost as he was to meaning.

Then she was pulling away from him, she wanted to be on her back. She settled herself squarely and drew a sharp breath. She rested the tips of the fingers of one hand on the lower part of her belly and massaged herself lightly. He remembered the pretty name, *effleurage.* With the other hand she clasped his, squeezing tighter as the contraction gained in intensity, in this way communicating its progress. She was prepared, she was controlling her breathing, making steady, rhythmic exhalations that accelerated into shallow panting as she approached the peak. She was off on this second journey alone, all he could do was run along the shore and call encouragement. She was going from him, lost to the process. Her fingers dug into his hand. His pulse was banging in his temples, disturbing his vision. He tried to keep the fear out of his voice. He had to remember his lines. "Ride it, ride this wave, don't fight it, float with it, float . . ." Then he joined in her panting, making a heavy emphasis on the breathing out, slowing down as the grip on his hand loosened. He suspected that the form of his participation had been devised by medical authorities to oppose the panic of paternal helplessness.

As the contraction passed they took a deep breath together. Julie cupped her hands over her mouth to counter the sickness of hyperventilation. She said something, but her words were muffled. He waited. She dropped her hands and smiled wryly. They returned to the room, and to themselves, as though emerging from shelter after a storm. He could not recall what they had been talking about, or whether they had been talking. It did not matter.

"Do you remember it all?" Julie said. She was not asking him to reminisce. She wanted to know if he knew what to do.

He nodded. He would have liked to take a peek at one of Julie's books. There were precise stages of labor, as he half remembered, different breathing techniques associated with them, time to hold back, time when it was important to let go. But there was a long day ahead. There would be leisure for that. And he remembered the last time clearly enough. He had been brow-mopper, telephonist, flower man, champagne pourer, midwife's dogsbody, and he had talked her through. Afterwards she had told him he had been useful. His impression was his value had been more symbolic.

He dressed, then crossed the room and found a pair of Julie's socks to put on. "Where's the midwife's number?"

"In my coat pocket, hanging behind the door. Put the kettle on as you go out. Make two hot-water bottles when you come back. And a pot of jasmine tea. Both the fires need building up." He remembered too these husky commands, the mother's absolute right to order her own domain.

Outside, the dawn was still confined to the eastern sky. The clouds had disappeared entirely and for the first time he saw stars. The moon was still the main source of light. He walked quickly up the brick path in his wet shoes, noticing that Julie had taken the precaution of sweeping the snow clear. The phone box on the corner had no light inside and he had to feel for the numbers. When he got through, he found he was talking to a receptionist in a medical center in the nearby town. He was not to worry. The midwife would be contacted, and would arrive within the hour.

On the way back, as he walked the short stretch of road he had run along less than an hour before, he slowed and tried to take the measure of the transformations; but he was incapable of reflection, he could think only of details — of tea, logs, and hot-water bottles.

The cottage was quiet when he returned. He prepared the tea tray, fetched wood from a lean-to outside, built up the downstairs fire, and filled a basket for the one upstairs. He scanned Julie's shelves without success for books on birth. To buck himself up with a show of competence, he stood at the kitchen sink for several minutes scrubbing his hands.

Balancing the tray on the basket and holding the hot-water bottles under his arm, he tottered upstairs. Julie was sprawled on her back. Her hair was damp and clung to her neck and forehead. She was agitated, querulous.

"You said you wouldn't be long. What have you been doing?"

He was about to dispute with her when he remembered that irritability could be part of the process, one of the markers along the route. But surely that should have come later. Had they missed out some stages? He gave her the tea and offered her a massage. She could not bear to be touched, however. He arranged the bedclothes for her. Recalling how furious she had been before when the midwife had spoken to her like a child, he adopted the tone of a soft-spoken football coach. "Move your leg, this way. Good. Everything's looking good. We're on course." And so on. She was not really mollified, but she complied, and she drank the tea.

He was blowing on the embers, encouraging a flame across a handful of twigs, when he heard her call his name. He hurried over. She was shaking her head. She made as if to place her fingers over her belly, and then gave up.

"I've been up all night. I'm too tired for this, I'm not ready."

His words of encouragement were cut off by a long shout. She fought to inhale, and there was another, a prolonged hoot of astonishment.

"Ride it out, ride the wave —" he began to say. Again his words were cut off. He had lost his place. Exhortations to rhythmic breathing were now inane. A gale had torn the instructions away from him. She held his forearm with both hands in a fierce grip. Her teeth were bared, the muscles and tendons of her neck were stretching to breaking point. He was lost. He could give her nothing more than his forearm.

He called out to her, "Julie, Julie, I'm here with you."

But she was alone. She was drawing breath and shouting again, this time wildly, as though in exhilaration, and when she had no more air in her lungs, it did not matter, the shout had to go on, and on. The contraction lifted her off her back and twisted her onto her side. The sheet was still gathered up to her waist and had knotted itself round her. He felt the bed frame tremble with her effort. There was a final click at the back of her throat and she was drawing breath again, tossing her head as she did so. When she looked at him, past him, her eyes were bright, wide with purpose. The brief despair had gone. She was back in control. He thought she was about to speak, but the grip on his arm was tightening again and she was away. Her lips shivered as they stretched tighter over her teeth and from deep in her chest came a strangled groan, a bottled-up, gurgling sound of colossal, straining effort. Then it tapered away, and she let her head fall back against the pillows.

She took deep breaths and spoke in a surprisingly normal

voice. "I need a cold drink, a glass of water." He was about
to stand when she restrained him. "But I don't want you to
go away. I think it might be coming."

"No, no. The midwife isn't here yet."

She smiled as if he had made a joke for her benefit. "Tell
me what you can see."

He had to reach under her to get the sheet clear.

There was a shock, a jarring, a slowing down as he entered
dream time. A quietness enveloped him. He had come before
a presence, a relevation. He was staring down at at the back
of a protruding head. No other part of the body was visible.
It faced down into the wet sheet. In its silence and complete
stillness there was an accusation. *Had you forgotten me? Did you
not realize it was me all along? I am here. I am not alive.* He was
looking at the whorl of wet hair about the crown. There was
no movement, no pulse, no breathing. It was not alive, it was
a head on the block, and yet the demand was clear and pressing.
This was my move. Now what is yours? Perhaps a second had
passed since he had lifted back the sheet. He put out his hand.
It was a blue-white marble sculpture he was touching, both
inert and full of intent. It was cold, the wetness was cold, and
beneath that there was a warmth, but too faint, the residual,
borrowed warmth of Julie's body. That it was suddenly and
obviously there, a person not from another town or from a
different country but from life itself, the simplicity of that,
was communicating to him a clarity and precision of purpose.
He heard himself say something reassuring to Julie, while he
himself was comforted by a memory, brief and clear like a
firework, of a sunlit country road, of wreckage and a head.
His thoughts were resolving into simple, elementary shapes.
This is really all we have got, this increase, this matter of life
loving itself; everything we have has to come from this.

Julie was not yet ready to push. She was recovering her strength. He slid his hand round to the face, found the mouth, and used his little finger to clear it of mucus. There was no breath. He moved his fingers down, below the lip of Julie's taut skin, to find the hidden shoulder. He could feel the cord there, thick and robust, a pulsing creature wound twice in a noose about the neck. He worked his forefinger round and pulled cautiously. The cord came easily, copiously, and as he lifted it clear of the head Julie gave birth — he saw in an instant how active and generous the verb was — she summoned her will and her physical strength and gave. With a creaking, waxy sound the child slid into his hands. He saw only the long back, powerful and slippery, with grooved, muscular spine. The cord, still beating, hung across the shoulder and tangled round a foot. He was only the catcher, not the home, and his one thought was to return the child to its mother. As he was lifting it across they heard a snuffling sound and a single lucid cry. It lay face down with an ear towards its mother's heart. They drew the covers over it. Because the hot-water bottles were too heavy and hot, Stephen climbed into bed beside Julie and they kept the baby warm between them. The breathing was settling into a rhythm, and a warmer color, a bloom of deep pink, was suffusing its skin.

It was only then that they began to exclaim and celebrate, and kiss and nuzzle the waxy head which smelled like a freshly baked bun. For minutes they were beyond forming sentences and could only make noises of triumph and wonder, and say each other's names aloud. Anchored by its cord, the baby lay with its head resting between its closed fists. It was a beautiful child. Its eyes were open, looking towards the mountain of Julie's breast. Beyond the bed was the window, through which they could see the moon sinking into a gap in the pines. Directly above the moon was a planet. It was Mars, Julie said. It was a reminder of a harsh world. For now, however, they were immune, it was before the beginning of time, and they lay watching planet and moon descend through a sky that was turning blue.

They did not know how much later it was when they heard the midwife's car stop outside the cottage. They heard the slam of its door and the tick of hard shoes on the brick path.

"Well," Julie said. "A girl or a boy?" And it was in acknowledgment of the world they were about to rejoin, and into which they hoped to take their love, that she reached down under the covers and felt.

ABOUT THE AUTHOR

Ian McEwan was born in 1948 and began writing in 1970. His first book, *First Love, Last Rites,* a collection of short stories, won the Somerset Maugham Award in 1976. His second collection of short stories, *In Between the Sheets,* was published in 1979, Among his other works are two novels, *The Cement Garden* (1978) and *The Comfort of Strangers* (1981), and a book of television dramas, *The Imitation Game & Other Plays* (1982).

Mr. McEwan lives in Oxford, England, with his wife and their four children.